TAKE IT OFFLINE

OUT OF OFFICE SERIES

BOOK 1

DANI MCLEAN

SET THE MOOD PUBLISHING

TAKE IT OFFLINE

CONTENT NOTE

While this story is a light-hearted contemporary romance, there are elements which may be difficult for some readers.

The protection of your safety and mental health is absolutely crucial to me. Please do what you need to look after yourself. If that means skipping scenes or the entire book, I fully support that.

If you have any questions about this list, don't hesitate to contact me via social media.

- Explicit language (there are approx. 208 fucks if that helps)
- Misogyny within a STEM field (tech) and the appropriate rage toward it
- References to growing up in the foster system and bad experiences therein
- Debt issues, specifically centred around parents who are terrible with money

- Detailed sexual content, with the following:
  bondage (cuffs), adult toys, sensory
  deprivation (blindfolds and headphones),
  elements of voyeurism (listening to a
  consented recording), switch dynamics (both
  parties enjoy taking and giving control),
  chastity cage (skip chapters 48 and 49 if you
  don't want to read this)

No, seriously.

Dad, **I mean it.**

CHAPTER 1
SURVIVAL OF THE 1%
EMMA

R ich bitch. Princess. Trust fund baby.

I've been called it all, and worse.

Lil heiress trying out a corporate job. Isn't that cute?

It doesn't matter that I've delivered everything asked of me, and I've done it early and under budget.

It doesn't matter that I work late and never take sick days.

It doesn't matter that I live paycheck to paycheck now, or that there could possibly be more to me than a last name and a pretty face.

Roberts (Karl, technically, but everyone calls him by his last name) stabs at the wall-mounted screen. "Change the colors. It's too harsh. Try blue. The percentages don't tell me anything, so change that back to full figures. And add filters for Discipline, Vendor, and Facility."

A part of me wants the screen to fall on him.

Would it count as manslaughter if I manifested harm to my own boss?

On a related note, if karma truly exists, then whoever inflicted Power BI on the world will only ever know pain.

Rolling my shoulders, I note the changes he wants, reversing the suggestions he insisted I make last week.

"I know you've been struggling with this level of advanced reporting," he says, as if he isn't the reason this report is taking three weeks to complete, instead of three days.

I focus on the bar chart, wishing he was joking. It's not the reporting that's difficult to understand, it's him.

He sits, clasping his hands on the table. The condescending pinch of his mouth makes my stomach drop. "But it's important that you learn. If you want to make up for your lack of experience, you need to invest in yourself. I won't be able to hold your hand next time."

I'm shocked he doesn't pat me on the head.

He's right about one thing. Though I've worked for Helix for five years now, it's still my first job.

But I'm determined to prove myself.

There's no separating me from the reputation that comes with my name, but I'm damn well going to try.

Roberts points back to the screen. "I'll need this finished before I present it to Emmanuel on Wednesday."

Two days from now. Fantastic.

I don't often dream about what my life would look like if my parents hadn't thrown away our eight-figure net worth, but when I do, it's because I'm stuck in one of the world's longest meetings, wishing I could scream at my boss.

It turns out that smiling and nodding at condescending older men is a fact of life, no matter how engorged my bank account is.

The retail therapy is infinitely better, though.

Reactions to my last name are always the same. *Conway? As in...? Yep.* I'm a second-generation nepo baby, so people never understand why I would choose to work a nine-to-five, especially at Helix of all places, the "gas giant gone green" as the news announced a decade ago, shocking the world.

Back when my world consisted of trunk shows and St. Barts, I wouldn't have pictured it either.

What nobody knows is that the great Conway legacy was gambled away on bad investments. The only reason my parents haven't declared bankruptcy is because I sold off as much as I could and took this job to pay off the rest.

But, as life regularly reminds me, hard work isn't always enough.

Karl Roberts, overseer of the Digital function and second-in-command to the CIO, seems to take pleasure in that.

Maybe if my parents had invested in Roberts's ability to constantly move the goalposts, I wouldn't have needed to take this job.

Another glance at the clock reminds me that Friday technically finished half an hour ago, but instead of curling up bra-free on my plush velvet couch and imagining how long I'd last in a zombie apocalypse, I'm once again working into the weekend.

"If you can get this right, it'll benefit you," he adds.

"The ability to effectively communicate our results to the leads team and beyond is integral if you want to move up."

Lately he's been hinting at a promotion.

I want it. I've earned it.

It's taken two years of overtime to get even a scrap of Roberts's approval. Then, after the catastrophe that was last year's staff briefing, I had to start over.

It still chafes. When I started working here five years ago, he asked for me specifically. Within weeks, I knew that Governance was the right place for me. Here, I get to lead change. Here, I create innovative solutions to real-world problems and—when I can convince Roberts —actually implement them.

And yet, despite all of that, I can't shake the feeling that he wants me to fail.

But what else can I do except grin and bear it? This is simply another test in a long line of them, and I'll rise to meet it, just as I have all the others.

I'm getting this promotion, and when I do, it won't be because anyone—including my boss—did me a favor. It'll be because I've earned it.

Me. Emma.

Not my parents. Not my net worth.

Me.

Then I'll finally have the recognition I've been working my ass off for, and a raise that will return to me a financial stability I haven't had since college.

———

"Two weeks," I say, having finally escaped to meet Ivy for a post-work drink. It's a credit to her powers as my best friend that I'm not currently: a) eating leftovers for dinner, and b) hunched over my keyboard while I do it. "That's how long I'd last in a zombie invasion." Maybe three if I used my Jimmy Choos as a weapon.

Ivy shakes her head, her long black ponytail swishing behind her. Around us, the bar is bustling with noise and activity, and the bartender has spent more time staring at Ivy's bright pink lipstick than she has on the drinks she's pouring.

"No way," Ivy says. "Together? We could get through a couple months, easy. Just have to make it to the Winchester."

I laugh, but the sound is cut short when my neck twinges. Too much stress, my mother would warn me. *Tell me something I don't know.* "I swear Roberts hates me. I was stuck in a Zoom meeting about the citizen developer update for two straight hours last night."

"That's because he knows you're smarter than him. No one knows the system the way you do." Ever so casually, she flicks her hair over her shoulder, exposing a dual turtle dove tattoo, and I have to stifle a laugh at how quickly the bartender's head turns toward her. The way Ivy is smiling tells me she's noticed it too.

I love her. For every person who stares and wonders what the hell I'm doing at Helix, Ivy's proven she couldn't care less about my past.

We bonded quickly during an all-day women in tech workshop I was *voluntold* to attend and I haven't let her go since. Like me, she's a senior document controller within the company. While I work in governance, Ivy's expertise is in development.

I wouldn't have survived at Helix without her.

At five-nine, I tower over her, but don't be fooled— she's far more cunning than I am.

I shake my head. "That's only because I spent eighteen months working on it with the enterprise team in the first place." A less than thankless task in the end, because the lead team cut anything from our scope that wasn't minimum viable product, signaling that the project was officially over budget and out of time.

Management didn't care what was implemented as long as they got a bonus.

Unsurprisingly, what we delivered was not all it could be. At the end of the day, all anyone cared about was where the system failed.

And guess who got the blame?

"People still message me about your training. Even the Subsea guys are happy, and they hate dealing with documents. Steve gave up his hard copies. Do you know how long that man has been complaining about digitization? Probably since he was born. But you walk him through it, and now it's 'Ivy, did you know I can reply to vendor comments directly in the system?' If I believed in the supernatural, I'd swear you hexed him." She laughs, sparing a flirty glance at the bartender when she returns for our glasses. "I know training people directly isn't in your job description, but—"

"But nothing," I say, even though she's right. Training like that is not my responsibility, and if Roberts knew, I'd be in trouble. But what he didn't know wouldn't hurt anyone. "I love you, and I'd do the same for anyone."

Well. Not anyone, but 99 percent of them.

"Don't look so worried," Ivy says. "You've got this."

"I've got this," I repeat. Maybe if I say it enough, I can force my will into being.

The issue with always putting everyone else's needs first is that there's no end in sight. I don't want to be the kind of person who doesn't care, but I also can't stop hearing the echoes of every authority figure in my life telling me to do as I'm told.

Fit the role. Play by the rules. Be a good girl.

If I could do all that, my life would be much easier. But some intrinsic part of me can't help but go left when everyone else goes right. To test my limits in new ways, whether that is teaching myself DAX basics to improve a report or holding a plank for ten seconds longer than I did last week.

Nothing excites me more than a challenge.

"This is your year, Em. Don't be afraid to be a little selfish. Step up and take what you've earned."

She's right. When I walk into work on Monday, I'll do exactly that.

CHAPTER 2
AND YOUR OPPONENT IS...
EMMA

Helix's headquarters took three years to build and boasts biometric entry, facial recognition, and a "defining carbon footprint."

Out of the four thousand people who call 1105 Martin Place home—and Helix does its best to make us live in the office—there's only one I truly hate.

Charlie Walker.

Which is why my stomach drops when I find the backstabbing pretty boy from Operations sitting shoulder to shoulder with my boss for the impromptu meeting I was summoned to.

The same meeting I am now desperately trying to decipher.

Because it can't be the promotion I've worked my ass off for, and since the smiling bane of my existence is here, it can't be anything good.

Roberts waves me into the room and gestures for me to close the door. This meeting room seats ten, but right now it feels uncomfortably small.

Charlie reclines extravagantly in his seat, head cocked, smirk firmly in place. So sure everything is about to go his way.

As always, he's perfectly put together. Tailored navy suit—a Zegna pinstripe that's making my mouth water —white shirt, dark tie. Paired with his pink pouty lips, silky brown hair, and blue, blue eyes, Charlie's a walking aphrodisiac.

It's a dangerous trap to admire.

I take a seat across from him, barely concealing my glare.

He winks.

Annoyance bubbles up inside me, but I can't flip him off like I want to. Not with Roberts here. Even so, I focus my loathing for him across the barren gray room with so much force there's no way Charlie doesn't get the message.

"Morning, sunshine," he says.

His smile sparkles like a diamond and leaves me twice as tipsy as champagne. I'd almost forgotten how attractive he is.

Oh, who am I kidding? I'd need to be dead to forget those dimples.

Roberts taps a cracked knuckle on the table, impatient. "I have a meeting in ten minutes, so I'll make this quick." He turns his body—along with the bulk of his attention—toward Charlie and rests his elbow casually on the table. I've always known Roberts to be an exacting man, with the cold, hard stare of airport security, but for Charlie, he's practically swooning.

"I've been given budget approval for an information

analyst. This will be a lead position, reporting directly to me, with responsibilities across corporate functions and projects. Now, as seniors with good track records, you're both eligible for the role. But before I can recommend one of you to the lead team, I have a project for you."

This is Roberts's preferred method of delivery. Drop a huge responsibility into my lap with little to no details, call it a development opportunity, and then rush out of the room before I can get my bearings.

So that's why the devil is here.

Across the table, Charlie's expression is as blank as the meeting room walls, and he's unusually quiet.

I've never seen him like this, but I'm too busy being annoyed that Roberts still doesn't trust me to complete this project alone. One step forward, seven steps back.

"At present," he says, "there are over thirty standards that govern our information at a corporate level. That number needs to come down drastically by the end of the year. I shouldn't need to tell either of you how important this is, especially after the reputational hit Digital took after the rollout of the system last year." Roberts sends me a pointed look.

Even though bile is stinging my throat, I hold his gaze and force a nod.

"We have an uphill battle ahead of us, and the person who lands the analyst role will need to spearhead a full sweep of our Governance footprint. For now, though, I need you to start with the top-level procedure. This is an opportunity not only for the function, but for you as well. You've both proven you can deliver high-quality results. You especially, Charlie."

My blood boils.

This is it. My promotion. The job I have earned with my tears, sweat, and thousands of unpaid hours of overtime.

I'm so, so close.

There's only Charlie in my way.

"The two of you will work together to simplify the procedure. I don't care how you manage it, but deliver that before the end of the quarter, and I'll decide who is the best candidate for the promotion."

Roberts checks his watch, then stands.

"I trust I can leave you to work out the details?"

"Of course," I answer quickly. The last thing I need is Roberts insinuating I'm not a team player. I might despise every part of the man sitting across from me, but I'm still a professional, dammit.

Charlie, on the other hand, turns his head to roll his eyes. If I were ever caught doing that, I'd be raked over the coals, but oh no, not him.

"Good. Send me your action plan by the end of the week."

With that, he's gone, and the room falls into a deadly silence.

If I could think, I'd make up an excuse and leave. A meeting or a document-related emergency. Instead, I'm wondering how in the hell my life has come to this.

"So," Charlie drawls from across the table.

Teeth gritted, I meet his gaze.

The first time I met Charlie Walker, he sauntered into my meeting room wearing a pinstripe McQueen blazer that did incredible things to his shoulders and waist, and the sight of him immediately banished every word in my head.

Tall, trim, pretty. A killer smile. In that moment, I wanted to know everything. I soon discovered he was as despicable as the devil himself.

No matter what I said, Charlie fought me every step of the way. As if I'd personally selected a system that only barely fit our needs. As though I hadn't already faced the wrath of every other department I'd trained.

If I'd known he'd follow up that glowing moment by taking credit for all of my hard work, I would have… well, I'm not sure what I could have done, but I wouldn't have wasted a single thought on how much I'd like to see what was under those expensive clothes.

The only thing we've ever agreed on?

We hate each other.

Charlie *fucking* Walker.

The smug son of a bitch I now have to work with.

"So," I fire back, lifting my chin. I'm not about to give him an inch.

Propping his elbow on the table, he taps once, twice, completely unbothered. "How do you want to handle this?"

I bite back a scoff. Of course he would expect me to do all the actual work.

"Well, considering I've only had sixty seconds to process it," I say, not bothering to hide my frustration— with anyone else, I would be on my best behavior, but

Charlie hasn't earned my best, "the current procedure is too prescriptive. It sits above every IM standard, so it shouldn't read like a work instruction. Instead, I'd strip it back. Outline what kind of information is the most valuable, how to identify it, and the critical requirements for managing it. All other details can be captured in the technical procedures." Which will also need to be updated, but one thing at a time. "I'll also make it system agnostic so that it's future-proof." Especially since everyone here hates the system already.

His response? A smirk. *Unbelievable.* "Am I supposed to just sit around and look pretty while you do all the work?"

"It wouldn't be the first time," I challenge.

He rocks back in his chair, hands on his thighs. "Stellar team ethic you've got there."

The frustration coursing through me is very quickly turning into rage. This is all a game to him. "Like yours is any better."

Any semblance of the loose, cocky man he was when I entered is slipping away now. His eyes go hard, and I swear a vein in his forehead pulses. "If you don't want me here—"

"I don't."

I don't want him getting in the way of what I've worked for. I don't want him anywhere near me.

We're at an impasse. If this was a simple matter of skill, I'm confident I could beat him. But Charlie's got the ear of some big players here at Helix, and I'm smart enough to know that popularity counts.

Rather than backing down, he sits forward, jaw

rigid, and says, "Then you better take it up with Roberts. I'm a part of this, whether you like me or not. So why don't you say what it is you want to say before we start?"

"Fine. If you really want to have this conversation, then let's have it."

CHAPTER 3
SORRY I WON (AND I'LL DO IT AGAIN)
CHARLIE

I know two things about Emma Conway.

One, she's Digital's superstar.

Rumor is, Roberts wouldn't even have his job under the CIO without the goodwill he received from an e-signature project she pulled off five years ago.

Two, she comes from money. Not billionaire big, but the designer threads and that icy attitude make it clear she thinks she's above everyone else.

Cosplaying as a civilian is a hell of a way to get your kicks, but I'm not going to give her a gold star for getting her hands a little dirty. Some of us had to climb our way out of that dirt just to be in the same room with her.

She eyes me down. "That moment was mine, and you stole it. I worked my ass off for over a year. Designed the workflows, tested every aspect, wrote every piece of training material for it. Did you know that? Every word of every work instruction, every training video, every tip and trick was me."

I didn't, but it doesn't change anything.

"Yeah, and then you zipped it together and handed it off to the rest of us to roll the damn thing out."

Everything about her is severe, from the cut of her trousers to the murder in her eyes.

It's infuriating how beautiful she is.

"I didn't have a choice," she says, crossing her arms over her white blazer. "I couldn't exactly meet with all four thousand employees and hold their hands while they complained a button was in the wrong place."

God forbid she do the real work. Instead, I was out there, grinding my ass, hand-holding engineers. "No, of course not. That's a job for us lesser humans."

Her glare intensifies. Guess she's not used to being called out on her shit. Well, tough.

"I'm not saying you didn't have to do your share of work," she starts.

"Funny, that's exactly how it sounds."

"*But,*" she stresses, slipping out of her professional tone into something grittier, "Do you have any idea what it felt like for me when the COO got up in front of every single person here and personally thanked *you* for your hard work on the rollout when my name wasn't even mentioned?"

"I earned that thank-you. After Digital dumped the system on us—"

She huffs at that, but I ignore it. I'm sick of corporate thinking they can mandate additional shit and then act surprised when we can't magically find extra time or people to complete it.

"I was the one who had to deliver it and all of your

training to every person working in Operations. Engineer by engineer, day in and day out, listening to all those complaints you didn't want to field. So yeah, when I had the chance to get a pat on the back, I took it." I stand, smoothing my tie. Was it bullshit? Yes. Am I going to flay myself so she can feel better? Hell no. We both wanted recognition. She's just pissed I beat her to it. "I assumed we'd both get thanked, but what the brass does is out of my control."

Emma slowly rises from her chair. God, even her watch screams money. Gold band, classic face, probably vintage. It makes my twenty-year-old Casio look like garbage.

"Nothing is ever your fault, is it?" she asks.

As an insult, it's so ridiculous, I could laugh. If she wants to hurt me, her aim is way off.

I can wear the right clothes and say all the right things, but I'll never stop expecting life to pull the rug out from under me. Good things don't come if I wait for them, and I have no interest in rolling over because she's upset about not being publicly applauded.

"Maybe next time your parents should send the CEO a nicer gift basket." For all I know, she's drinking buddies with the guy. The rich play a different game.

The way her jaw drops feels like victory.

"You don't know anything about me."

True. But I know all I need to know.

Rich, beautiful, talented. Forget the silver platter, Emma's life is probably dipped in gold.

Only one of us has opportunity in short supply, and it's not her.

"Yeah, well, ditto." I stuff my hands in my pockets and rock back on my heels. "But I bet it's real rough sailing through life with a black card and a handshake."

Emma flinches, and pain flashes in her eyes. Fuck. I've been in enough fights to know when a hit lands. Great, now I feel like an asshole.

I scrub a hand down my face. "Look, I'm trying to apologize here."

Trying and failing spectacularly. If Reese were here, the look of disappointment she'd give me would be enough to take a good ten years off my life.

I'm only twenty-nine. I'm not ready to watch my salt intake and say shit like "back in my day…"

"Oh," Emma says, her eyes cold. "Will the apology be joining us?"

I let out a breath and consider quitting. Anything's gotta be better than offering myself up as Emma's personal punching bag for the rest of the year.

If I hadn't earned my shot at this role, I would just walk away.

But if I backed off every time someone didn't like me, I wouldn't have made it out of middle school. Foster kids with smart mouths don't win a lot of favors, but that's what made victory so sweet when I finally learned how to beat the bastards at their own game.

Now I can walk into a room and have anyone I want chasing me like I'm a cheerleader in a frat house.

The moment hangs in the air, tight and tense between us.

When I don't respond, she lets out a frustrated huff. "Excellent apology. No, really. Ten out of ten."

When Emma walked into that meeting room a year ago, I was too pissed about corporate once again dumping its changes on Ops to stop myself from mouthing off. By the time I got my head out of my ass, I'd ruined any chance I had of changing her mind about me.

And now I've ruined the apology on top of that.

She should have been named during the company briefing. Even if the system sucked, the e-signature work was a lifesaver, and some of the staunchest of guys in Ops are still grumbling their thanks about that project, which is practically akin to professing their undying love.

Honestly, I can name half a dozen improvements her name has been attached to, so I don't know why she's treating this role like it's a life-and-death situation.

Her time will come again.

Meanwhile, if I'm promoted, I can finally stop checking my bank balance fifty times a day. I want to take a damn vacation and stop fake laughing at jokes told by sulfur-fueled jackasses in upper management.

I want to stop pretending I like golf, for fuck's sake.

"You're right," I say, because I'm a lot of things, but I've never wanted scumbag to be one of them. "I'm sorry."

Her eyes widen and her lips part, and there's a moment where we're just two people forced into the same crappy situation.

"Thank you," she says quietly, a hint of softness peeking through.

Damn, what I wouldn't give to crack her wide open. See if there's more under there.

"Though I would have appreciated it more if you'd said it months ago."

So much for that.

"Well." I clap my hands once. "This has been great, but I still have my actual job to do."

"I look forward to working with you," she says, looking as pained as I feel.

I sigh. No matter what Roberts says, there won't be any working together. Emma might have grown up with a silver spoon in her mouth, but I was born with a pair of brass knuckles; I won't go down without a fight.

With that, she turns on her heel and leaves.

I ignore how much colder the room feels after she's gone.

CHAPTER 4
YOU CAN TAKE THE STRAY OUT OF THE SHELTER...
CHARLIE

Nights and weekends, I swap cuffs for collars.

All because my sister is living her dream of running a rescue shelter.

We might not be related by blood, but I'll do anything for Reese, and at least three nights a week, *anything* translates to *whatever she volunteers me for*.

I love it almost as much as I love her, and that's a hell of a lot. I'll gladly take shoveling this shit over the hot air Roberts spews, and also, what kind of monster doesn't want to spend their spare time around puppies?

They're *puppies*.

I brace myself beside Reese, who's staring down a tabby named Saffron. "Ready?" I ask.

She nods.

"I'll open on three," I say. "You grab her."

"Careful, she's scrappy."

Saffron eyes me like it's high noon, poised and ready to strike. It's the exact same look a teenage Reese used to give me when I'd drag her out of bed before nine a.m.

"I can handle you, can't I?"

Chuckling, I duck out of the way before her elbow can hit me.

Once the stubborn kitty is safely out of the way, we get to work freshening up the kennels. The small inner-city pet rescue only has space for six dogs and eight cats, but Reese and Mae work their asses off to find a loving home for every single animal that joins us.

Reese follows after me, replacing blankets and water as we go. "Let me get this straight. You'll still be doing your old job, plus working on this new project, and they aren't even giving you a raise?"

"Not a cent. They're calling it a stretch project," I say, rolling my eyes. "Free labor, basically."

"I will never regret going to vet school. Screw corporate life. Even if you earn twice what I do, I'll take four legs over two any day." She wrangles her chaos of red curls into a bun.

I throw my arm around her shoulders. "That's because you're the smart one."

Reese shakes her head, but it's true. I made my bed when I took this job. Would I rather be doing something I enjoyed, instead of drowning in emails every day? Damn right I would. But the pay's good and the money paved the way for my sister, so it's really no choice at all.

This is all Reese and I dreamed of as kids.

Pets meant forever, or as close to forever as two misfits in the foster system could imagine. Before Reese, the closest thing I could get to unconditional love came from animals. As long as I looked after them and loved them back, they'd never leave. They'd never decide there was something better out there.

Never dump me on the doorstep of a stranger and walk away.

Reese is the only person I trusted to stay by my side.

All the years we struggled, crammed into tiny apartments with neighbors who were extremely vocal and usually fighting, were worth it for this.

She's gotten her happy ending, and no one deserves it more.

It's been a long time since I dared to dream of my own ride-off-together-into-the-sunset ending, but as long as Reese has it, that's all I need.

She stills, hugging a blanket to her chest. "I feel responsible."

"Don't," I say, my tone firm. We've had this conversation too many times since Reese needed help getting this place off the ground. If only one of us gets to do right by the world, I'm glad it's her.

I can suck it up and take the hits. That's just what I do.

Besides, the locals love Pet Pawsitive. It's the best thing either of us has ever done, and I'm so fucking proud of her.

"Once I get this role, it'll get easier," I say.

She arches a brow. "That's what you said before you became a senior."

Don't I know it. I'm a broken record at this point, but that's why I'm going to make sure I make lead.

"Yeah, well. They said it would take five years before I would get promoted again, but I've done it in three."

Beside me, she shakes out the throw and lays it inside the cage, mouth pursed to the side. Classic thinking face. "And they really have you competing for it? Isn't that a little cruel?"

My pulse jumps at the thought of *her*, but I ignore it. "It's only cruel if we play into their game."

Her short laugh echoes off the cinderblock walls. "You're the most competitive person I know. I've seen you make grown men cry."

I smile at her.

Some of my proudest moments involve taking misogynistic dude bros to task. I may have broken a few knuckles, but it always felt like righting the wrongs of the universe, one left hook at a time.

These days I keep my fists holstered, but that doesn't mean I won't use everything else at my disposal to stand up for myself.

"Just be careful," Reese adds. "This chick's probably got it out for you, and for good reason, after what happened last year. I'm glad you apologized, at least."

Emma definitely has it out for me, but at the moment, I have bigger issues.

Ops couldn't care less that I'm being tasked with extra work. They hate that I was moved up to the twenty-fourth floor without their stamp of approval.

I don't blame them. The work won't stop just because I have ambitions. Throw in trying to outmaneuver Cruella, and it was already damn exhausting.

Beds, blankets, toys, bowls. Reese and I move like a

well-oiled machine until each kennel is fresh and clean and every paw is accounted for.

"Nice," she says, giving me a high five. "Thanks again for taking Saint last night. How did she do on her walk?"

I scratch behind the Great Dane's ears, and she wags her tail. "She's a trooper. Made it all the way to the second corner before we had to slow down. Should be able to visit her boyfriend next week."

"No limping?"

"None."

Reese sags in pure relief. Her heart is too pure for this world. "Fantastic. And you're still good to take Nugget for a doggie sleepover on Tuesday?"

"Of course. You know it's not a problem. Whatever—"

"Yeah, yeah. Anytime I need you, whatever I need," Reese teases.

Good to know I've gotten predictable.

"So," she drags out in a tone I know all too well. I brace myself. "Are you free Friday night?"

I eye her warily. "Should be, why?"

"Mae mentioned her cousin—"

I hold up a hand. "I'm gonna stop you right there." If I had a nickel for every time my sister set me up, I'd be richer than the Conways.

"She's a historian, Charlie, and she's super cute."

I set my hands on my hips. "Then you date her."

Mae—with perfect timing—chooses that moment to walk in with Nugget. Reese waits as her girlfriend and business partner secures the fluffy Maltese in the last kennel before catching her finger in Mae's belt loop, pulling her close, and slinging an arm around her waist.

"If Mae wasn't the love of my life, maybe I would," Reese says. "One date, Charlie. What's the harm?"

We've been having this conversation for two years. Ever since Lucy left and I decided relationships were too much trouble.

Yeah, it hurt, but it's not like I'm still pining for her. Last I heard, she's engaged. I'm happy for her. She dodged a bullet, honestly. I've never been good at anything I couldn't walk away from.

Breaking up was the best thing for both of us.

Who cares that every damn time I think about the future, Lucy's voice echoes in my mind, saying, "I don't think I ever loved you."

She wasn't the first to throw me aside, but I'll make sure she's the last.

Mae, as always, plays backup. "Bar hookups are fun and all, but don't you want something more?" She brushes her bangs out of her eyes, and the chain mail of earrings cascading around her ear glitter against her spiky black hair.

"No. I'm good with what I have right now."

And I am. For once in my godforsaken life, things are fine. There are no creditors after me, and our bills are paid.

Hell, I even have savings.

Things are fine.

"Don't get me wrong, I love how much you help us out around here, but you deserve to find love again. After what happened with Lucy—"

I toss my head back with a huff. "Enough of the chick flick moments. That was years ago. I'm over it. I'm perfectly happy getting what I need when I need it, no strings attached. I like it this way."

Reese throws her hands in the air. "Well, I tried. Now, get out of here. Go spend time in that empty apartment by yourself."

CHAPTER 5
AN EX-ISTENTIAL CRISIS
EMMA

Saturdays are sacred.

An hour of Ivy and me sweating our way through a weekly Pilates class, followed by an even longer gossip session over lattes.

But today? Today is special.

As of this morning (and half of this month's salary), my parents are officially debt free, so Ivy and I have come to Mint. Sure, I could eat for a week on what the chicken piccata costs, and the combination of moss-myrtle-lime décor is making my eyes sore, but the food is so good that I can almost, *almost*, forgive the pretentious atmosphere.

"That's ridiculous," Ivy groans, stabbing her fork into her mesclun salad. "You've earned that job four times over."

"I know." I exhale out the frustration. I lay my napkin over my plate and thank the waiter who comes to collect it. "And don't even get me started on Charlie."

Months of hard work unrecognized, but apparently, it's not Charlie's fault because "boys will be boys." The scream I want to let out could probably count as a renewable resource.

"At least he apologized."

It's true. Those are words I never thought I'd hear from him. Though I'm not sure how to feel about it. I should accept it, but the memory of being passed over still stings like an ice burn on the tip of my tongue.

A better person would forgive and forget.

But I'm not ready.

How can a simple apology make up for what he did?

Why does forgiveness feel more like a sacrifice than a blessing?

"You know, he and I started at the same time," Ivy says. "No one has a bad word to say about him."

"Of course they don't. Apparently, I'm the only one he's rude to."

It's dangerous to let Charlie get under my skin, but I can't help it. He couldn't even say sorry without insulting me. And when he brought up money, all I wanted was to hurt him back.

There's no way Charlie could know how deep that cut runs. The whole point of giving up everything I had was to ensure no one found out how much trouble my parents were in.

To the rest of the world, I'm still the perfectly privileged daughter on a field trip to see how the 99 percent live.

Truth is, I love my job. I wouldn't give it up for all the zeros in the world.

"Emma?"

I turn at the sound of the familiar voice, a thrill running through me.

Logan Williamson Cross.

Ex-boyfriend. Manager of special projects (a.k.a. fancy intern) at his dad's firm. Can usually be found enjoying a meal at any one of the fine dining restaurants throughout the city. Currently standing in front of me, blond hair falling casually over his forehead and beckoning my fingers to tame it, looking just as good as he did when we split up three months ago.

Possibly better.

Fond hearts aren't trouble for no reason. And mine thumps heavily as I take him in.

"Logan, wow. What a surprise." Cue the polite hug and kiss. "You look great." Memories of us tumble out of the closet I crammed them into, crashing into me with a force that makes my knees go weak.

There's day-old scruff darkening his jaw. It's a look I've never seen from Logan before. In the year we dated, he was meticulous about grooming. Even now, it's clear it's deliberate. It makes him more distinguished. A replica of his father.

Logan Senior must be delighted.

"Fancy seeing you here," he says.

Yes, what a complete coincidence that I in no way hoped for.

I duck my head. "I remember how much you love it."

He leans in and lowers his voice conspiratorially. "Let me guess, you had the piccata."

"Guilty as charged," I admit, pleased he remembered. "It's too good to pass up."

Logan appraises me, his expression intent. "Some things are."

My skin heats. Oh, how I've missed this. "How was Europe?"

He shrugs, casual. "The same. Ate too much pasta, drank too much wine…"

"Raised your father's blood pressure by not working enough," I finish for him and am delighted when he laughs.

There's been a lonely ache in my life since he broke it off, and while I've tried to ignore it, it's the reason I picked this place for lunch. Seeing him again and making him smile only makes it more obvious I've missed him.

Is it too much to hope he misses me too?

"How are you?" he asks. "Your folks are all right?"

"I'm good," I say, breezing past the second question. I never told Logan the truth about my parents' financial state, and I still feel guilty about it. "At least as good as I can be before the 'event season' starts."

He smiles knowingly. Our parents have been friends for over a decade and have worked together on my parents' foundation, hosting every party under the sun. "I'm sorry I missed the garden party last month. It was always more enjoyable with you. Although Mom mentions the upcoming fundraiser every chance she gets."

"Will you come this year? My parents would love to see you." *Please say yes.* "So would I."

He doesn't respond right away. Just studies me.

My breathing picks up as I wait. In the year we were together, it was easy to read him, but now I can only wonder... and hope.

God, if he gives me the standard "let's catch up soon" line—otherwise known as the polite way of saying "I hate you and never want to see you again"—I might melt into the carpet out of humiliation.

His eyes fill with a mix of sympathy and pity. I'm suddenly sure he's about to let me down gently, and after this week, I can't stand to hear it.

"Besides, it'll be good to show our parents that we've both moved on," I rush out, and before I know it, I'm adding, "Especially now that I'm seeing someone."

Oh, hello. There is the hungry look I remember.

"That's news," he says in a neutral voice, but my pulse is skipping. Maybe I shouldn't have lied, but the proof is there. He hasn't forgotten us either.

I might stand a chance of getting him back.

"It's early, but it's going well. Really well."

"I'm glad." But the strain in his smile says otherwise. "I guess I'll see you soon, then. You really do look good."

As he kisses my cheek, I'm enveloped in his thick, woodsy aftershave. I breathe deeply, as though there might be a way to hold a piece of him when he leaves, some faint connection to tide me over until I can get him back.

When he turns to leave, I force myself not to watch him go.

Ivy clears her throat. "Have you been hiding a boyfriend I don't know about?"

"Yes," I say, sliding back into my seat. "I let him out Tuesdays and Thursdays. It keeps him from getting stale."

Ivy tosses her head back and laughs. "Logan didn't look very happy about it."

My gaze drifts to the door, but all that's left of him is the tingling where his lips brushed my cheek. "He didn't, did he?"

And like all good document controllers, Ivy has an acute attention for detail. "You still miss him."

I turn back to her and sink a little in my seat. "Is that ridiculous? It's been three months since we ended things."

I've been afraid to admit it. Gutsy and glamorous, she's the greatest friend I've ever had. I can't stand the idea of disappointing her.

Ivy sets a hand flat on the table and leans forward. "How you feel is not ridiculous. I just don't want to see you get hurt."

What a precious gem of a human. "I know, and I love you for that."

"He did seem genuinely happy to see you."

Hope springs up inside me. "Do you think so?" I really want to believe her. We left things unfinished, ending with a *maybe later* that I wasn't sure would ever come. But now… "I was supposed to use this time to work things out, and I'm no closer to an answer."

"You're being too hard on yourself. If he really cares about you, it won't matter to him that you can't—"

"It matters to me," I say. I want him back, but I can't handle disappointing us both a second time. "Whatever is stalling me in the bedroom needs to be fixed. If I can do that before the fundraiser, then we stand a chance at making it work."

"If you're sure," Ivy says.

I am. I've never been more certain of anything.

All problems have solutions, even intimate ones. When Logan and I were together, I hoped all I needed was time, but the issue grew like mold, invisible to the eye until it was too late.

Now I'm determined.

If I'm going to get Logan back, I need to solve this. And as monumental as it feels, it'll be a hell of a lot easier than the Charlie-sized obstacle I have.

CHAPTER 6
SETTING THE STANDARD
EMMA

Let the record show that I do not enjoy being deceptive. Or unhelpful.

Despite what I promised Ivy and myself—and the mantra I repeated ten times while applying mascara this morning—I'm not sure I can be ruthless when it comes to Charlie.

Where do I even start?

Probably not with the coffee I bought as a peace offering.

As I place the piping-hot hazelnut mocha on his empty desk, I know Ivy is somewhere, shaking her head at me.

May my parents rejoice in years of etiquette lessons finally having taken root, I guess. At least I know they never managed to put out the fire in me.

See? I may be accommodating and unfailingly polite even when I'm imagining where a pencil could do the most damage (it's probably the neck, but the testicles would be so much more satisfying), but polite does not mean passive.

So when Charlie greets my olive branch with nothing but an amused brow raise, I know one thing for sure.

He better be ready for a fight.

———

Calling the procedure bloated and illegible is being kind.

It'd be a hell of a lot easier if we were simply tweaking a few sentences and deleting references to the old system before patting ourselves on the back for a job half-done.

But I refuse to let the opportunity to really make a change slip through my fingers. As far as I can tell, all anyone's ever done with this procedure is patch it with Band-Aids and duct tape for years.

That stops now.

If they want future proofing, I'll give it to them. Worst-case scenario, all of my ideas are shot down and we keep using the same old standard we've been dragging behind us for at least a decade.

Best-case scenario? I finally earn my promotion.

In lieu of working *with* Charlie, I've split the document in half. On the surface, it's an even division of labor between the two of us, a minor lie that Roberts accepted.

In reality, I've given Charlie the thankless job of covering retention and engineering metadata—the former is a wasteland of regulatory red tape, and the latter a series of unending contentious arguments with Projects.

That'll keep him busy while I focus on the real work.

There's no missing the moment he's read my email.

"What the hell?" Charlie grits out, looming over his computer.

"Keep your voice down," I hiss.

His blue eyes are blazing. "Oh, I'm sorry," he says in a stage-whisper, "are you worried someone will over-hear how well we're working together?"

I stand and meet his accusing stare, then throw a glance over his shoulder toward Roberts's office. The door's open, but I can't tell whether he's inside.

Quickly, I stalk into the nearest empty meeting room, waving madly and glaring back at Charlie until he follows me inside.

Most days, wearing heels puts me on top of the world, but today I am a sovereign.

Ruler of Charlie's goddamn *universe*, and he better be ready to take a knee.

"Okay, you've got me alone now." He stuffs his hands into his pockets. "Care to explain?"

It's the first time we've stood this close, and as I'm staring him down, all I can think is *I never realized how tall he is*. He's only got a few inches on me, and it puts him at what Ivy would call a "perfectly kissable" height.

No one's lips can be that naturally plump.

Charlie, of all people, should *not* be allowed.

I inch forward, refusing to back down. "Weren't you

the one complaining about having a real job to do? I'm simply taking the bulk of responsibility off you."

With a disbelieving huff, he fixes his tie and steps even closer.

I've always adored neckties. Watching someone put them on, take them off, finding other fun uses for them… well. There's a lot to love.

Except when it comes to Charlie Walker.

Especially while he stands there in a charcoal waistcoat and narrow black tie, pretending to be sorry for risking my career.

Given the chance, I'd like to wring his neck with it.

He has the audacity to smile. "You know, if you really wanted to beat me, you'd give me something harder."

A bark of laughter escapes me. "Oh, I'm sure you'd love something hard to beat."

He slides a little closer, propping one hand on the wall beside me. His cologne is the deep, intense sort that I usually love.

It's like he was designed in a lab to bother me on every level. His suits, his scent, those damn lips—

"Got something on your mind, sweetheart?"

Heart skipping, I pull my gaze from his mouth.

"You wish." I glare, ignoring the goose bumps that have spread along my spine. "We have a deadline. If you can't do your part—"

He pushes off the wall and steps back, slipping his hands into his pockets. "I'm not the one who has a problem here. Unlike some, I don't always need to be in control."

The jibe lodges itself between my ribs, twisting until the back of my throat stings.

It's true, in more ways than he can possibly understand. Letting go isn't easy for me, but I need to try.

What's ironic is that my entire life feels out of my control. My parents, my body, my job.

And here comes Charlie, swanning in at the last minute, accusing me of what? Wanting to be in charge of my own destiny?

What a horrific fate for a woman.

Well, he can take that opinion and shove it up his extremely attractive ass. I'm not backing down.

I doubt he'd feel any guilt if our situations were reversed. Hell, he probably doesn't feel anything at all.

I'm getting this promotion. And not only that; I'm getting Logan back.

"Roberts has already approved it. So I'll do my thing and you can do yours, and we won't have to even talk to each other."

"Fine."

"Great," I grit out.

CHAPTER 7
FIRE VS. FLAME
EMMA

As the turnstile flashes green, I step through the open bi-fold gates, then stride across the polished marble floor toward the bank of elevators.

By the time I spot the traitorous head of brown hair, it's already too late to hide.

Charlie steps onto the elevator, and I pray it closes before I reach it, but why would I get lucky now? His eyes meet mine as soon as he turns around, and he smiles as he throws an arm out to hold the doors.

"Don't," I grumble, tightening my hands into fists. "Don't you dare hold the elevator for me, Charlie."

I'm not sure I can survive standing close to him again.

"Better hurry up, Emma," he sings out, and the butterflies in my stomach take flight.

Two weeks in and I'm still not used to him.

I huff. Debate it. Hate him a little more.

The doors chime a warning.

I shoot him a glare as I step in. Not that Charlie

cares. He looks happier and more attractive than ever, leaning back against the rail, ankles crossed, a cobalt cashmere sweater making his eyes sing brightly as they lay into me.

What I'd give to wipe that smirk right off his face.

Bad luck used to be sold-out shows and parking tickets and not finding the shoes I love in my size.

Now it's two little words, dripping with sarcasm and a twang I cannot escape, even in my dreams.

"Morning, sunshine."

I say nothing, keeping my eyes fixed on the number panel.

He hums. It's a deep rumble. "Not a morning person?"

"I'm not talking to you."

Even his laugh is smug: rich and loud and confident. "Could've fooled me."

It takes willpower, but I won't look at him. Even though I can feel the heat of his gaze on my skin as sure as if he were touching me.

It's been two torturous weeks of Charlie Walker and that damn smile sitting opposite me.

There used to be a buffer of eight floors between us.

I miss that buffer.

"Good morning," I say, sounding anything but good.

"Did you wake up on the wrong side of the bed again? I know a few tricks for that."

I finally give in to temptation, and dammit, he looks good.

Do they still give keys to the city as rewards for

community contributions? Because whoever tailored Charlie's pants deserves one. Or an honorary knighthood.

If a petition is needed, I have no doubt that everyone in this building would sign it.

"I'm shocked anyone sticks around that long." The instant the words are out, I want to take them back. I shouldn't even be thinking about his love life. It's none of my business. But it shuts him up.

I stare at the elevator doors, my stomach churning with guilt.

Now that I've seen him interact with other people, I understand exactly what Ivy was talking about. The man is so charming, I doubt he needs any help warming his bed. Hell, knowing my luck, he secretly has a heart of gold and saves puppies in his spare time.

Yeah, and I'm the next queen of Atlantis.

————

Subject: RE: Document group terminology

Emma, I've reviewed the wording you sent through. I'm disappointed. The goal of simplifying the process appears to mean "remove all boundaries," and while I'm sure Engineering will be pleased that Controlled Documents are relatively unscathed, there seems to be a large disconnect where highly sensitive contractual information exists. I would have expected you to understand this, but perhaps we need to get everyone in a room to realign expectations.

· · ·

The response from the Procurements lead is damning and, frankly, confusing. If he'd read the procedure, he would have seen the detailed note I left in the second paragraph, outlining how contractual information is universally considered as a confidential class document, and thus, is the sole exception to the managed rule.

So why does his email—with Roberts cc'd in, because why not make this worse?—sound like I threatened to take his firstborn son?

Five years in, and it still shocks me how often women in this field receive emails like this.

We don't get grace for errors. We don't get friendly reminders. We get ignored, talked over, debated, corrected, explained to. *Managed.*

Returning to my original email, I open the link to the document and immediately see the problem.

That very important paragraph I wrote is gone.

One guess who is responsible.

Speaking of evil, Charlie's voice catches my attention from outside of Roberts's office. Look at them, chatting away, all buddy-buddy. Whatever Charlie is saying, Roberts is pleased. The man is smiling. I didn't even know his face could do that.

It's been less than a month, and he's already got Roberts eating out of the palm of his hand.

I hate how Charlie has no trouble being heard. I hate how easy it is for him to be respected. If he sits quietly in a meeting, he's assessing and thoughtful.

If I do it, I'm not paying attention.

"Speak up more" are three words I never want to

hear again. It's the "you'd be pretty if you smiled" of the corporate world. I want to rage quit every time it's uttered.

But speaking up is a gamble. If I could say the right thing, that unknowable correct answer, I'd be golden, like Mr. Walker over there. Free entry into the club. Pass GO. Collect two hundred dollars.

But say the wrong thing, and suddenly I'm too opinionated, too emotional.

My ire only increases when I view the document's edit history and find the last person who accessed it and made changes is none other than Roberts.

I bite down on the scream building inside me.

The audacity of men might be the only thing more endless than the known universe. Larger than we can fathom, always expanding, and guaranteed to eventually decimate all forms of life.

They end their conversation by Charlie's desk, and Roberts turns to me. By the way he instantly sobers, I know he's read the email.

"Emma. I hope you'll be clearing up that misunderstanding with Procurement today."

Shame washes over me, and I swallow past the tightness in my throat. "Yes, sir."

Oh, I'll be clearing it up. And then I'll be locking my document down.

All I want is to do my job, without interference.

Of course that would rely on Charlie abiding by the rules.

. . .

"You talked to legal without me?" I ask two hours later, after my meeting invite comes back declined with a curt "this has already been discussed."

Charlie only shrugs. "You told me to take on retention, and it led me to legal. I'm just doing as I'm told."

Like hell he is.

I'm starting to think he enjoys getting under my skin.

No matter. Charlie might be good, but I'm better.

"Fine. Since you're already working with them, you can take over the security labels, but I'm taking back metadata requirements."

He raises a brow. "You better not cut projects out of the loop on that one."

I sigh. I had really hoped I wouldn't have to talk with them, but he's right.

"I can handle projects," I say, and I'm only half lying.

———

I had hoped that in a building this big, I'd have no problem avoiding the one person I don't want to see.

So, imagine my surprise when I arrive at my next meeting to find Charlie perched happily beside the Project lead, Samir.

"Emma, it's good to finally meet you." He stands and holds out a hand. "I hope you don't mind that I invited Charlie to sit in. He knows our requirements backward and forward."

"Of course," I lie, sliding my hand into his. "The more the merrier."

Across the table, Charlie winks.

CHAPTER 8
THE PROBLEM WITH FIGHTING IS I LOVE IT
CHARLIE

It's too late to say this, but capitalism was definitely a mistake.

And I say that as a man who's spent more than I'm comfortable admitting on ties and wingtip shoes.

Every day, my patience is tested by companies whose profits could fund humanitarian causes, but instead line the pockets of eccentric millionaires.

"Sea-tec?" I ask Drue.

He nods. There's a sunburn peeking out from above his collar and a twitch in his eye that he always gets when he's almost certain he's fucked something up and needs me to save him.

"No," I say, "they'll hold their IP hostage until after final investment. You'll only get the renditions for now. Don't even try for the natives unless you want to be trapped in a room with Pegrum while he drills their confidentiality clause into your skull."

"Yeah, no thanks." He lets out an uneasy chuckle. "Okay, so I should just map the PDFs for migration?"

I feel for him. Drue is the only other DC in Operations, and he's the only one on level twelve now, which means he's fielding the majority of face-to-face visits from disgruntled engineers. Not that half of them haven't found their way up to see me despite that.

"Send me the doc schedule. I'll tee up something with pre-ops and the DAT team and flick you an invite. They won't be happy about the tag to doc stuff, but they're good guys. And if we can't get them over the line, a few beers will."

"Thanks, Charlie. I owe you."

He owes me a few, but I won't hold him to it.

"Course, man. I've got your back."

———

The new building feels like a spaceship.

Each desk curves like the monitors we use. They all rise to standing and are set up with Bluetooth accessories and built-in phone chargers.

There's even ambient noise playing overhead. All day, every day.

HR calls it sound-scaping, which is just about the wankiest title I've ever heard. Reese and I have spent hours debating what kinds of sounds Starfleet would use.

Her money's on black noise, but I like to think Kirk's a Slash fan.

The building is nice, but all the fancy technology in the world can't disguise how impersonal it is.

No artwork or color of any kind. No name tags or

photos to tell us whose desk is whose. No forgetting that we're replaceable.

All it would take is a few strong-armed security guards and a wet wipe, and bam. Clean slate.

Of course, there is one perk to my new location. The view.

Emma's layers come off at the start of the day, when she has the most steam. By three p.m., they're back on, and when she thinks no one is watching, she'll warm her fingers by trapping them under her thighs.

It's enough to give a man ideas.

There are other things I'm noticing too.

She never takes a lunch break unless Ivy forces her to. Most days, the only time she'll stop working is when she makes her habitual trips to the kitchen. Often, I'll find her, arms crossed, staring out at the city skyline, lost in thought, during the three minutes it takes for the coffee machine to finish.

I've taken to not looking out the window too much while working here. Too much temptation, too many exit roads.

I've worked in Operations for six years, which makes it the longest I've spent anywhere. It's making me antsy, eager for a change.

I'm convinced I'm not the settling down type. No matter how much Reese and I talked about it as kids, I've never been able to shake the itch to pick up and go.

Where the hell does someone like Emma go? And why do my feet ache with the urge to follow her there?

Back at her desk, she throws her head back and groans. It elongates the mile-long stretch of her neck, which I've been distracted by all morning. Glamorous is the only way to describe her. Sharp, serious, infuriating… and utterly sexy.

"Do you have to chew so loudly?" she asks.

There's nothing sexier than getting Emma flustered. Her breathing speeds up, and her cheeks flare pink, and I finally get a glimpse of something real. It makes my heart rate take off every damn time.

"Sure. I can stop breathing as well, if you want?"

She narrows her eyes. "That boyish charm might win Roberts over, but it won't work on me."

"You think I'm charming?" I give her a winning smile.

It always makes her glare harder.

During every meeting, she's a pro. Prepared, polite. In complete control.

So knowing I can crack open that calm exterior to the brimstone underneath?

Well…

It's like a big red button taunting me—*Don't press.*

Of course I'm going to want to.

"Anything else I can do for you, boss?"

Her mouth tightens. "Don't you have a meeting with Technology to get to?"

Interesting. Someone's keeping an eye on my calendar. I'm not even surprised. Every time I update her doc —and Christ, she's even got me calling it *her* doc now— my sections have been reworded.

The lack of subtlety pisses me off even more than the blatant micromanagement, because come on, if you're going to screw me over, at least try to be sneaky about it.

Surely she's better than this.

On top of that, I can immediately see every gaping sinkhole our vendors are gonna use to get out of jail free, since charging us extra for our fuckups is their favorite pastime.

It's disappointing.

I can see some promise in the parts she's written, but it doesn't change the fact that we're competing. Emma doesn't seem to have forgotten, that's for sure.

So I'll follow her rules… to a point. It's not my business if she underestimates me. I'm used to that.

———

"I've already talked to Emma about this. You really didn't need to waste your time."

Jocelyn is younger than I'm expecting, which throws me off balance for a whopping five seconds before the version of Reese in my head slaps me for being *that guy*.

But I'm nothing if not adaptable.

So I quickly throw out the speech I prepared, because if I'm right—and I usually am about these things—I've been set up to disprove what was supposed to be a landslide victory for Tech. Now, in order to do that without burning this bridge, I'll have to get creative.

I smooth down my tie and give her the kind of charming smile that works on just about everyone but Emma. "Indulge me."

She nods. Good, now to sell it.

"Have you ever been out to site?"

With a shake of her head, she says, "No, I haven't had the chance yet."

"That's a shame. It's worth the trip. Although the helicopter training is a doozy."

She smiles, right on cue.

Look, if hell and heaven and all that crap actually existed, meetings like this are without a doubt someone's cosmic idea of torture. What's the saying? Death by a thousand cuts? Yeah, like that, but in expensive business wear.

"Did you realize that the system runs 40 percent slower on average at our sites than at headquarters?"

She presses her lips together. "I didn't."

"I only mention it because when we remove the—granted, arbitrary—file-size limit, we risk allowing files so large they can't actually be opened. If that document was, say, a safety-critical piping diagram during a shutdown, well…"

I let the implications paint their own picture.

The real solution would be to improve the site tech, but that'll never get across the line. It makes zero sense to me and will be the first debate I have with management once I'm the lead.

But I can sell the best solution later. Right now, I only need to get her to agree with me.

"Look, I'll be honest," I continue, "there's only a slim chance of a safety incident, because regulations state that hard copies of all critical documents must be on site, but do you really want to take a risk on a slim chance?"

By the way her lips purse, it's obvious I've landed it. No one wants their name coming up in an audit.

"No, I don't. All right, what would you say is the best option?"

And sold, to the scrappy fighter from the north.

———

After eight hours of back-to-back meetings and dealing with half a dozen engineers who can't understand what Do Not Disturb means, all I want is to shove something greasy down my throat before I pass out. Add a few beers, and I'm good. I'll drink them lying down. I don't care.

The only good part about my job is the paycheck. Every cent I haven't saved has been spent on the essentials—clothes that make people take me seriously, and a memory foam mattress I'd commit crimes for.

It's not much, but it's mine.

Reese doesn't know what she's talking about. I'm not lonely; I'm fine.

I've got a decent life.

Gym, work, home. Visit the shelter a few times a week or a bar if it's the weekend. If I'm lucky, I get laid.

It's not as bleak as she makes it out to be. I've come a long way since the days of electricity roulette, hoping we wouldn't short out the building if we rolled the dice and used the microwave at the same time as the toaster.

I bet Emma has never had to worry about that sort of thing.

Weeks of working together, and still, nothing about her makes any damn sense.

With a name like Conway and the sort of money she comes from, she should have a seat on the board, not be sweating her ass off in a low-level position.

I, however, have scraped every win together with my teeth and fingernails.

With me, she's everything she's always been—cold, harsh, entitled—but to everyone else, she's a different person. Sweeter, joyful. It rubs. What the hell do I have to do to get her to smile at me like that?

(Unfuck that briefing, probably).

I just wish I could stop thinking about her damn eyes.

CHAPTER 9
THESE HEELS WERE MADE FOR CRUSHING YOU
EMMA

Yesterday, when Charlie joked that I couldn't last a day without caffeine, I was cocky. This morning, I regret everything.

Holding my eyes open has become a feat as challenging as separating the jaws of life. I can't remember ever being this tired before, including the nights spent panic-cramming for exams.

I should never have agreed to his bet, but any time I think about him, every time he throws me a teasing wink, an inferno rises within me, urging me closer, to fight fire with fire. It's like nothing I've ever known before.

Charlie wears a gleeful smile as I stalk into the office, those damn blue eyes dancing.

I'm tired, cranky, and fifteen minutes late.

I've never been late in my life.

I'm going to kill him.

"Morning, s—"

I slap a hand to his desk, the sound loud in the quiet space. "Don't even think about finishing that sentence."

He smiles wider. "I keep telling you, you drink too much caffeine for your own good."

If I plan it right, they'll never find the body.

I cross my arms and attempt to glare, but it's ruined by a long yawn. "I did it, all right? Proved your little point. Now hand over the beans."

He leans back in his chair, legs spread and a pleased fucking grin on his face. *I hate him I hate him I hate him.* All James Dean swagger in a six-button waistcoat.

God, he's gorgeous.

"I don't know," he says, rocking back. "It's only been one day. Don't you want to see how long you can go? Anticipation is the best part."

Very carefully, I lower my foot onto his, slowly increasing the pressure until his smile falters. "Charlie." My voice is low, sharp as a steel blade. "Hand it over."

There's a heated moment where our eyes are locked and I'm certain he's going to make me suffer. But the way he licks his lips and flexes his toes makes me pause.

I press a little harder in challenge, and his eyes darken. It hits me like lightning, flashing bright and hot through me.

Oh.

He's enjoying this.

Even worse, so am I.

With his focus steadily trained on me, he opens the drawer to his right and pulls out my bag of ambrosia. The instant he places it in my hand, I let out a sigh. I blame withdrawal for the way I snatch it up and immediately bury my nose in the package, moaning as the smell of sweet, sweet coffee hits me.

All right, I'll admit it: I might have a problem.

Charlie says nothing, and his expression gives away even less.

I spend ten minutes slowing my heart rate down and the rest of the day trying to forget how much I wanted to crawl into his lap.

CHAPTER 10

IN THE ROBOT UPRISING, THEY'LL COME AFTER ME FIRST

EMMA

"What," I grit out, clenching my hand, my nails digging painfully into my palm, "the hell is wrong with you? You heinous piece of programming… I hope you catch a virus."

I hit save. *Error.*

I lean down to hiss at the machine. "I hope the guy who coded you never knows a moment of peace in his entire—" Again. *Error.* "Fucking—" Third time's the charm. *Error.* The screen freezes. "Life. Ugh."

I fight the urge to cry. I'm about to lose hours of work, and I really don't think I have the energy to start over today. Not without a bottle of something strong.

A shadow appears over my screen. "Oh, good. Roberts is locked out of the procedure and needs a copy, and here I was, worried you were in a bad mood."

Right, yes, of course. Why stick me in hell without the devil being present?

No matter how badly I need a break from this man, every time I turn around, there Charlie is. If I send files to the printer on the other side of the floor, he still finds me. I can't escape him.

I clear the cache and try again. *Failed.* A scream dies in my throat.

This laptop and I officially have beef.

"There is a fire that will burn until eternity circles around on itself," I mutter, ignoring Charlie. This computer will not be the end of me.

"And it will be fueled," I whisper, "by my never-ending hatred for you."

This morning, this white pantsuit made me feel powerful, but here I am, only a few hours later, being bested by a microchip.

I will not destroy company property. Not after what happened with the teleconference screen last year.

"That's an impressive speech. Do I say amen now or wait for the choir?" Without asking, Charlie plants himself on my desk.

In protest, I don't let myself notice how tightly stretched his pants are at the thighs.

I definitely notice.

I'll say one thing—he makes Tom Ford look good. Broad lines, sharp angles… all perfectly contrasting that pout. Charlie is a lesson in distraction.

But I will not be moved.

"Go away, Charlie."

"I'd love to do that, sweetheart," he says, grasping the edge of the desk on either side of his obscenely muscular thighs. "But boss's orders are to find out what's holding up the review draft. So why don't you hand it over, and I'll put you out of your misery?"

To do that, he'd need something a lot sharper than that wit of his.

"Don't you think that if I could, I would have already? Why do you think I'm yelling at this piece of useless, incompetent, broken—"

In one quick move, Charlie straightens and spins me away from the keyboard, his touch making my pulse jump. "Whoa, whoa, whoa. Let's take a breath. Come on, in and out, just follow me."

The heat of his hands radiates through my linen shirt. *Spark, meet flame.* This close, the deep, intoxicating smell of his cologne is unavoidable. It's nice. Like stepping under a waterfall or digging my toes into cool sand.

"That's better," he says.

It's only when I come back to myself that I realize he's rubbing circles on the inside of my wrist. It's incredibly soothing.

As I blink up at him, he clears his throat and quickly drops my hand.

"Thank you," I say softly, lightness fluttering in my belly. Maybe he can be helpful. *Occasionally.*

"There's morning tea for everyone in the kitchen. I figured you'd be too busy overthinking, so I brought you a bit of everything."

I blink again and zero in on a plate filled with an assortment of treats. Another of Charlie's skills is apparently sniffing out free food.

"Are you secretly a beagle? Or did Amy tip you off again?"

"First thing I learned growing up was if you wanna

eat, you gotta get in quick. The second thing I learned," he says, sliding the plate closer, "is to never turn down good pie."

The golden flaky crust is practically calling my name. My stomach rumbles. "And this is good, is it?"

"Top five." He grins around his own mouthful. "The best is PJ's on fifth. Their pecan will make you question things."

It's annoying how adorable he is, and I'm smiling before I can stop myself.

"If I promise to try the pie, will you let me get back to work?"

"Sure." He winks. "Now eat something."

I roll my eyes, but I do as he says and shove a bite into my mouth. *Dammit*, it's incredible. I make a note to tell Amy about PJ's.

Beside me, Charlie waits for a response, but I don't want to give him the satisfaction.

"You can get back to work now."

"I think the phrase you're looking for is, *thank you, Charlie. You were right*. This pie is as delicious as you are."

I'd rather kiss Roberts's feet than tell Charlie he's right.

Affecting my best glare, I say, "How about, *shut up and let me work?*"

He laughs as he returns to his own desk, where I can see he's hiding more pie. "Oh," he adds, "and send the damn email already."

———

I've never seen Charlie stressed until today. It's disconcerting.

Operations can't seem to function without him.

First Trevor appears, complaining about a review deadline, then Kush, pleading with him to push a project through, even though it doesn't follow any of the format requirements. At least that request came with an invite to lunch next week. After that is Sheldon, Ingmar, and a slew of others whose names I don't catch.

Engineers appear at all times of the day to complain—the system is infamous there, which is fun to hear repeatedly from four feet away—and while Charlie is nothing but friendly when they're around, his shoulders continue to bunch and tighten as the day wears on.

Maybe I've been too hard on him. He did apologize.

I'm used to seeing him in action, not... behind enemy lines like this. It's taking some getting used to.

It's clear he works out. It's stitched into the line of his jaw, his hands, even the ease of his walk. Like he knows where he's going, and heaven help anyone who gets in his way.

For a moment, I watch him through the break between our screens. His sleeves are rolled up, exposing his toned forearms and a set of black leather bracelets. It's a habit he saves for when a task needs his undivided attention.

Now that I've started, I can't stop noticing small details about him. The way he always stretches his back at two p.m., hands lifted overhead and ending with a little groan. How different his "I win" smile is from his

"I'm trying to win you over" one. How much brighter his eyes are in a navy pinstripe.

It's messing with me.

"So," I say, letting the word hang between us. My curiosity is piqued, practically seeping from every pore.

Charlie doesn't look over, but the slow curl of his smile tells me he's listening. "So."

I trace the letter *C* on my keyboard. "You and Amy."

Charlie stills his fingers over the keys. His smile deepens, showing off a dimple I want to hate but can't.

"Something you wanna know?"

Yes. "No."

He catches me watching him, and my heart jumps into my throat. "We had a couple dates about a year ago, but it didn't work out."

Relief washes over me, which is ridiculous, because I don't care.

I stare down at my computer. "It's none of my business."

"How about you?" he asks.

"I've never dated Amy."

He laughs, easy and smooth. I ignore how good it sounds.

"Maybe you should," he teases. "She's pretty great."

Like I haven't worked with her for years. I already know how great she is.

"I appreciate the advice," not that I asked for it, "but I'm not interested."

"Because you already have a partner?"

"No."

"Huh."

I lay my hands flat on the desk and inhale slowly. *Don't do it. He's trying to get a reaction.* "What?"

He shrugs one shoulder. "I'm surprised, is all."

Right. Charlie probably couldn't imagine anyone being interested in me.

"Not all of us need to constantly have our ego stroked." Among other things.

I'm met with a silence that makes my stomach sink. Shit. It's clear we're both stressed, and fighting won't help. Besides, wasn't I the one who said we would be better to simply leave each other alone?

I stand, hoping he's waved it off, cool and calm as always, but no luck. Though he's trying to hide it behind a smile, his entire body is tense and his face is drawn in exhaustion.

"I'm sorry. That was inappropriate. It isn't an excuse, but today has been a bad day in an even worse week." I release a long breath. "Regardless, I shouldn't take it out on you, and I really shouldn't have commented on your personal life like that."

In five years, I haven't spoken to anyone in anger, but Charlie seems to be the exception to every rule.

Even now, he doesn't act the way I expect him to. "Hey," he says, and though there's no fight in his voice, his smile is brittle. "Don't worry about it."

With nothing left to say, I go back to work. But I feel off-kilter the rest of the afternoon.

"Emma?"

And with that, Roberts remains the undefeated champion of "how to ruin my day with one word." But I plaster on a smile as he calls me into his office.

"How is progress coming along?" he asks when I'm seated.

Better now that I've saved the document offline. But I suspect he knows that already.

"It's still too early to tell, but I've had some good conversations with Legal—"

"Because I'm sensing some friction between you and Charlie. If you don't think you can work together, it might be a good idea for you to receive some coaching on emotional intelligence."

No.

My stomach sinks down to my Jimmy Choos.

Awful, *awful* man. So awful it's almost impressive. If there was a league of awful, he could go pro. Fan club, sponsorships, the works.

Instead, Roberts is determined to practice on me. Who knows, maybe during the offseason, he catches up with Scrooge and the Grinch to swap tactics.

"No. No friction," I lie, my throat tight.

"Would Charlie agree if I asked him?"

Would he? Unlikely.

In fact, the idea of Charlie agreeing with me about *anything* is so comical I have to dig my nails into my thigh to stop myself from smiling.

"I would certainly hope he would have spoken to me about it if he didn't."

———

Home is a first-floor studio with a small bath and a sink that doubles as part of the "kitchen" (quotation marks necessary). The walls are thin, at least half the outlets are broken, and I'm woken up every day by angry truck drivers. It's half the size of any guest room at my parents' house, but it might as well be the penthouse suite at the Ritz, because it has one key feature I won't ever give up…

It's mine.

Well, technically it's the landlord's, but I pay for it with money I've *earned*, not inherited, and to me, the distinction matters.

Ivy calls it my bachelorette pad. Logan called it quaint.

Honestly? It's cold and has terrible water pressure, but it's only a half-hour walk from the office. This little place is my sanctuary on days when I want to throw up my hands and quit.

Small spaces don't need much to fill them, which is good, because I've spent the last five years selling off everything I can stand to part with to help cover what my parents owe. Everything bar my couch and a capsule wardrobe.

Maybe now I can finally start again, fill in the gaps with new memories.

If I survive this project.

ME: no promotion can be worth this

IVY: what the hell did i miss today?

ME: Roberts being Roberts and Charlie messing with my head. Today it was a gray worsted suit. With French cuffs. And a completely distracting red checkered tie. Can you believe that?

IVY: oh no (laughing emoji)

ME: It's bad enough I have to see him every day. I miss cubicle walls

My phone lights up with Ivy's call.

"No, you don't," she says before I can greet her. "You love the open plan office."

I do. There's so much more natural light.

"If it's a choice between that and Charlie's face, the decision is easy," I say, reaching for another fry.

I don't know if there's an angel of food and beverage service, but the fast-food chain on the corner must be blessed. It's the only church I've ever come close to walking into, and like a good charitable organization should be, it's open twenty-four seven and no one is turned away.

Charlie might love his pies, but today, I need grease and salt.

Good days deserve good treats, like a glass of Pol Roger vintage Rosé and dark chocolate truffles. On bad days, it's any pasta drowning in parmesan paired with my favorite tempranillo.

On truly awful days, like today, it's a box of large fries dipped in a thick chocolate shake.

"Any news yet?" I ask, keen to think about anything that isn't work. "Your sister must be exhausted."

"The baby is as stubborn as she is. Pretty sure it's karma, but I value my life too much to tell her that. Mom's about five seconds away from storming the hospital, but Ciara will throw hands to keep her out of the delivery room, so I'm keeping the peace."

"And we thought she was bad during the wedding."

"That was a play date compared to this," she says.

"Also, stop changing the subject. You were waxing poetic about Charlie's suits."

My favorite topic of conversation.

"No matter how well he dresses, he's still a demon."

"Oh, of course," she says, laying the sarcasm on so thick I could dip my fries in it.

With the first real smile I've managed all day, I curl into the couch a little more. "I miss you. Lunch tomorrow?"

"Definitely. And don't let Charlie get to you. You don't have anything to worry about."

I wish I had her certainty.

CHAPTER 11
WRECK-LESS BEHAVIOUR
CHARLIE

There's no two ways about it. Emma Conway hits like an anvil to the chest.

Straight to the solar plexus, putting me on my ass every goddamn time.

So maybe it's karma that I almost hit her back. With my goddamn car, no less.

I slam the brakes hard, and the squeal of the tires finally pulls her attention away from her fucking phone —which would have helped before she stepped out into the street—my seatbelt clotheslining me as the car stops.

Fuck.

Between the brakes and my reflexes, I stop only inches from her, but the shock of it still sends her tumbling to the ground.

I throw the car in park and jump out. Emma's flat on her back on the asphalt, her chest heaving.

"Are you trying to get yourself killed? What the hell were you thinking?" I ask.

Wide eyes blink up at me. Shit, she's in shock.

I crouch down, ignoring the horns and complaints of the cars behind me. "Hey," I say, keeping my tone light. Her skin is cold, and she jolts when I touch her shoulder, but at least there's a spark of recognition. I release a breath. "There you are."

I keep trying to convince myself she'll get less beautiful each time I see her.

Maybe next time I'll see the shock of blond hair and fierce eyes and not want to say a little prayer to a deity I don't believe in.

Maybe she'll stop being so insistently competent, and I'll get through a single fucking day without having to picture an octogenarian's wrinkly, sweaty ball sac to cut off the salute my dick wants to give her.

Maybe the little shit will remember Emma hates me and wouldn't touch either of us, even if it guaranteed world peace.

It hasn't happened yet, but I always hope.

I'm a fool because Emma Conway only ever manages to get more beautiful.

"I can't believe you almost hit me," she pouts. "What, annoying me to death wasn't working fast enough, so you thought you'd finish me off with your car?"

Thank fuck the question is rhetorical, because as she dusts her hands off on her knees, all I can do is stare.

She's in pale blue tights and a matching crop that draw spectacular attention to her trim waist and full, beautiful breasts. Holy shit, is this what she's been hiding under her clothes? I can't work out where to look first, my eyes greedy as always to drink in as much of her as possible.

"You're the one wish a death wish, sweetheart."

Her chest rises and falls dramatically with every harsh breath.

She's still blinking too rapidly for my liking.

"Fuck. I didn't even see you," she says.

Yeah, no shit. I bite back my frustration in favor of helping her up. I haul myself back up to my feet and reach down, but she just stares at my hand like she doesn't know what to do with it.

"Not trying to kill you, I promise."

Tentatively, she slips her hand in mine. The instant we touch, the world around us slows.

"You sure you're all right?" I ask as I carefully pull her up and scan for cuts. My heart is flipping like a fish out of water. "Nothing sprained? No broken bones?"

Emma stands, grimacing. "Only a bruised ego."

I take a step back and look her over, not bothering to hide my appreciation. "You look pretty good to me."

The eye roll she gives me is 100 percent expected, even though it lacks its usual bite. The shock must be worse than I thought.

Maybe it's the adrenaline coursing through me or the way those leggings make my head spin, but I find myself saying, "Let me drive you home."

She stalls, frowning at me.

"No, thank you."

I sigh. Sure, *I get it*. We aren't friends. But when Emma takes a step and winces, I can't leave her to walk home like this.

"At least order a ride," I say.

She looks away, chewing her lip, and I'm starting to think I should just walk away. If she'd rather hurt herself than be near me, then so be it. That's a game I'll never win.

When she finally meets my eye, I raise a brow in question.

"Don't make me regret this," she says, shuffling to the passenger side of my car.

If anyone's going to have regrets, it'll be me.

"Wouldn't dream of it." I can't hide my smile, though, as I slip into the driver's seat.

It's no secret Emma hates me.

I can't exactly blame her. She made her reasons clear and there's a hell of a high chance I'll never change her mind.

What she doesn't know is that I don't feel the same way.

———

The farther I drive, the more I'm convinced she's pulling my leg. "You really want me to believe you were gonna walk all this way? Did your driver get the weekend off or what?"

She side-eyes me, her jaw ticking. "Believe what you want. I walk it every day. To and from work. I don't have a driver, or a car, and I'm not allergic to public transportation. Any other aspersions you want to throw at me? Because I'll get out at the next light."

I knew a guy like that once. He'd never had the need

for a license because he never learned to drive. But Lang was an environmental activist. I'm not sure Emma's reasons are the same.

Or maybe they are, since I've already established that *nothing* about her makes sense to me.

I risk a glance over and find her watching me, brows raised like she's waiting for a response.

What? Does she want a gold star?

When I turn back to the road without answering, Emma shifts to look out her window.

It's another two blocks before she speaks again. "One good deed hardly makes up for what you did."

My chest tightens. Christ, I can't win. "Hey, I'm trying here. What are you doing?"

She lets out a disgruntled sound and crosses her arms over her chest. It pushes her tits up, and I have to focus not to crash the car. "I don't have anything to apologize for."

I scoff. Treating me like filth doesn't count, I guess. "Of course you'd see it that way."

She continues to scowl out the window.

Fuck. Everything about her is clenched so tight I could probably farm diamonds out of her molars. There's never a strand of her icy blond hair out of place.

Perfectly straight, middle part, no fun allowed.

Reese spent most of her junior year of high school in the world's ugliest purple hat after an impromptu undercut from a curling iron.

Emma's hair—permanently soft and always glowing under the fluorescents in the office—could win best in show.

"Look," I try, gripping the steering wheel. "I know you don't like me much, and I know I deserve it, but I'm trying to make it up to you. Do you think you could give me a chance to prove I'm not the monster you think I am?"

"I don't know how Roberts thought this was going to work," she sighs.

It's a question I've been asking myself for weeks.

"It would be easier if you weren't locking me out of the document I'm supposed to be helping you write," I say.

She twists in her seat to face me. "I wouldn't have to if you and Roberts stopped rewording everything."

Daddy's little princess must be so used to getting everything she wants. Emma probably assumed that she'd walk in and immediately be put in charge. I bet she hates that she has to compete for this promotion. Even more so because I'm the one she's up against.

"Look, you might know the system backward, but maybe if you got off your pedestal—"

She raises her voice three notches. "Excuse me?"

"—and listened to the people who are actually using it, as lowly as you might consider us—"

"Stop the car. I'll walk."

I hit the lock button.

She whips around in her seat. "You're seriously trapping me in here? I think this technically counts as kidnapping."

So much for being nice. This is the last time I offer to help her.

"You'd rather risk your life than talk to me, but I'm the problem?"

She crosses her legs and glares out the window. Thank fuck I need to keep my eyes on the road. I can't even decide whether I'm more mad about her attitude or how perfect her ass looks in those pants.

The damn smoke alarm between my thighs has been throbbing, low and constant, since she got in the car, an annoying and unnecessary reminder. *Don't know what you want from me, buddy. I see the fire, but I can't do shit about it.*

There's no way to touch without getting burned, and yet I can't help but want to anyway.

"I don't think I'm better than you," she bites out, as if it's costing her to admit it. "It's obvious you've made up your mind about me, and I can assure you that regardless of what you want to call me, I've already heard it. I've known guys like you my whole life."

I doubt that.

"Sweetheart, there are no guys like me."

She barks a laugh that borders on ugly. "You think that because you're attractive, you can say anything you want. For an opportunistic dick, at least you're stylish. Does the Zegna come with a hypocrisy discount, or is that a bonus?"

I white-knuckle the steering wheel in frustration. "You really wanna go there? When you're hauling around a watch like that, even in your gym gear? What is it anyway, a Rolex?"

She covers it with her hand as though I'm about to reach over and take it. "Cartier."

Of course.

I hold back a scoff, and an uneasy silence descends for another block.

Roberts couldn't have known what he was getting by pitting us against each other, but I'm starting to wonder if it's more pain than it's worth.

It takes a solid minute before I realize she's shaking. Son of a bitch. First, I almost hit her with my car (even if it was her own damn fault), and here I am, arguing with her and making it worse.

At the next red light, I reach between the front seats and grab one of the blankets I keep in the back for the dogs. Emma takes it without a word and pulls it around her shoulders.

Every few minutes, she gives me a new direction, and the closer we get, the more curious I am to see where she lives. It's not every day I play chauffeur to an heiress.

It's not until I've parked that I realize where we are. Dormside is a nickname for the part of town where just about every college kid I knew—including Reese and me—bunked for cheap when we first moved here.

Why the hell would she direct me here? To play a sick joke at my expense?

Anger has my heart pounding like a vicious drummer. Emma might be cold, but I never took her for cruel.

Then again, I've been wrong before.

"You can't live here," I say, each word jagged and harsh. How does someone like Emma Conway even know this dump exists?

"Screw you," she hisses, then she's unlocking her door and climbing out. "Thanks for the ride."

Polite to a fault. I almost laugh. She's barely three steps away before I'm out and following her. As I catch up, she stops, turning on her heel.

Brows pinched, she glares at me. "What are you doing?"

"Proving something." Like the fact that she's a damn liar.

She lifts her chin. "I've got nothing to prove to you."

I step closer. "Look. I don't know who told you about this place"—or that I used to live here, and *fuck,* who at work would even know that?—"but I know this neighborhood, and if you really do live here, like you say, then I'll feel a hell of a lot better walking you to your door." Shoving my hands into my jeans, I step closer. "Now, are you going to let me be a gentleman, or should I drive you to your actual apartment?"

There's that murderous look again. Many people have leveled that at me, none of them half as stunning as she is.

Shit, she's gonna give me some kind of hate kink, isn't she?

"Fine."

She stalks ahead so fast I have to jog to catch up.

Everywhere I look, I'm hit with nostalgia. It's been years, but I can still point out the pipe the super bent when he parked his truck too close and the water damage spot that looks like a two-headed llama on the ceiling. The hallway still smells like smoke, and I would bet money that the fire alarms don't work.

"Christ, this place hasn't changed a bit."

We stop at a door on the first floor, and that twisting in my stomach has turned to dread. She's so damn close to the stairwell. It'd be easy for someone to break in.

Then Emma slides her key smoothy into the lock and opens the door.

Holy shit.

"Well?" she says, still looking angry and beautiful. "Get inside. I'm not doing this in the hall."

I step over the threshold, my heart thundering in my chest. "I bet you say that to all your dates."

None of this makes sense, and not in the sexy, mysterious way I've come to associate with her. No, the apartment is cramped and dark, transporting me to a time in my life I've worked for years to move past. A place I never would have pictured her in a million years.

I rub the back of my neck, scrambling to connect this place with the Emma I thought I knew.

"Are you happy now? Have I passed your test?"

Honestly, I don't know what I am.

What the hell happened? Last I checked—and I'd never admit to googling her, but I absolutely have—the Conways were still considered part of the upper class. So what's Emma doing slumming it in a studio with more scuffs than a monster truck?

As I take in the forest green couch, the espresso machine crowding the kitchen counter, the cotton candy sweater she wears on Fridays hanging over the back of a chair, it's clear. This isn't a prank.

And *fuck*, maybe I've been wrong about her.

"You actually live here."

It's the wrong thing to say.

Her eyes go ice cold. "Yes, I do. Now that you've seen it, you can go back and laugh about it with your golfing buddies. I'm sure all the people at work who have called me a princess will enjoy creating a new nickname."

No one would ever accuse me of having tact, but in this moment, my mouth definitely loses the plot.

"Did you run away from home? Mom and Dad cut you off or something? Or is this another part of your community outreach?"

"You know what, Charlie? Fuck you." Emma's on me before I can blink, both hands gripping my shirt and pushing. She matches me, step for step, so close I could count every lash. Her eyes spark in surprise when my back hits the wall and our chests touch, our breaths tangling together. "Is that all you've got?"

Be careful what you wish for.

And like the beggar and thief I've always been, I slide my hand around her neck and pull her the rest of the way, stealing the kiss that's been driving me to distraction since I met her.

It's filthy and deep. A battle of teeth and tongue and every bit of brimstone I've seen let loose.

If this is burning, then I'll cross hot coals to get to her. Beg her to incinerate me and thank her for the pleasure.

God, she tastes better than I imagined she would.

Emma kisses the same way she works—with passion and determination. It's devastating. The brutal way she attacks my mouth, her tongue battling mine, makes my blood sing.

Fuck, no one's consumed me like this before.

The world exists as nothing except the hungry sweep of her tongue, her vicious grip on my neck. Our teeth clash, and I'm greedy for more, pushing my thigh between hers, leaning in with my whole body. When she gasps and rocks against me, I suck on her bottom lip with a growl.

She's better than any dessert, hot and sweet and already so fucking addicting.

No ice bath on earth could be cold enough to replicate how it feels when Emma steps back, her eyes wide again with shock.

"This is wrong," she says, her voice shaky. "You should go."

Fuck. Leave it to me to make everything so much worse.

So that's that. She'll never be able to see past what I did or who I am. Good to know.

CHAPTER 12
MY WAY, OR THE CONWAYS
EMMA

A quick internet search will tell you the facts. Abigail Conway (née Seymour) launched Conway Connects when she was just twenty-two years old. What started as a collective of a dozen accessory designers quickly grew into a luxury group best known for cultivating niche small goods.

The key was exclusivity. Nothing was franchised. Releases were limited in number, and every piece was handmade and astronomically priced.

Nana called it "hyper luxury." By her fortieth birthday, she'd sold the company for one hundred million dollars and promptly retired.

On the face of it, her journey was impressive, yet simple enough. The entirety of it was barely enough of a story to take up my daily commute to work, let alone the weekly trek to my parents' house.

She was never featured in a list, and her life wouldn't warrant a biopic. While her success was grander than she expected, it was a combination of savvy and luck.

What the internet doesn't say is that my father, Lawrence Conway, has never had need for money, and thus, has never worked a day in his life. Instead, he's chosen to dedicate himself to family and lifelong retirement.

Similarly, my mother has limited work experience. Her career includes some modeling in her teen years before marrying young and becoming a mother.

Even though none of the family has been involved with the company in decades, the name has lived on. Within the upper classes, in the minds of my schoolteachers and classmates, and on the tongues of my coworkers.

But there's only one tongue that kept me awake last night.

Charlie's lips are softer than I imagined, full and insistent. I can't stop thinking about the heat of his hands on me, in my hair, down my back, digging in, as unrelenting as his mouth.

Kissing him was a mistake.

One I can't stop thinking about making again.

Just as the cab pulls up to my parents' house, the front door opens, and Harvey Casemiro exits, looking ruffled. At the sight of him, my heart drops into my stomach. He's been their accountant since I've been alive, and if he's here, there's trouble.

"Good afternoon, Emma," he says, flattening his tie and buttoning his jacket. The man is built like a linebacker Ivy once dated, and he's always in his Sunday best.

I'm afraid to ask how good it can be if he's here. "Is this a social visit?" I ask, desperately hoping, even though his visits have never been social.

Harvey has a fantastic poker face. Though his eyes are kind, it's difficult to get a read on the deep frown lines carved into his brow. "A small consultation. Nothing to worry about. Your father has been getting some new trading tips, but I was able to steer him away before he committed to anything. Everything else has been cleared away now, and you'll be the first to know if anything changes."

The relief makes my knees weak. Harvey has single-handedly saved us from impending doom, and at this point, I trust him with my life.

"It was Logan senior, wasn't it?" I ask. Logan's dad is always filling my father's head with "finance tips." The man hasn't heard of a pyramid scheme he doesn't admire.

Harvey tips his head. "Mr. Williamson Cross might have been mentioned. But he's only a symptom of the larger issue." He exhales, long and slow, his mouth pinched in the corners. "They need to be realistic in their situation, Emma. If they make a big move without my knowledge, even I won't be able to save the house."

The estate looms behind him, and my gut twists.

It's exactly what I'm scared of.

He slides a hand into his pocket, his broad shoulders testing the stress limit of his jacket buttons. "Keep working to convince them to dissolve their investment in the foundation. It's a good place to start. Though I really want to reiterate that moving—"

"I know." Downsizing is the only way to get my parents out of their circle of friends and far away from the peer pressure to keep up with them financially. More than ever, I wish I could convince them to sell. The price it would get could take care of them for two lifetimes, and it would save me a lot of sleepless nights. "I'll talk to them again."

His face softens so profoundly that I think that if I gave him a hug right now, it would throw him into a tailspin, so I pat his arm instead.

"Thank you, Harvey. We're in your debt."

There's twice as much gray hair at his temples than there was the last time I saw him. My parents have probably taken years off his life. "It's all part of the job. Don't worry yourself too much. You pulled them out of the worst of it. We'll make sure it works out. It's under control."

What a kind lie. "I don't deserve you."

He surprises me with a gentle smile. "I think you'll find you do, and more importantly, it's your parents who are indebted to you. Remember that."

———

Once upon a time, I had designer clothes, front row tickets, first class flights, almost everything I could want.

It was wonderful.

It was also an illusion.

The first time my parents dipped into my inheritance, I was a freshman in college. By sophomore year, they had drained every last cent through bad investments and overspending.

Though it's a constant fear, they haven't had to file for bankruptcy. But that's only due to Harvey's smart accounting, along with two Renoirs, a Signac, two summer homes, an apartment in New York, and every other item I could convince my parents to give up.

We disguised it as retirement—as much as two people who hadn't ever really worked could retire—downsizing from four houses to one, and ensuring all financial decisions had to be approved by Harvey or me first.

After all the stress and heartache, they refuse to give up their lifestyle or this house. Anything to keep up appearances, as though nothing has changed.

Walking through the house is like playing spot the difference, except the differences are glaringly obvious. That blank spot is where the Chagall hung. Over there, the Renoir. Two Ligne Roset sofas, the Hermes throw, a library's worth of rare books and first editions (none of them read).

When I was a kid, every room was filled to the brim, either with things or people. Parties for the foundation were thrown in different rooms, each with its own theme, and no expense was spared.

Back then, my parents were magicians, capable of conjuring up every wish I imagined and more.

As an adult, I've learned the lie that hides behind

the spectacle, and it's written in every empty space in this house.

Despite Harvey's reassurances, I'm dismayed to discover Mom in what's left of the wine cellar. She's holding a checklist in one hand and a '95 P2 in the other.

I steel myself as I come down the stairs. "Where's Dad?"

"Oh, hi, honey. In his office, last I saw. Something, something Ethereum, something, something Logan…" she says with a *yada, yada, yada* kind of wave of her clipboard. "He disappeared after breakfast, and I thought it would be an excellent time to tackle some administrative tasks before you arrived."

With a nod at the P2, she makes the decision she's clearly been pondering, and the foreboding churn in my gut sinks deeper.

"Whatever you're planning, we can't afford it," I remind her.

She looks up at me, her sigh echoing in the dim space. "Next you'll be asking me to serve box wine to our guests."

Wrong. I don't want her to serve anything at all.

My heart sinks. "Mom, you promised me."

"I know, but—"

"No. No buts. No ifs, buts, or maybes. You promised no more parties." If I have to camp out in this wine cellar to stop her, I'll do it.

She quietly slides the wine back into place, rotating it until she's satisfied. "I always host the annual gala.

We raise more funds in one day than we do the rest of the year."

I hate bursting her bubble like this. The foundation has been her second child for years, and I wouldn't ask her to give it up if it wasn't absolutely necessary.

But it's become increasingly necessary.

"Let somebody else host," I plead. Though she might never admit it, Logan's mother has been angling to take over the foundation for years.

"Emma," she says softly as she tucks my hair behind my ear. "And how would that look? I've been hosting since its inception. Everybody would think we can't afford it."

"We can't."

Every Sunday, I hop on a train, then into a cab so I can visit. And every Sunday, without fail, I'm reminded that the world of the rich does not exist on the same scale as the rest of the world.

If only I could make my parents accept that.

"Stop your stressing. Violet is taking care of everything this year."

Oh, thank god for that. I let the relief settle as she returns to her notes. The cellar has always been cool and damp, a cavern of dark delights, but now half the racks are bare, and it's another somber reminder of what used to be.

I swallow past the lump in my throat. "How is Violet?"

"Oh, you know Vi. There's an issue with her house on the coast, but she's glad to have Logan back. Have you heard that he's been offered partner?"

I pretend to check my nails. "No, but that's impressive."

Though I'm surprised he didn't mention it at lunch.

"I suppose he'll be joining her at the fundraiser, now that he's home." I shoot for a casual tone.

The knowing look Mom gives me says I missed the mark. "Are you sure you'd be comfortable with that? I know how upset you were when it ended."

I drop the act. "Logan and I are adults, and besides, we've already seen each other, and it was perfectly fine."

"Oh?" she asks, eager for all the details I won't be giving her.

Thankfully, Dad chooses the perfect moment to appear.

I swear if you saw him on the street—six foot six, long limbs extending from equally long khaki shorts and polo—you'd never know he once spent more than my annual salary on a garden gnome.

"Oh, perfect. I thought I heard you come in." His thick mustache tickles when he kisses me on both cheeks. It's remained black, even as his hair has grayed, and I've never seen him without it. "A case of GSM arrived from that new vineyard I was telling you about. The one that ferments in terracotta amphora rather than oak."

He holds the bottle like a trophy in one hand, three glasses in the other. "Sulfate free, vegan, and a steal for the price."

I don't even want to know what my father considers "a steal."

As he pours, I frown at him. "Dad, it's barely one p.m."

He pauses, looks up. "You're right. We need nibbles."

Mom perks up and is already moving toward the door. "I'll cut up some cheeses."

I should sell tickets to this show.

"Perfect," he says, holding a glass out to me as she disappears. As always, his broad smile melts away the last of my concern. "Cheers, pumpkin."

As out of touch as my parents are from the real world, there's one responsibility they always came at with enthusiasm, and that's me. There were times it was too much—when I was fourteen, I spent every weekend at a different friend's house to get some peace—but I also know how lucky I am.

They're stubborn and quirky, and I adore them.

"A little earthy," he says, swirling his glass. "You can taste the richness of the minerals, but it's still young. Open her up a little, and she'll be a great aperitif. What do you think?"

I savor the first sip. It's an extremely smooth blend, and soon, I'm reaching for the bottle to find out more. A second sip brings out the dark fruits, with a hint of spice. "I can see what you mean. There's something almost rustic about it. Did you just open this?"

He nods.

"It's lovely. Did you really need more wine, though?" I gesture around us. Three hundred bottles at his disposal, and he's always showing me something new.

"We're trying to secure the vineyard for an event. It seemed unseemly to not buy a case."

Change has been difficult for all of us, but teaching my dad to be frugal is almost impossible.

I sigh. "Don't you think it's time to hand the foundation over to someone else? You could find a new hobby." Something less likely to keep me up at night.

Mom returns carrying a platter overflowing with more cheese, nuts, and fruit than we could possibly eat in one sitting.

"If we didn't have the foundation to keep us busy, what would we do with ourselves? I'd rather see you step in than hand it over to anyone else," Dad says, causing Mom to look at me in triumph.

"No," I remind them for the fiftieth time. I can't imagine a task I want less. "I love my job"—*mostly*—"and I'm happy." Again, *mostly*. "I'm not interested in running a nonprofit that makes your rich friends feel good about maintaining the wealth gap."

They frown like they always do and drop it in favor of asking about work. Dad's always been fascinated by my job, and maybe it's ridiculous to still want his approval at twenty-seven, but when he looks at me with something akin to awe and tells me he's proud of me, it makes up for all the times I've wanted to give Roberts the finger and storm out.

"This is exactly why you would be such an asset to the foundation. You're a natural problem solver."

"He's right, honey," Mom chimes in. "While I enjoy the social aspects, you'd be much better suited to keeping everything organized."

At this point, I'm beginning to think taking over might be the only way to convince them to retire for good, and it terrifies me that one day, I might have to choose between my happiness and their livelihoods. Because I already know my answer.

Every kid considers the turning point where they need to care for their parents instead of vice versa, but I never thought it would happen so soon.

I love them more than life itself. I only wish I didn't have to worry about them so much.

Dad's refilling my glass for the third time when he eyes me with curiosity and asks the last question I'd ever expect from him. "Are you going to tell us about this new boyfriend of yours, or must we wait for the official newsletter?"

It takes everything I have not to choke on my wine.

"Who told you about that?"

"Violet was very curious," Mom says.

One look at how happy the two of them are, and I almost regret lying to Logan.

Almost.

"There's nothing to tell." *Literally, because he doesn't exist.*

"The most important thing is, does he make you happy?" Dad asks.

What do I even say to that? I only made him up in hopes of getting Logan back, but I can't bring myself to disappoint them.

"He keeps life interesting" is what I land on.

They look like they just found out Santa is real, and my stomach churns. I hate lying to them.

"We expect to see him at the fundraiser, at least," Mom says.

Uh… hell no.

"He's not sure if he can make it," I try.

It's no use. Mom is already cupping my cheek and smiling, and I know I can't take it back now.

"Then you'll just have to bring him around to meet us when you visit next Sunday."

Shit. Shit, shit, shit, shit.

I should have known the gossip mill would get back to them, but the flare of jealousy I caught in Logan's eyes was too good to pass up. Too bad I now need to find myself a fake boyfriend for a night.

Mom clinks her glass to mine. "Don't forget to tell him it's black tie."

"I'll let him know."

Once I have a *him* to invite.

CHAPTER 13
OH, YOU THOUGHT THIS WOULD BE FAIR?
CHARLIE

Monday mornings are a bitch. Yeah, yeah, what's new.

Today is a new kind of kick in the ass, though, because the taste of Emma has lasted all weekend, and if she was cold to me before, I'm expecting subzero temperatures now.

Look, I didn't make it this far in life believing in fairy tales. I know it's not going to happen again, but I can't stop thinking about it, thinking about *her*.

How incredible she tasted.

How right she felt in my arms, gripping me tight, her lips opening beautifully under mine.

How quickly she's ruined me for anyone else.

Reliving it is maddening, but finding even a minute to talk to her in private is an impossible task. Her calendar is booked solid with meetings I expect are code for "I'm busy, don't bother me."

Then when she does finally return to her desk, Drue appears.

"Hey, so, Malcolm needs six hundred new numbers, and the distribution matrix didn't load correctly, so it all has to be redone." By the time the poor guy spits it all out, he's so tense his shoulders are next to his ears.

"Okay, deep breaths. You can bulk load the numbers, and I can fix the distribution."

He sags in relief. "Are you sure? I know how swamped you are."

"Don't worry about it." I say, waving him off. This new project is already running me ragged, and that's while Ops isn't imploding. But what's one more thing on my plate?

"Thanks, Charlie."

He leaves me to a fresh clusterfuck that completely derails any other plans I have for the day.

It's only when I'm dick deep in the data that I realize how quiet it is.

Emma's at her desk, but the furious chorus of her typing is missing from behind my screen, so I wait, holding my breath, knowing she's got something to say.

It doesn't take long.

"Is the distribution likely to take a while?" she asks, her tone curious.

It's enough to make me suspicious. "All day, probably."

She stands, and I don't even try to hide how quickly my attention jumps to her. Emma's always beautiful, but this morning, she's a walking fantasy. White button-down under a body-hugging black dress, hair long and loose.

"I know a trick for that if you'd like. It might save some time."

The chance that this is another wild goose chase is small, but I'm still wary. "What do I have to do?"

It's a good thing I'm sitting down, because the way her eyes light up as she rounds her desk to mine knocks me on my ass. The smell of blossoms and sunshine follow her like she's a cartoon princess.

Goddamn. Reese would have a field day if she saw me.

"Do you have the original list?" she asks.

As I open the file, she inches closer, her chest brushing my shoulder. I want to bury my nose in her neck and drown in her.

"Why are you so helpful all of a sudden?"

I feel the exact moment she freezes, and fuck, I really need to stop putting my foot in it.

She pulls away, ducking her head. "If you don't want it—"

Spinning in my chair, I peer up at her, pleading. "I do." I'd sell my right arm for a solution right now, but even if it doesn't work, this is the nicest Emma's ever been to me. I'm not about to mess that up.

"Charlie," she sighs after several quiet seconds. "About the other day. I'm sorry for the things I said. I was frustrated, and I took it out on you, which wasn't fair."

Well, fuck me. I spent the weekend kicking myself for crossing the line, and here she is, beating me to an apology. Once again, nothing about Emma makes any goddamn sense.

"It was rude and unprofessional," she continues. "And I'm genuinely sorry."

Christ. If I never have to hear those words out of her mouth again, I'll die happy.

"No." I take a chance and place my hand on hers. "I was a jerk. I didn't mean to—shit, I thought you were taking a shot at me, and then I wasn't really thinking at all. If we're gonna talk about being unprofessional, I think I got you beat."

Emma ducks her head, hiding behind a curtain of blond hair, but not before I catch the blush on her cheeks.

"We don't have to talk about that," she says, her voice softer than I've ever heard it.

My worn, pessimistic heart aches. "I think we do."

Her hand slips out from under mine. "Things got heated, and we got carried away. It's…"

She looks around, lips pressed together, as if she's searching for what to say, but I'm too focused on what she's not saying. There's no sorry, no screaming about how I took advantage. No, it's *we* got carried away. Both of us. Together.

My chest tightens, remembering the sting of her teeth and the lash of her tongue and—

"It's fine," she finally says. "It won't happen again."

My heart sinks. Damn. "Okay."

She nods, and I immediately want to take it back. I also want to kiss her again, but I'm pretty sure I just lost my chance.

———

For eight years, I've busted my ass at this company. Around the six-year mark, I almost quit. I've never been good at standing still, and in a place like this, where they've crushed the hopes of people twice as smart as me? I didn't want to go out that way.

But time disappeared in a blink. Now, they must know I'm getting the itch again, because this promotion is the first opportunity I've been offered to move out of Ops, and I need it, or else I'll never get out.

I hate feeling stuck, but without a degree, it'll only get harder if I leave. Landing a job here without one was a miracle. I'm not going to have the same luck twice.

Experience only goes so far, and I'm still waiting for the other shoe to drop.

So when Roberts pulls me into his office because he wants to "check in on progress," I'm immediately suspicious.

Of course, I'm proven right, but it's so much worse than I expected.

"How would you say the project is going so far?"

Roberts might as well be a stock image. Ill-fitting button-down, black pants, and the same bulk-billed haircut as every other middle-aged man in a middle management position.

Needless to say, I don't trust him.

"Great," I say, lying through my teeth. Until I know what his angle is, I'm not giving him anything.

By the frown marring his face, that's not what he wanted to hear.

"Because if there are any roadblocks, I want you to

tell me. No matter how slight you think they might be."
He rests his elbows on his desk and clasps his hands.
"You know, I've been looking forward to working with
you. After last year, your name has been getting
around. That's good. That's exactly what we need in
Digital. Make sure you keep that proactive attitude; it's
going to get you far in this business."

Does he have any idea how easy he is to read? He is
everything I've heard people say about him behind his
back. Opportunistic. Chauvinistic. Charmless.

Then he gets to the meat of the conversation, and, oh
boy, is it juicy.

"To be honest with you, Charlie, if it were up to me,
I'd give the lead job to you right now. Forget all this red
tape."

The fuck? A muscle in my jaw twitches when I
clench it too hard. "So why the test?"

He smirks, and cold, hard realization slams into me.

This isn't a test. It's a game.

A check-in-the-box bullshit exercise masquerading
as fair play.

But a real game—an honest one—has rules, and
every opponent has an equal shot.

Not this one.

Because Emma never stood a chance.

I grip the armrests as pure, unadulterated fury
burns in my veins. It takes all my energy to keep my
face clear of it, to think before I act for once.

Roberts gives me a smarmy smile when he's sure
I've caught on. As if we're in this together. Buddies,
sharing an inside joke. "Don't worry about that. It's

merely a formality. You've already impressed the lead team, and you can't ask for a better reference than a personal shout-out by the COO."

Fuck.

He continues, every word cutting into my skin, a hundred nails sealing my guilt in with heavy finality. "Emma is a fine worker, but she can be… difficult. This role demands a leader, and I see a lot of potential in you. I want you to think about your future here. When you're the lead, I'm going to delegate some responsibilities to you that I'm already confident you can handle. Enough time with me, and you'll be ready to take on my job when I move up."

Not if. When.

"What will happen to Emma?"

"Nothing." He leans back in his chair with a flippant shrug. "She'll remain a senior, although I'll suggest to Emmanuel that we rotate her into a different function. She doesn't have any direct experience in a project team, not like you, so that'll be a good start. And, of course, as the lead, you're welcome to offer your feedback on her development."

What the actual fuck?

He can't be serious.

He is.

He's fucking serious.

My stomach has practically fallen through the floor, yet Roberts takes my silence as agreement. He smiles and pats my shoulder, and it's only years of practice that keep me from peeling his hand away.

"Emma doesn't have the visibility you have. All the

hard work in the world won't get you half as far as getting your name in the minds of the right people, and that's something Emma has continually failed to do."

That damn briefing is going to haunt me for the rest of my life.

Decisions, meet consequences.

Of course that's what this boils down to. I wanted to earn this role fair and square, not cut her from the running and kill her career in single hit.

I can't decide whether I hate myself or Roberts more.

Fuck it, it's me.

"I disagree," I say, finally, pushing the words past the lump in my throat. "I don't know many people who aren't aware of Emma's name."

"But is it for the right reasons?"

Bullies are bad enough. Give a mean guy power and a target, and he's dangerous. But the truly despicable ones attack in the shadows, where no one can see them.

I force my breaths to remain slow and even. "Her work stands for itself. Introducing digital signatures, rolling out a companywide system upgrade, and that's just in the last two years."

By the patronizing look on his face, it's clear he won't be convinced. "How long have you worked for us, Charlie?"

"Eight years and some change."

"And in that time, you've garnered the respect of several important people. That's not easy to do. Don't waste it. It takes all types to make a business successful, and if you play this right, you can share in that success. This role is a big win, both for you and the company."

For him, he means.

"The Emmas of the world are necessary, of course," he goes on, waving a dismissive hand, "but that doesn't make her the right choice. 'Kay, son?"

Life flashes before my eyes. Not mine. His. Because I'm about to end it. I hope he's said his goodbyes.

There's a pen on the desk in front of me. Fountain tip. Solid. Not the best weapon, but it'll work in a pinch. Reluctantly, I drag my eyes away, shoving my hands into my pockets.

"Yes, sir." *Heard you loud and clear, asshole.*

This is what Emma's had to put up with for five years? I've seen some shit in my time, but to have to work for a man who actively hates you (and let's face it, probably has some mommy issues) might rank right up there with "reserved for my worst enemy."

If Reese were in Emma's position, I'd be reevaluating my stance on workplace conflicts. And I'd be preparing a new résumé in my head because I'd be gearing up to give a speech that'd no doubt get me fired.

And really, it shouldn't matter that it's not my sister in the hot seat. No one should have to fucking work like this, even Emma. She may hate me, but she's worked as hard as I have and shouldn't be wasting her talents trying to please an asshole who's actively working against her.

So fuck it.

I'm going to fix this. Somehow, I'm going to make it up to her.

CHAPTER 14
WAVING MY WHITE (COLLAR) FLAG
CHARLIE

I've never had time for regrets. Happiness is tough enough to collect on.

I'd rather act and learn than wait and wonder.

When I originally apologized to Emma, I meant it. There was no reason for me to believe she'd be cut out of being recognized for her hard work. At least not until Roberts's awful speech yesterday.

My blood's still boiling.

It's bullshit, plain and simple. There's no changing the past, but I can damn well make sure that I'm not a part of his plan to cut her out again.

Until I can prove Roberts is playing favorites, I'll have to convince Emma to work with me. The harder it is for him to separate us individually from the results, the more time I'll have to make it a fair competition.

I just have to hope Emma doesn't castrate me before then.

"What are you doing here?" she asks with a scowl.

It's a fair question. I'm sure the last thing she

expected when she woke up this morning was to find me parked outside her apartment, offering her a ride to work.

But we need to talk, and I have a habit of pressing my luck when it comes to her.

"Giving you a lift. Now get in."

She looks incredible, as always. Hair slicked back today, with a black turtleneck belted over a deep green skirt that flows like water around her long, gorgeous legs.

She crosses her arms. "I don't need your pity."

"Not what this is. But if you really want to walk in those shoes, that's up to you."

She taps one her heel on the ground. "I've managed it every day for years," she retorts, raising a brow in a way that's far sexier than it should be.

I've seen her rubbing her feet under the desk when she thinks no one is around. So I watch her, silent, waiting.

Eventually, she drops her arms. "Thank you," she says as she slips into the passenger seat, looking regal and untouchable.

Around me, her soft, sweet perfume is a lure, the kind I imagine could easily tempt wayward sailors who spend too many nights fighting the ocean, dreaming of sparkling eyes and red lips.

I've never wanted anyone more.

Biting back a groan, I grip the wheel and take off before I get any wild ideas. "Don't mention it. You're on my way."

The journey is familiar, taking me back to when

Reese and I moved here. So much has changed since then, including me.

Now I have the flashy apartment, and suits more expensive than my rent was in those days. That kid with a hell-on-wheels attitude probably wouldn't even recognize me now.

What would he think of where our life is going?

When we're two blocks from the office, I bite the bullet. "As fun as this whole game has been, I think we need a new plan."

"Do you." It's not a question.

"Look, this isn't working." I glance over, careful not to be distracted by the way her smooth skin glows in the morning light. "We either put our personal shit aside and get this done or spend the next six months in hell."

I can survive hell. Been there, done that.

But I'd rather see what else is lurking underneath those long lashes and sharp claws. Make her smile for real or, fuck, make her laugh.

Maybe even be friends. Crazier things have happened.

Plus, I really want to stick it to Roberts.

Emma's silent for another block, though when I peer over, her expression is thoughtful rather than angry. That's a good sign.

"Let's say I agree," she finally says, shifting so she's angled my direction as I pull up to a stoplight. "How do I know you aren't going to stab me in the back again?"

"My word."

I haven't given her much reason to trust me, but when I make a promise, I damn well keep it.

She shoots me a look I can't hold because the light changes, but her gaze burns into me as I accelerate. Assessing my virtue, probably. I've been found wanting plenty in my life, but I don't want now to be one of those times.

"We do this together," I say. "Equal. I care about getting this procedure right. Whatever you think about me, I know you want that just as much as I do. We have the opportunity to make changes that will make the job easier. Don't you think that's worth it?"

I want to make up for the Robertses of the world.

I want to earn her trust.

I want her to want me back.

But I'll take her partnership.

As soon as the car is parked, she holds out her hand, a peace offering if ever I've seen one. If only she knew that peace is the last thing I have any experience with.

We shake, her hold as firm as her gaze, demanding my commitment.

And that's how it begins.

———

"So. Where are we at?" I ask.

Emma's squared us away in a meeting room as far away from Roberts's office as we can get, and she's now commandeering the AV system like she owns it.

Honestly, I gotta hand it to whoever made that

keyboard. With the ferocious way she types when she's really mad, I'm shocked it holds up this well.

One of the best parts of my day is the inevitable scowl she gives me when she finally catches me admiring her angry tapping.

Emma connects her laptop to the screen and opens an offline file. *Ahh.* So that's where she's been hiding it.

"Roberts just reviewed it," she says.

I wait for more. There's none.

"Okay," I say, dragging out the word. "And? On a scale of *Marvel* to *Game of Thrones*, how bloody is it?"

She looks me straight in the eye. "An episode of *The Boys.*"

Shit. "That bad, huh?" Bonus point for her taste in shows, though.

"It's a disaster. No, worse. A catastrophe." She pinches the bridge of her nose. It's too fucking cute. "No one can agree. I'm ready to throw everyone in a room and—"

I grasp her forearm to stop her. "Terrible idea. Only do that if you want to waste a day and lose all faith in humanity."

"Great," she deadpans.

I can't help but smile at her. The project is probably fucked, but suddenly, working together is looking a hell of a lot more fun.

Why didn't I think of this sooner?

Up on the big screen, the doc looks bloodier than a *Carrie* remake. Roberts clearly took glee in redlining all of Emma's sections and leaving pedantic arguments over any bullshit thing he could think of.

Fucking hell. "What an ass."

"He's not all bad," she says far too politely. She'll need to be a better liar than that if she wants to last in management.

"You hate him," I say.

Emma keeps typing.

I duck lower and angle in. "Admit it."

Her breath catches. "I'd rather not."

Ridiculous. I can't believe she'd protect Roberts's feelings over mine. I rock back. "You never seem to have any problems saying you hate me. Am I special?"

Briefly, the corner of her lips curls up, but she stifles it. *Almost got her.* "You're different."

Not exactly how I'd hoped to hear it, but it doesn't stop the traitorous little jump in my chest. Good or bad, being anything to Emma will always be better than nothing.

"You want to know how I know you don't like him?" I ask.

There's no denying the flicker of interest in her eyes as she finally peers over at me. "Okay, tell me."

"You get a little wrinkle," I say. Slowly, because I'm a fan of keeping my limbs, I reach out and bop her nose. "Right here."

She's fighting a smile, but it peeks out at the corners.

"Am I wrong?" I ask, raising a single brow, and fuck, when she grins, she's downright dangerous.

I'm seriously screwed.

"Is that why you're being nice to me now?" she asks.

Ouch. I probably deserve that. "Maybe I just want to be your friend. Ever think of that?"

"I know you don't respect me—"

"Whoa, back up." That comment hits me like a punch to the gut. How the hell does she think I don't respect her? "When have I ever said that?"

"You didn't have to."

"Then let me be clear. I respect the hell out of you, Emma."

She gives me a frown, clearly unconvinced.

"Fine, don't believe me." I drop my pen to the table and run a hand over my face. "Anyway, forget Roberts. Tell me how you wanna save this, and we'll go from there."

The first wave of the plan—and, of course, she's already thought ahead for waves two and three—is to strip everything back. Document management 101.

"Off the top of your head," she says, standing.

I'm almost 100 percent sure if I make a teacher joke, she'll tear one of my limbs off, but I can't help it when she looks so damn good like this. Passionate. Competent.

"What is the difference," she continues, "between the Document Control Standard and the Document Governance Standard?"

It's a trick question. There isn't one, at least not one that can be worked out between its pages of overwritten, self-aggrandizing nonsense. "Showmanship?"

"See?" she asks, exasperated. "If the best document controller in the business can't tell the difference, what hope does a layman have?"

Well, fuck. I'm grinning wide now, and if I had a damn tail, it'd be wagging.

Emma continues. "I'm not saying do away with the details, but there are too many here. And too many rules." Now *that's* a phrase I never thought I'd hear from her. "It's forty-five pages long when it could be ten. It serves as the foundation, so it needs to be an overarching, easy-to-read document that outlines why we do what we do. The how comes later. Then every document underneath should start with identifying who it's aimed at. One for internal users, one for external, and an instruction for DCs."

Fuck, she's smart. And damn if I don't find myself getting swept up in her. Roberts is dead wrong. There is a leader in her. A damn good one, who cuts through the bullshit and—despite what I've thought in the past— genuinely cares about the people impacted by her work. She might come across as unmoving, but in reality, she's a force to be reckoned with.

There's a badass under all that politeness, and she's electrifying.

"What about you?" she asks, and goddamn, the full force of her attention is like a shot of adrenaline. Even more surprising, she seems to really want to know my opinion. "What would you change?"

"The way I see it, we can't change the regulation stuff, so we should focus on the areas we can. But too much change is going to make people panic. If we start with changing the shit that already annoys people, it'll be easier to convince them to adopt it."

She smiles. "Go on."

My heart does a weird little flip. Goddamn, why

does it feel like I just impressed the teacher? Fuck. *Get it together, man.*

"Fewer rules might not be the answer. Our processes aren't really the issue. They're just confusing as hell to follow, so people find the path of least resistance."

"You're right."

I think it takes a full minute to process what I just heard.

Leaning into her space, I grin. "Wait, say that again. I wasn't recording."

And holy fuck, she laughs, real and loud, before dropping back into her chair with a looseness that's got to be the sexiest thing I've ever seen.

"Well, as you've reiterated to me many times, vendors either don't want to follow our procedures, or the project scope is too small to warrant rigorous compliance."

Never have I ever been turned on by a thesaurus until now.

"And honestly, I can understand it. I've been wanting to untangle the mess around uncontrolled documents since the day I started here. It's ridiculous the amount of energy we spend on supporting information that only needs to be kept internal or confidential but not referenced for operations."

"Do that, and they may throw you a parade," I say. "But we need to be careful. If we make it a free-for-all, it'll be carnage, and site will have the bad kind of field day." I sit back and press my hands against the armrests of my chair. "The last thing we need is to piss off the guys on the ground. They complain, and it's straight to the boss's ears."

She sags back in her chair, her hands falling away from her laptop with a sigh. "Back to the drawing board, then."

And just like that, I know things have changed.

A month ago, there was no way Emma would have admitted I was right or listened long enough to let me change her mind about anything.

It shouldn't be as hot as it is. I've sat in day-long meetings with red-faced guys with bald spots discussing comment processes and turnarounds, and this is the first time I've ever gotten hot under the collar.

"If we can make compliance invisible," she says, her eyes brimming with an intense focus. "Build it in so it's automatically there as people create content. They'd have to go out of their way to go against it. The harder the system works for us, the better the experience for the people using it."

Fuck. She is *so* much better suited to this than I am. Roberts shouldn't have even asked me to do this. I work my ass off, and I know everything there is to know about how it works, but I don't have these kinds of ideas. And here Emma is with a multi-step plan. Talking about keeping things system agnostic so we don't have to rewrite the rules every time we so much as think of changing a button.

In short, she's incredible.

"Sounds like a plan." I tap my pen against my lips, and her attention drops there, shooting a thrill down my spine. "But if you really want this to work, you'll need to convince a couple of key people. Ford in Ops, Samir in Projects, and Kamile and Jeremy Baxter across Engineering."

Emma's joy recedes. "You should be the one to talk to Baxter. He won't listen to me."

Funny, I didn't take her for a quitter. "Giving up already?"

There's a flash of fire in her eyes, and she straightens, pulling her shoulders back. Fuck, I love a woman in a power pose. "I'm not giving up. Baxter automatically vetoes every change I suggest. Has for years. I want to give us the best chance we have. And that's you."

That's the kind of compliment that'll make a man get down on one knee. And maybe I would if I didn't think Emma would kick me while I was down there.

But then, I could be into that.

"I've worked with him for a while now," I say. "And I don't see any reason why you couldn't convince him."

She slow blinks, her lips parted, looking at me like I'm crazy. "Oh, really? Not one reason?"

If she gives me any more sass, I'm going to have to kiss her again. "Not the one you're thinking of. Look, I know you get flack for your background, and Jeremy Baxter is a tough nut to crack, but he's not the kind of guy who'll give a shit about your last name. If you're prepared to walk in there, explain why these changes will benefit him, and not take no for an answer, he'll agree."

She lowers her head. "I don't think I can change his mind about this."

"Why not? You've changed mine." I lean forward, elbows on the table.

I've never seen anyone blush so beautifully.

"Oh," I add. "We'll need to get Emmanuel Fletcher on board."

"Roberts's boss? Do you really think he'll care?"

Not yet, but… "We'll make him care."

And better yet, Roberts won't be able to do a damn thing about it.

CHAPTER 15
PROS AND CONS
EMMA

Everyone has flaws.

One of mine is finding Charlie Walker attractive.

It's the dimples that appear when he smiles.

The charm that oozes from him.

Those blue, blue eyes.

I don't particularly *like* that he's sexy, but I'm not blind to it. I almost wish I was. It would be easier.

Today he's in a bespoke suit so distracting I've locked myself out of my laptop three times already. Standing out from the sea of gray and black, he looks resplendent in a three-piece overcheck brown tweed that melts my brain and most of my inhibitions every time he comes into view.

Yesterday was Loewe. The day before, Paul Smith. Then Boss.

His wardrobe is impressive, but it's not simply the clothes that turn me on.

He moves with purpose. The man doesn't walk; he

strides. He doesn't merely sit but presides. There's power in every smile, wink, nod.

And his voice?

As smooth as silk and twice as seductive. He could probably disarm a bomb with a simple flirtation and a flash of his dimples.

From the bespoke suits, all the way to his polished brogues, Charlie is formidable in a way I've never mastered but have always aspired to be.

There's more to him than I anticipated, and the curiosity is leading me into dangerous territory.

———

I spent years trying to be a perfect child.

Straight As, gymnastics, volunteer work, entry into a prestigious college—even my love life wasn't spared.

At the end of every failed date and broken relationship, I've sat down and asked myself, why? What didn't work, and how I can fix it?

No matter the man, it kept coming back to one little problem. *Me.*

I have an issue sealing the deal, as it were.

Or, more specifically, I have a problem finishing. Climaxing. Coming. And it drove them all away.

Life is about more than sex, and it's certainly about more than money. Life is about laughter and friends and family. Wine and burgers at midnight. Chocolate and slim-fit waistcoats and crying at movies. Solving a problem that's been bothering me for weeks.

But I want a life *with* sex.

I like sex. I think. I love orgasms when I have them. I adore the sleepy, lazy afterglow where all I want to do is curl up, skin to skin, next to somebody.

I want so badly to enjoy sex. But unless I'm alone, I can't come.

And I don't know why.

I talked to a sex therapist. I talked to a regular therapist. And too many times, I've tried to think my way out of the issue, going round and round in my head over what could be stopping me.

And no, it's not overstimulation from toys. It's not porn or the number of kegels I haven't done or any number of the other reasons men have offered me.

Honestly? Good porn paired with a clit vibe has done more for me than anything else has.

It's like being hungry but never feeling full unless you're eating Oreos in a closed pantry with the lights out. It's good, but sometimes I want to eat a full meal. Plus dessert.

So, like every other problem I've come up against in life, I refuse to let this stop me.

If there's a way to work this out, I'll find it. It's all in the approach.

I've gotten extremely good at getting myself off. I have a box full of toys, a subscription to Quinn, and the results of multiple kink quizzes.

I've done my research.

Hours upon hours of extensive research.

And I think I know what the problem is.

I'm not insecure about my looks or personality. I'll say it… I'm a catch. I have given men some of the best orgasms of their life. Emphasis on *their* orgasms.

I focus on meeting their needs while putting myself aside. And boy, am I phenomenal at putting myself aside.

I'm so focused on them, it's impossible to stop thinking and relax.

Are they enjoying themselves? Are they getting annoyed that this is taking too long? Am I moaning enough? Can I scratch that itch, or will it ruin the mood? Should I just tell them to tap out before they get lock jaw?

Every one of those guys who swore in the beginning it was okay that I didn't come became frustrated in the end. Even Logan, who lasted the longest.

But what if there is a way to break through the dam by sleeping with someone whose pleasure I'm not invested in?

Someone I don't particularly care about?

Someone that I might not even *like*?

———

Every Thursday at two p.m., there is an hour blocked off in my calendar titled *update weekly report*. It's Ivy's idea. There's no report. It's our go-to code for "I need you."

Right now, I'm using it to show her my list of pros and cons.

"Think of it this way," I tell her. "He's already screwed me over once. He might as well finish the job."

Ivy looks like all her birthdays have come at once. Eyes bright, an impossible-to-stifle smile. "I don't know, Em. The way you talk about him—"

I know that look. "Whatever you're thinking—"

"It sounds an awful lot like when you had a crush on Dominic."

Heat creeps into my cheeks. "It's nothing like that. I hate Charlie."

Ivy nods, still smiling, clearly not believing me.

I amend my previous statement. "*We* hate Charlie."

She raises her hands in surrender. "Okay, we hate him. He fucked you over, and I have your back no matter what. Just give me a heads-up before there's a body to dispose of, and don't search poisons on a work computer."

"No promises on that last one."

Ivy is sitting on my desk, feet swinging, the distressed cuffs of her jeans hanging over her sneakers. Her attitude toward work attire has always been "my brain works the same in jeans as it does in a pencil skirt, but only one of those options is comfortable."

She's a wondrous, sassy prism of light, and I love her.

"If you hate him so much, why even ask him?" she asks.

Because as much as I hate to admit it, I'm curious. And I can't stop thinking about him. The kiss we shared replays in my fantasies often enough to prove that. "It's a gut feeling, I guess. I think he can help me fix it."

Her feet still, and she tilts her head, homing in on me. "You're not broken, Em."

"I know," I lie. It's so much easier to say than believe. "It was a bad choice of words. But I've tried just about everything, and I miss sex. Right now, all I have are my vibrators, and last night, two of them died on me before I could finish. I'm all for edging, but that's just ridiculous."

Ivy throws her head back with a laugh, gripping the edge of the desk.

"It's not funny," I say, but I'm already giggling.

A throat clears, loud and exaggerated, and my heart spikes with panic. *Shit. Please, please don't be Roberts.*

It's not.

It's infinitely worse.

When I can muster the courage to look at Charlie, I stuff my embarrassment all the way down to my So Kates and fight to keep my voice even. "Is there a problem?"

"You tell me." He's smiling gleefully. I imagine this is how the Coyote would have looked had he ever caught Road Runner. "Do I need to inform Pam to keep an eye on the stationery cupboard? The batteries are for office use only."

"Oh, would you look at that." Ivy hops off the desk. "It's time for me to get back to work." As she strides off, she blows me a kiss.

It's deathly silent after she's left. I still haven't responded to Charlie's comment, but if he's bothered by it, it doesn't show. Sometimes, I think he just likes trying to get a reaction out of me.

"You know," he adds as he saunters back to his desk. He removed his jacket about an hour ago, but he hasn't yet rolled his cuffs. The pale blue of his shirt makes his eyes ethereally bright. "There are other options, if you're interested. For example, I never run out."

I think I could roast marshmallows on my cheeks.

"I'll keep it in mind," I croak out, my pulse pounding in my ears.

I look back at my list.

The pros are numerous.

On the cons side, there are two words.

One name.

Charlie Walker.

Hours later, when Charlie drives me home, I decide it's not a con at all.

CHAPTER 16
PRESENTING A DEAL TO THE DEVIL

EMMA

The first time I remember enjoying sex, or more specifically, the first time I understood why *other people* enjoy sex, I was alone.

It was a relief at the time, to finally get it, but I really, really want to enjoy it with someone else.

Kissing and touching. Lips and fingers trailing my neck and a hot body over or under, in front or behind me. Somebody else's skin under my hands, the salt and sweat and taste of them on my tongue. The hot press of them inside me.

It's all so wonderful… until it's not.

Because sex is a journey with a destination. A destination I can never arrive at when I'm traveling with a partner.

I'm sick of explaining it. Of thinking about it. Of wishing I was different.

I'm going to guess that, in Charlie's life, the count of unsatisfied women is zero.

How could it not be? Look at him. This is a guy with

techniques. He's going to hear "I can't come," and take it as a personal challenge. New objective unlocked.

I only hope that if (when) it fails, he doesn't hate me more than he already does.

———

"Isn't this cozy," Charlie says. He's casually sprawled on my sofa, his arm out, one foot balanced on his knee, looking like an invitation. Corner of his smile clicked into place like taking the safety off a gun.

No doubt he still tastes of danger and coffee.

He's still in his suit, but this is the most relaxed I've seen him. Collar undone, tie loose, cuffs rolled. It's giving him a rugged, off-duty look. Combined with his leather bracelets and tanned forearms, he is the definition of delicious.

"Would you like a drink?" I ask, stalling.

Charlie declines with a shake of his head, which is good, because I only have water and coffee.

I don't host. It isn't a skill I ever took to, something I'm sure keeps my mother awake at night. And in the last several years, I've had little opportunity. Logan always preferred his apartment, and Ivy comes prepared.

Hands sweaty and courage fading, I clear my throat. This is it.

If I go ahead with this, our relationship won't be the same.

Time to rip off the Band-Aid. "I have a proposal."

Charlie immediately nods. "I'll do it."

"Can you be quiet for five seconds?" I retort, smiling against my will. "You don't even know what it is yet."

"You invited me over, it's late, and you haven't stopped staring at my mouth since I got here," he says, wiggling his brows. "I'm in."

Those damn dimples are going to be my downfall. I just know it.

Flushing, I force my eyes back up to his. "Are you finished, or should I come back later?"

"It won't change my answer, but sure." He waves a hand. "Go ahead."

I sigh. Maybe this is a terrible idea.

"I…" Shit. Okay. "I have a problem that I can't solve by myself." I sincerely never imagined admitting this to him, but here we are. "It's… personal."

He shifts forward, lowering his foot, eyes intense. "How personal?"

"Intimately."

Charlie takes a long, slow breath as the implication lands. "I see. And you want my help with it."

Heat creeps up the back of my neck as I nod.

"For the last few years, I haven't been able to come during sex."

I dive into how it's not a problem on my own, how it's ruined my relationships, and how, if I could just work out why, I could get Logan back. How much time I've spent trying and failing.

"I don't know what else to do."

My mouth is suddenly dry. It's one thing to admit it to someone I'm already involved with, naked in every way I could be. Why did I think it would be easier with clothes on?

"Hey," Charlie says, his voice softer than I've ever heard before. Christ, he's being gentle with me. I didn't know Charlie could be gentle.

It's only when he touches me that I realize he's moved. He's hovering in front of me, cupping my elbows in his palms and stroking calmly with his thumbs. It's grounding.

"Hey," he repeats, ducking down until our eyes meet. His are so bright. "You don't have to tell me any of this if you don't want to."

"I do," I rasp. "Want to."

It's easier to match his breathing now that he's closer.

I'm not sure what fixing myself even looks like. Freedom, I guess. Or peace, maybe. Letting go. Being present. Being intimate without constantly worrying that I'm going to fuck it up. Or worse, be disappointing.

"Why me?" he asks.

Ah. The difficult part. He'll either storm out or… I don't know. Maybe there is no other option. If our positions were reversed and he said what I'm about to, I'd have a hard time not committing a crime.

"Okay," I say. My heart is beating so fast I can hear it humming. "It's going to sound bad, but I need you to listen and let me explain. Then if you want to yell at me, you can."

His grip on my elbows tightens. He's bracing himself. "Okay."

Okay.

"It's just…" I close my eyes. "I get caught up in thinking about making it good for them, so I thought it might be easier with someone I don't care about."

Charlie's hands go still for an instant before he drops them altogether.

My heart clenches. This was a disastrous idea. We're finally getting along, and I go and insult him. Great.

"Emma, look at me."

The command sends a shiver down my spine. If I asked, would he grab me again? Leave marks behind? How far does his gentleness go?

"It must be pretty serious if you have to ask me."

"It is." So serious, in fact, I wonder if this is a huge mistake.

He's quiet. Too quiet. His expression is intent as he studies my face.

Truth be told, this feels like my last hope. Logan tried to make it work, but by the end, he barely wanted to touch me because it was inevitable that sex would lead to disappointment.

If I can't solve this, I don't know what I'll do.

I don't want to spend forever alone.

Charlie returns to the couch, his earlier smile long gone. "Tell me more about this proposal. What would you need from me?"

I treat it like a business deal. That, at least, I know how to handle.

"We meet once a week for sex. You'll come here and leave when we're done. You should review the list of things I've tried so that you can see what hasn't worked and what I don't like. If it's not working or either of us is uncomfortable, we end it."

He arches a single brow. "And if it works?"

Oh, Charlie. So confident.

"Then that's it. Arrangement over."

He's quiet again, but his attention is laser focused on me.

Finally, he nods once. "I accept."

My breath catches in my chest. All week, I've been preparing for rejection. It's hard to believe he's interested at all. "That's it?" I ask.

His smile spreads slow and easy, and I'm so captivated by his lips I almost forget to listen.

"You got an NDA you need me to sign? T&Cs I should know about?"

I must be more nervous than I thought if Charlie is making me smile right now.

He leans forward, elbows on his knees, eyes never leaving mine. It's intoxicating. "I'm in."

He's in.

We're really doing this.

"Not that I'm not grateful," I say, "But why would you agree to this?"

It's a lot to ask. It feels selfish, to crave someone's undivided attention while I switch off for a little while.

Maybe I shouldn't have asked. If he's only saying yes because he pities me, I'm not sure I can stand it.

His brow furrows in frustration. The look he's giving me is one I'm used to receiving from him. "Why?" he scoffs. "Because you're incredibly sexy, I'm attracted to you, and I want to."

Well. Okay.

Lucky for me, this sweater hides the goose bumps he just gave me.

"It sounds simple when you put it like that."

He lifts one shoulder. "It is."

It doesn't feel simple, but there he is, with determination in his eyes, and goddamn if it isn't enough to make me hope.

CHAPTER 17
SISTER KNOWS BEST
CHARLIE

I say yes. Of course I say yes. I'm a masochist, apparently, and when it comes to Emma, I'll take every scrap I can.

"You need to be careful."

Reese unclips Ziggy's lead, jingling like Santa's sleigh as she follows me into the kitchen. Pants with pockets at the knees should be illegal, but she refuses to throw them out no matter how often I've threatened her with breaking in and doing her the favor of burning them. At least she's got my good taste in music.

I take the lead from her and place it on the counter. Meanwhile, the Mastiff-German Shepherd pup has already located the dog bed and toys I keep here for doggie sleepovers like this.

"Calm down, Sally Jessy Raphael. I'll be fine."

There's absolutely nothing to worry about.

The key to not getting hurt? Not needing anyone. And since Emma's only asking me because she hates me so much, I doubt it'll be a problem.

Maybe there's something funky in my DNA, but Emma's anger only makes her hotter. There's brimstone in her green eyes when she gets riled up, and if there's one thing I'm happy to be, it's a sinner.

I'll eagerly enter every circle of her hell.

"It'll get messy," Reese says.

"It can't. She hates me."

She levels me with a look. "Maybe if you stopped being such a jackass to her, she'd stop saying that. If you let her see the real you—"

Here we go again.

"Then she'd realize that you're nothing but a giant teddy bear."

Right. There's a higher chance of Hollywood releasing a decent remake.

"It wouldn't matter. She's only doing this to get her ex back. I'm just the practice run."

"I don't buy it." Reese frowns. "No way she doesn't like you a little bit."

It sure felt like it when we kissed. But going down that road is bound for disaster. I'm already cruising down shit highway without a map. Hoping for more would be like cutting my own damn brakes as well.

There's only so much self-destruction I can take.

Reese casts a critical eye over the bare spaces of my apartment. "Seriously, Charlie, it's been two years. I don't care how you do it, but if you don't at least get a fake plant in here by my birthday, I'm buying you every Funko pop in existence."

"You wouldn't."

"Even bicycle girl," she threatens.

Over my cold, dead body. Reese and her odd fascination with zombie movies. Ghosts, she doesn't fuck with, but apparently cannibalistic dead people are A-okay.

"You're a monster," I joke, though as I watch Ziggy sniff around the vast nothingness, I can admit that she's not exactly wrong.

She crosses her arms over her chest. "Should I even ask why you're doing this to yourself?"

"What's the problem if we both get what we want?" I rummage around the kitchen for dog food so I don't have to look at the judgment on Reese's face. "Get in, get out, and no one gets hurt. I'm a man of limited skill, but this is one of them. I know what I'm getting myself into."

"Do you?" she asks, her tone too knowing for my liking. "Because all I'm hearing is that you're sleeping with someone who has told you on multiple occasions that she hates your guts."

As if I need the reminder.

It's better this way. Less chance of getting my hopes up. I'm a means to an end for Emma, even if I think her problem isn't a problem at all. Even though I'm sure this asshat she wants to get back with needs his head examined for making her feel that way.

"Charlie."

"What?"

There's a sigh behind me.

I don't need the lecture. I'm walking into this with my eyes wide open.

Hell, I'm sure Emma already has a plan drafted.

With a hundred points and a performance review at the end of every session.

When I can't avoid Reese's judgment any longer, I turn. "It'll be fine. It's just sex."

"You know what? I don't think it is. I've seen you with your one-night stands. And the way you talk about her is different. You actually like her."

I rear back, my pulse jumping. "Whoa, don't go putting words in my mouth. She's hot, all right? So it's not exactly a hardship to be the one helping her out. But that's it."

With her lips pressed together and her arms still crossed, she stares me down. It's no use fighting it. Reese will wait me out all night if she has to.

"Fine. Maybe I like her a little."

Reese rolls her eyes, but I barrel right through it.

"But I'm a big boy. I know there's no chance of anything happening."

Her eyes shine with a hint of sympathy I don't like. "This has disaster written all over it. I want that noted for the record."

"Yeah, yeah. I heard you the first seven thousand times."

With a hum, she pulls out her phone and types furiously. I don't have to ask to know she's talking to Mae. "This goes down as the most ridiculous game of Duck, Duck, Gray Duck, you've played yet."

It's fascinating to watch her type while holding eye contact.

"Can you even see what you're writing?"

Reese smiles, her thumbs still moving. "I don't need to see it. It's called muscle memory."

"It's called a worrying addiction to social media."

She manages to flip me off without stopping. A heartbeat later, she's got Mae on speakerphone.

"She's right," Mae says. "If you really like her, you should be up-front about your feelings."

"I don't have feelings," I say, offended.

Reese snorts. I definitely walked into that one.

"Anyway," I say, barreling on, "you're her girlfriend. You're legally obligated to agree with her."

"Yes, it's the first law of lesbians," Mae says, so dryly I could age a steak with it. Reese couldn't have chosen someone whose personality was less like hers, but they're the most solid couple I've ever known. There's a U-Haul joke in there somewhere I'm not qualified to make.

With the wave of a hand, I get back to feeding Ziggy. Fuck, it's time to change the subject.

They coo at each other a bit before Reese finally hangs up.

"Beer?" I offer.

She throws herself across my couch. "You need to ask?"

I grab two and fill Ziggy's water bowl. "Are you sleeping any better?"

She shrugs instead of answering. I get it. It's a good night if I get a solid six hours. I don't press her.

As soon as I've sat down, a cold, wet nose is bumping my knee, and two big puppy dog eyes beg me for couch time. Ziggy's drool will be impossible to get out of the sofa, but I pat the seat anyway. Fuck it. I'll buy a new one.

He settles with his head on my knee, so I'm helpless to pull the remote away from Reese when she finds it and starts another terrible *Exorcist* sequel.

"Promise me," Reese says later, pausing at my front door. "If this turns into more than casual sex, don't run from it. I know how terrible you think it is, dragging someone into our mess. I did too. Our childhood was chaos, and you can't hurt anyone from the other side of the glass. But you deserve to find something real."

For me, dreams have never been happy. When I fall asleep, I'm getting turned down, dumped, fired, or worse. I've watched Reese fall down a flight of stairs so many times I still have to stand in front of her on an escalator.

Where other people get their wildest wishes granted, I'm waiting in lines or trying to jump high enough to get off the ground.

The fact is, my subconscious knows the truth.

Good things don't happen to me.

CHAPTER 18
TRUST IS THE GREATEST COMPLIMENT I COULD GIVE YOU

EMMA

It's midnight the first time Charlie calls, and I'm so surprised, I answer out of pure curiosity.

"Charlie?"

All I get in return is rustling and a curse. Then a curious "Emma?"

"Am I interrupting?"

There's a small groan. "My phone fell on my face and called you by accident."

Laughter bubbles up through my chest like fresh fizz. The image alone is going to make me giggle for months.

"Yeah, yeah, laugh at my pain."

It's different like this. A little softer, his voice more like wool than steel. There's a flicker of excitement in my chest, a side effect of the smile I can't hold back and don't bother trying to hide because he can't see me.

"This is one hell of a list, sweetheart."

Oh. Right.

Ivy gave me the idea while I was three margaritas

deep into my grief over Logan ending things. Why not try some new things for myself? Like kinky user testing.

Spanking? Not interested. *Blindfolds?* Yes. *Bondage?* Yes (ties and cuffs). *Pain?* No. *Humiliation?* No. *Toys?* Yes, please, and thank you. Followed by a list of maybes I want to try.

I *did* ask him to read the list, but discussing it while I'm in bed, his voice deep and rumbling in my ear, never crossed my mind.

I kick the sheets off, suddenly too warm.

"I didn't give you my number so you could call me in the middle of the night."

"Would you rather I sent you a Teams message tomorrow?" He chuckles. "The guys in cyber security might have some questions."

Was it meant to be humid tonight? A light sweat is breaking out behind my knees.

I sprawl out, desperate for relief from the fire heating me from the inside out. "No, this is fine."

That's a lie. It doesn't feel fine. It feels… confusing.

Which is ridiculous. I'm the one who asked him to help me.

Music swells from the television, reminding me I was mid-movie before he called, and I quickly lower the sound.

Charlie, who notices everything and can never help himself, asks, "What are you watching?"

I curl up on my side, stuffing one hand under my pillow. "*To Catch A Thief.*" It was Nana's favorite, so it's mine as well.

"Give me a minute, and I'll catch up."

Why not? Things are already strange enough. And I'm not ready to discuss the real reason he called.

"Cary wore his own wardrobe here, you know. Nan was obsessed with his style, Kelly too, of course."

Charlie hums, the sound low and soothing.

I find myself trying to picture him. Today he was sporting a slim charcoal wool suit that I would bet money is a three-piece, even though he wasn't wearing a waistcoat. "Your wardrobe would have impressed her."

"Thanks, but I'm much more interested in your opinion."

My pulse rabbits in my throat. "You already know how good I think you look."

"I don't, actually," he purrs, and the air around me grows thick. "Tell me again."

Christ.

"You're ridiculous," I sigh, but secretly I'm happy. With the phone cradled against my ear and the soft sheets under me, it's easier to let go. Like we've pressed pause on the outside world, and now it's only us.

"This movie is a little ridiculous," he says. "But I can see what you like about it."

"It's a guilty pleasure. Nana loved the clothes. Every chance she could, she'd come over, put a movie on, and teach me everything she knew." Suits were her favorite. She really would have loved k-dramas. "Edith Head, Eiko Ishioka, Ruth Carter. She loved costume designers. Have you ever seen *Mahogany*? The clothes are gorgeous. The whole reason Nana studied fashion was to get into wardrobe. That's how her business started."

It's been ten years since she passed, and I miss her every single day. "Watching them now always makes me feel like she's with me."

Every time I finish a project at work, I hope she'd be proud of me. "If you're looking for suits, I really love Loulou Bontemp's work. Oh, we should watch *The Untouchables*. I don't think I've ever seen a version of Eliot Ness I didn't want to—" I stop.

"Want to what?" he asks, practically purring down the line.

It shouldn't be seductive. But my body doesn't care. Charlie's little rumble instantly sparks a wave of goose bumps.

I clear my throat. "Why did you call?"

"I'm curious about this ex of yours," he says without hesitation. "What's so great that you want him back?"

"Logan is—"

He snorts.

"What?"

"No, nothing." But his voice is laced with humor. "Is he Logan the Second or the Third? I wouldn't want to offend."

"Second."

Charlie's low laugh skitters through the phone and down my spine.

"Shut up," I add, but I'm smiling.

"Okay, so Sir Logan the Second makes your heart go pitter pat. Fine. What's his deal? If he's so amazing, why didn't it work out?"

I take a deep breath as unease swirls in my stomach. Where do I even begin? So much of our story is wrapped up in how we grew up and what's always been expected of us. I know exactly how Charlie feels about my last name—he's not alone—but with Logan, I could forget all that.

"We dated for a year, and for the most part, it was great. Our parents are close, and I really wanted it to work with him. But eventually, he stopped wanting to try. I went to a doctor to find out what could be causing it, but there wasn't anything physical stopping me. That only made me feel guiltier. He was right to leave. I can only imagine how frustrating it must have been."

As patient as Logan was with me, I can't blame him for wanting a partner who can satisfy him in every way. Knowing that I could have saved us, *can* save us, if only I could fix myself, nags at me.

"That's complete and utter bullshit. He didn't want to stay because he was, what? Mad he couldn't get you there? Did he even give a shit about how you felt?"

"He tried," I force out, pain lancing my chest with the memories. But what I really mean is *I tried. And I failed.*

"Not hard enough, in my opinion. If he really cared about you, don't you think he would want you to enjoy yourself no matter the outcome? That he'd want to be with you in any way he could? He sounds like an asshole, and honestly, you deserve better."

He sounds like Ivy.

"So that's the sex. What else?"

"What do you mean?"

"You dated for a year, right? Relationships don't just end because of that."

Um.

Charlie curses down the phone.

The movie ends, and I find myself suggesting *A Streetcar Named Desire* next.

"If I tell you something, will you promise not to judge me?" I don't even know why I'm asking; I know the answer before he says it.

"Of course," he says.

I'm starting to suspect Charlie's a hell of a lot sweeter than he'd let anyone believe.

"I really don't like this movie. I'm only a fan of how Brando looks in that shirt and those double-pleated chinos."

He laughs. "You're a lecherous perv under all that glam, aren't you?"

My cheeks are starting to hurt from smiling. "It's my darkest secret."

It's not until Blanche calls Stanley a forceful Aries that Charlie brings up Logan again.

"I still don't understand why you want this guy back. Anyone worth their salt would be able to satisfy you whether you come or not. You're putting too much importance on it."

"Not everyone is as enlightened as you."

"No," he says. "But I'll get you there."

I hope so.

"I have to admit, when you sent me this list, I was expecting it to come with a PowerPoint presentation and a roadmap."

"Why? Are you worried you can't find your way?"

He chuckles. "That's not gonna be a problem."

Goose bumps wash over me, and I'm suddenly aware of how little I'm wearing, as well as the reality that soon, Charlie will be seeing me in a lot less. Touching me.

I slip back under the covers. "My plans haven't worked out so well, so I'd rather try something new."

"You sure?"

"Yes, I'm sure. Are you going to argue with me the entire time?" I ask, although, honestly, why am I even surprised? Charlie loves to antagonize me. "Because I can find someone else."

"Consent is a thing, you know. I'm not an asshole."

I wince. *Right, yes.* "Of course, I'm sorry. Um, I need to be out of my head. Give up control. So, it's up to you."

"Sure thing, boss."

"Stop calling me that," I say, even though it thrills me to hear. I'm supposed to be taking a back seat here.

"All right, sweetheart."

The shiver that runs through me is so strong I almost drop my phone.

There's a rustle of sheets on his end of the phone, mingled with his steady breathing, as if he's shifting, making himself comfortable. Suddenly, I want to know; what does someone like Charlie wear to bed? Sweats? Boxers? Nothing at all?

"All up to me, huh?" he asks, and it's clear he's smiling.

Giddiness kicks up in my belly. I hum, hiding my smile in my pillow. "Don't make me regret it."

"Or what?"

He's a menace. "Have you always been this contrary? Your toddler years must have been on par with the Herculean labors."

"Yeah, well," he says, his tone gruff, "when you get tossed around the foster system from before you can talk, you learn to give back as good as you get."

Oh.

"Charlie, I'm so s—"

"Hey," he says, cutting me off. "It's late. Don't worry about it. We should sleep. I'll see you in the morning."

A click, and I'm alone again, miserable because I'm starting to see just how much I've misjudged him.

CHAPTER 19
ROUND ONE
EMMA

There's no need to be nervous. I asked him here. He said yes. This is probably a regular Tuesday night for Charlie.

Nothing special. Wake up, go to work, give a girl an orgasm.

The usual.

I've already spent an hour tidying my apartment, and it's too late to hide the stuffed raven I won in last year's Secret Santa. If Charlie's afraid of claws, even plush ones, maybe he can't be trusted with my pussy.

A sharp knock makes me jolt and sends my heart racing.

Okay.

When I pull the door open, Charlie's as easygoing as I've ever seen him. The suit jacket's gone again, tie loose, collar undone. There's a tan line I've never seen before, whispering clues about who he is underneath the suit. I shouldn't be as tempted as I am to find out.

This isn't supposed to be about him.

"Come in."

As he saunters past, I'm treated to Charlie's impeccable ass. Whoever tailors his pants either deserves an award or a sexual harassment lawsuit.

I'm so busy admiring that I almost walk into him when he turns around and leans in, his hands settling on my hips.

I turn my head quickly, and his lips graze my cheek. "One more thing. I don't think we should kiss. This is purely physical, and I don't want either of us to confuse things."

He doesn't move away, and I'm left staring at his baby blues blinking back at me, his long lashes sweeping his cheekbones. I'm not sure how long the moment lasts, only that it feels natural to be here. Close. Connected.

As though, when we're apart, gravity is constantly urging us back together.

"So," I force out, already rethinking my own rule. "What now?"

"Straight to it, huh? I think I'm starting to see the problem," he says.

"Sorr—"

Charlie cups my cheek and traps my lips with his thumb, stunning me into silence.

"No apologies. That's *my* rule."

When his thumb strokes my bottom lip, I resist the urge to dart my tongue out to taste him. As if he can tell just how affected I am, he slows down, taking his time and lighting my body up.

It's been so long since anyone touched me like this.

"Your kissing rule, does it apply everywhere?" he asks, gaze firmly on my lips.

It should. It would certainly be the smarter option. Charlie's mouth is trouble enough without the imprint of his lips on my skin.

But temptation is a cunning beast.

"No," I breathe. "Everywhere else is good."

"Good." Before I know what's happening, he's sucking a mark on my throat, and I have to grip his arms to keep myself standing.

The best part of living in a studio apartment is that my bed is ten steps away at any given moment, and Charlie proves himself very clever as he quickly and quietly gets us there.

"Strip down to your underwear," he orders, sending a thrill through me. "Then lie down."

He rolls his sleeves up to his elbows as I do as I'm told. He's gearing up for something, preparing himself, and I'm grateful he's not making light of this. I told him I wanted to let go, and he's taking that seriously.

"Jesus fucking Christ, those are sexy," he says, appraising my lingerie, his blue eyes burning into me. "Where are these toys of yours?"

Heat spreads through me as I pull my lipstick vibe out from under the covers.

Charlie gives me a wicked smile. "Anything else?"

"There's a box under the bed."

Propped up on my elbows, I lie back and wait while he finds it, takes a look, nods to himself. That's it. No indication of what he's thinking. Just the rapidly rising sound of my heartbeat in my ears while he puts the box back and stands over me.

"You ever use that with someone else around?"

I'm still holding my vibrator, doing my best not to let my hand tremble. "No."

"Good. I'll be your first." The bed dips at my feet as he kneels on the mattress, and although he isn't touching me yet, the weight of him above me, covering me, is palpable. I shiver as he runs his palms up my legs. "Show me."

All the nerves I've been holding back come rushing forward, like a wave of fans rushing the stage, screaming for my attention.

This is what I wanted. He's directing me. Taking control. I need to lie back and do what he says. He's not here for himself.

"You're thinking too hard." He leans down, places a gentle kiss on my knee, then the other one. "Relax." He runs his hands down my calves gingerly, soothing me. His palms are soft and warm. "Do I need to distract you?"

Yes. "Please."

It's simultaneously too quiet and too loud.

The bed dips again as he stands. I reach out to stop him, but quickly pull my hand back. Christ, he's right. I need to relax.

Then he places a small black speaker on the bureau, and music fills the room.

"Of course you have a sex playlist," I say, but I'm smiling.

"I'm a man of many talents."

I sure hope so.

"Close your eyes," he says as he lowers himself back to the mattress and lies beside me.

I obey.

Our soft breaths mingle in the quiet, and then tingles flood my skin as he starts to touch me.

Starting at my shoulder, he runs his hand along my arm, down to my hand, before guiding it and the toy between my legs.

This probably won't even work, and isn't that more embarrassing?

Even the smooth bass and seductive tones of the music aren't enough to drown out the pounding of my racing heart.

"Relax, I've got you," he says, his voice a low caress. "Show me what you like."

With a deep breath, I turn it on.

The buzzing is suddenly louder than it's ever been. Has it always been this deafening? I hold the vibe against my clit, but I'm too aware of the air hitting my skin and Charlie next to me, watching.

Maybe this was a mistake.

"I feel like I'm watching a medical exam," he says.

I'm so frustrated it shocks a laugh out of me. "Fuck you," I say, but I'm smiling too hard to sell it. The tension begins to bleed out of my shoulders.

With a click, I turn the toy off and look at him.

He's smiling back. "Maybe next time. I've got a better idea."

Then he's sitting up and undoing his tie, slipping it

off slow and sexy. He looks so damn good like this I think he just rebooted my nervous system.

"You know, you're not as subtle as you think you are," he says, straddling me, his tie wrapped around one hand. "I've seen you looking. You like the red ones especially." He touches the inside of my elbows, trails his fingertips to my wrists, leaving goose bumps like breadcrumbs along his path. "Have you've pictured it?" he asks, trapping my wrists above my head, clamped in his grip. Charlie leans down, so close he could kiss me.

So close.

But he doesn't.

"You have, haven't you?" He wraps the tie loosely around my wrists. "Tied up, completely at my mercy." Still holding tight, he drags his lips along my jaw. "I bet you're getting wet just thinking about it."

I'm lucky to remember my own name right now, with his low growl in my ear, the heat of him blanketing me.

I want him. I've done everything I could to ignore it, but I can't. Not now.

"Please," I beg, even though I don't know what I'm asking for.

"Shh," he whispers, freeing my wrists and sitting up. Immediately, I want him back, but he doesn't go far, slipping the tie over my eyes instead.

"Good?" he asks.

Yes, it's good. It's exactly what I wanted.

I nod, and then his weight disappears. A moment later, his heat returns at my side as he lies down.

"Now. Make yourself come for me."

This time, I ignore the buzz of the toy, focusing instead on the feel of it, the hundreds of times I've done this before.

It's better. I tease my clit with the tip, running the flared edge over the lace of my underwear, exploring every inch of my pussy. The tension seeps away, and I spread my legs wider and slowly writhe against my hand.

Charlie ghosts his lips over my shoulder, the sensation shocking me back to reality.

I pull the vibe away, leaving my clit throbbing.

"I thought you were only going to watch."

His lips brush my ear. "And I thought you wanted me in charge."

He's right. With a shuddering breath, I relax. "I do."

"Then, respectfully," he whispers, and the butterflies start up again, "shut up and let me work," he says, throwing my own words back at me with a smile I can't see but know in my bones is there.

This time he isn't tentative as he trails wet kisses along my neck. The nick of teeth against his earlier mark pulls a whimper from me, and I twist my free hand in the sheet.

Oh, fuck. Yes. That works. That really works.

I glide the vibrator across my clit with a whimper.

With a low, rumbling hum, he lays his palm on my collarbone, a steady weight. My throat sits in the curve of his hand, barely touching. But the pressure and breadth of his skin against my chest calls to me, calms me.

With my eyes covered, he could be anyone, but it's

hard to picture anyone else while I'm surrounded by the deep, cool scent of his cologne.

I moan as Charlie mouths down my chest, sucking one of my nipples into his mouth. It's hot and wet, and I arch my back, desperate for more.

"That's it," he purrs, pulling my leg over his, spreading me further. He leaves his hand on my thigh, not close enough to touch my pussy but enough that I want him to.

He continues to touch me, never where I can predict it. Fuck, it's wildly sexy.

I focus on breathing, on the slow movement of his fingers along my side, up my arm, then back again. New tingles start, good ones, running up and down my spine, until I can't stop writhing. I want more. I *need* more.

It takes me all the way to the cliff edge, but as I hover and hover and hover at the peak, willing my body to just fall, *go over*, do it… I can't.

Like always, it's there, just out of reach, mocking me.

Every breath is thick, hot, like trying to inhale smoke. My lungs are squeezed, and all I want to do is get some space so I can take a breath. I drop my head back against the pillow with a frustrated thud, and I point my fear away from him so Charlie won't see it.

Why does this always have to happen?

It's the closest I've ever come to climaxing with someone else, like standing on one side of an unlocked door I can't open. All I have to do is move. But I can't. I'm frozen in place, on the precipice, frustrated.

I want to cry. Scream. Find the receipt for this broken body and demand a refund. I settle for turning the toy off and throwing it to the side.

I hate this.

I was so close.

"Why?" I ask, desperate.

Why can't I come like this?

Why can't this part of me work the way I want it to?

There's so much noise in my head—*stop; don't stop; tell him to leave; oh god, he's going to hate me; shut up and pretend; why did I even ask for this?*—that for a second, I don't realize Charlie has removed the tie and covered me with the sheet.

I blink up at his face. His eyes are creased in concern, jumping around mine, searching for something, and, oh god, he's gorgeous like this. Hair ruffled, lips red.

My frustrated clit throbs.

Yeah, yeah. Get in line. We're all disappointed at this turn of events.

"Don't you dare apologize," he says, as serious as when he's debating with me about document categories. If I wasn't still so keyed up, I'd probably laugh.

"Okay, I won't."

It's only when his trademark smile slips back into place that I exhale my relief.

When his gaze drops to my mouth, my breath catches. I want his lips back on me. I want to watch as he teases marks into my pale skin. But I say nothing.

Charlie clears his throat and rolls away.

————

At first, I'd put it down to bad sex.

Then the data stacked up, and I realized the common denominator was me.

Sometimes, I warn men beforehand, but mostly I've learned not to, because when I do, they either think I'm being coy, or they think I'm playing a game.

If it is a game, it's a terrible one where everyone loses.

And they tried. Really, they did. But that always made it worse.

The way they'd look up at me, doing their absolute best, eyes hopeful, then dejected, then annoyed.

I couldn't stand it.

Making them the focus became the easier option. Make them come before they get frustrated and wave them off afterward. Say I'm tired. Send them home.

So when Charlie stands at the foot of my bed, heel of one hand dug into the base of his erection, I hold my breath, waiting for him to ask me to return the favor.

He doesn't.

Neither of us speaks while I slip into fresh clothes. My gut is churning with a tension I can't work out how to address. How do I say "thank you for trying to give me an orgasm"? Is there a card?

I'm still working it over in my head when I find Charlie packed up and standing by the door. Right. Of course he isn't going to stay. Why would he?

"Usually, I'd give you one last breathtaking kiss

before leaving, but uh," he says as he scratches the back of his neck. "I guess that's off the table."

I swallow down the urge to put it back on the table. And then throw myself on there, too, and give tonight another go.

Me and my ridiculous rules.

"I guess so."

He turns to leave, and I can't let that be it. Not if I have any hope of sleeping tonight.

"Wait," I croak out. "I wanted to say thank you for tonight." It's exactly as awkward as I expected it to be, but he's been so cool about all of this, and truthfully, I can't imagine anyone else would be. "It was good, really good, before…"

He leans in and softly kisses my cheek. God, he smells amazing. "Pleasure was all mine, trust me."

I run out the battery on my vibrator after he's gone.

CHAPTER 20
IS THIS FLIRTING I SEE?
CHARLIE

Doubling our efforts at work means double the meetings, destroying any chance I had of balancing my workload, but honestly, I need the distraction.

Ever since I watched Emma play with herself, writhing next to me in pink lace with that toy between her legs, I can't think of anything else.

"We should just sleep here," I say, dumping my bag on the desk at ass o'clock in the morning.

The back of my shirt is still damp from rushing out of the shower this morning, and if Emma so much as smiles at me, I'm going to throw her onto the desk and wake myself up with her tongue.

It takes a little shuffling to see her face, but it's worth it for the view. "You know, I'm shocked you've never camped out in the sleep pods, just in case you get document-related inspiration in the middle of the night."

She scoffs, her eyes dancing. "And give this place more of my life?"

"What, you don't like EPCOT Jr.?"

Her laugh morphs into a yawn. So the woman is human after all. "Don't give them any ideas. If they could sell us the idea of living here as a new form of working from home, they'd do it."

Christ, they would too. "State-of-the-art depression with a side of lifelong servitude."

"Don't forget the annual 2 percent pay rise," she adds with a smile, and my traitorous heart thumps away in my chest.

I spend the next five minutes reminding myself that kissing her is off limits. If I do anything ridiculous, she'll probably cut off my dick.

I'm thinking it so hard, I don't even notice she's moved until she's at my side, holding out a coffee and looking like a dream come to life. I don't need to ask to know she's gotten my order perfect again. Hazelnut mocha, extra whip.

"Marry me," I say, gently taking my prize from her. Our hands touch briefly, causing lightning to shoot through my veins.

When I look up, Emma's watching with a mix of exasperation and fondness that is desperately fucking with my ability to not kiss her right now.

"You better be talking to the coffee," she says. Fuck, she's gorgeous.

I shoot her a grin. "Only because you wouldn't have me."

I'm locked in place as she looks me up and down, hungry for every drop of her attention and desperately waiting for her next move.

Whatever she's thinking, she doesn't share, but the soft smile on her lips as she walks back to her desk haunts the rest of my day.

———

"You do realize that if we don't tell them where to save anything, they'll just make it up as they go."

Emma sighs out loud. "Yes, thank you for pointing that out. I did, in fact, phrase it that way on purpose. Any document that doesn't require strict approval or revision control can be saved in any other company-provided system. If anything, we're over-saving information. Do you know how much money the company spends on storage?"

"No, but enlighten me."

"Well, actually, I don't know. But I'm sure it's millions." She crosses her arms, waiting for me to challenge her. I like her like this: headstrong, unapologetic.

I swear if she embraced that side of herself more, there'd be no stopping her.

"Okay, I trust you. I'm merely playing—"

"If you say devil's advocate, I'll kick your ass."

I waggle my brows at her. "Promise?"

She huffs a laugh, finally losing the tension that's kept her shoulders up by her ears. The collar of her candy-colored sweater dips low enough I'll be lucky to concentrate if Ford ever shows up.

We're meant to be meeting with the Operations lead, Geoffrey Ford, but there's no sign of him. Yeah, he's a busy guy, and if he couldn't make the meeting, his admin should have canceled. But that's not what's bothering me.

It's that Emma is treating this so casually. Like this shit happens to her all the time.

Fifteen minutes later, she's fidgeting, clearly as desperate for a break as I am, but her stubborn streak is stronger than I thought.

Giving up all pretense of working, I lean back, hands clasped over my stomach. "Dear diary, my fucks have vanished. There wasn't a note, but they changed the Hulu password so I can't watch *The Bear*."

The look she gives me is full of contained glee. I want to rip open that vault door so wide the hinges can never be repaired.

For weeks, I've been attempting to get under her skin, to itch, to pick. But now I want to look closer, find what's really underneath the buttoned-up front she wears so well. I want to know what makes her tick.

Finally, she pushes her laptop away. The buttons across her chest fight for their lives as she crosses her arms. I know the feeling.

"You don't like to take life too seriously, do you?" she asks.

"I'll take things that are overrated for four hundred."

Her brow raises. "I didn't take you for a *Jeopardy* fan."

I shrug. "My parents love it. Reese and I made a game of it when we were kids."

"Reese is your...?"

"Sister. A year younger in age and half decade older

in maturity."

There's a question in her eyes. In the way she sinks her teeth into her bottom lip. One she's wanted to ask since that phone call. It's the same question Reese and I always get. What was it like? Are you okay?

As if our childhood is a true-crime story ripe for amateur investigation.

I let her chew on it for a moment, waiting to see what she'll do.

"You said something," she says, "when you drove me home the first time. Before we…"

Before we kissed. Oh, I remember.

"You knew that building," she finishes.

Trust Emma to find a new angle. I should know better than to underestimate her.

Talking about my past is a surefire mood killer, which is why I rarely bring it up. Shit happened, I lived through it, the end.

A few weeks ago, no amount of money could have convinced me to open up to her. But she's been brave enough to bare herself, fucking literally, so I give fear the finger and answer the question.

"I lived there a few years back, though it seems like forever ago now. Bit of a tight fit with the two of us. Reese snores like a freight train, so be grateful you don't have to deal with that. But it was ours, and that made it better than anywhere else. I didn't mean to be an ass about it. Of all the places I'd imagined you living," and now she knows I've been thinking about it, "that was the last one I expected."

"Most people wouldn't imagine me there." She lifts

a shoulder, going for casual, but the way she's staring at her hands tells me it's a sore subject. "So, you and Reese moved here together?"

It was the first time I felt like I was moving toward something good. No more jumping around, trying to fit in. We had each other, and we were going to make our own home.

"Yeah. Reese got into vet school here, so the decision was easy, even if the living conditions were a little cramped."

Her expression softens. "I'm sorry for getting defensive about it. It's certainly not because I have a problem living there. Though it'd be nice if the little knob thingy in the tub wasn't broken so I could remember what it's like to wash my hair standing up, but—"

"The little knob thingy?"

I swear she blushes all the way to her temples. "The thing," she says again, as if that will make it clearer, "that changes it from tub to shower. I don't know what it's called."

If we'd had this conversation a few weeks ago, I would have scoffed, like an asshole. My gut twists.

"If it helps, I don't know what it's called either."

She ducks her head with a smile. "Thanks for not making me feel bad about it."

I want to cuss out anyone who would, but I'd have to start with myself. Hadn't I been ready to chuckle over where Digital's reigning superstar hung up her cape at night?

"Any of it," she finishes, and yeah, I can't blame her for hating me, if all I've done is give her the impression that I'd take the trust she's placed in me and throw it back at her.

If I really wanted to make it up to her, I'd be on my knees right now. God knows I'd go willingly, but she's already on her feet, packing up.

As I reach for our empty coffee cups, Emma catches my hand.

"Where's this from?"

She grazes the groove next to my thumb, a jagged pink scar, over and over, softly tracing the ridges. It's mesmerizing. sparking electricity down my arm, through my spine, straight to my cock.

I want her so much I'm about to lose my mind.

Doing my best to ignore how fucking good she smells, I keep my breathing steady. "Tried to pick a lock with a screwdriver and cut myself."

"I thought maybe you'd been in a fight."

It's a good guess.

"More than my fair share, actually, but this was me trying to outrun one for a change. I can show you those scars if you want."

She rolls her eyes but keeps her voice soft. "Keep your shirt on." I wonder if she knows she's still holding my hand. "How old were you?"

"Young." I don't want to say more than that.

"And those other fights?"

"A little less young."

With a hum, she finally drops my hand.

I clench my fist to fight the urge to reach for her.

With a shy smile, she says, "I'd hate to see the other guys."

"Yeah, well, I was a bit of a dick as a kid."

"I'll take Things that Aren't Surprising for two hundred," she replies, dry as the Sahara, mischief in her eyes.

Reese was right. This is absolutely going to get messy.

CHAPTER 21
(UN)DENIABLE CHEMISTRY
EMMA

When I was a kid, the future glowed rosy with the fantasy of late lunches, shopping trips, and weekend vacations.

It glittered with spontaneity.

And sure, material things are nice, and first class is a superior way of traveling, but real wealth?

Real wealth is measured in time.

Time to think, breathe, relax—thousands of hours at my disposal to spend on anything and nothing.

I'd take limitless time over a hundred Cartier bracelets any day.

Now, as I wait outside the meeting room I've booked and watch the guys inside laugh and stretch and, more importantly, waste my time, it's clear I'll never get half the respect Charlie gets.

Speak of the devil. Without even pausing, Charlie walks past me, opens the door and pokes his head in. "Finish up, would you, fellas?"

No stress in his tone. Just a short, sharp command.

Immediately, they're up and out with a smile. Jojo even claps him on the shoulder and suggests they meet for drinks soon.

I swallow my annoyance.

How nice it is to be heard and obeyed.

It's what I envy about Charlie. His confidence walks into the room before he does. It's all there, bright and sparkling and undeniable. He dazzles. Slips under people's defenses with a grin, slips out with his prize and a thank-you. Even I can see he's a shoo-in for this promotion.

The man is a leader, where I've only ever been told to follow.

———

"What did that keyboard ever do to you?" Charlie teases.

It's been half an hour since I saw anyone but us in the office. It's not so late that it's dark outside, but I do feel bad for keeping Charlie here so long.

Luckily, I'm at the end of my notes, because I can feel my brain shutting down.

Ivy's been on my case for years to stop working overtime, but there are too many people watching me. Too many people waiting for the second I stop working this hard so they can point out that I'm resting on my family's money.

I won't let them.

"I'm almost done. You don't need to wait."

Charlie groans as he stretches, the movement pulling his shirt taut over his chest, shoulders, biceps. It's a visual feast of long, lean muscle, and my hungry eyes devour every inch.

"Don't you ever get tired?" he asks. "You're always working. Even when you're not here, you're thinking about it."

I tear my eyes away from his chest, flushing. "Of course I do. Most nights, I'm lucky to eat a meal that isn't ordered or microwaved."

"You don't cook?" he asks, frowning thoughtfully.

I shoot him a grin. "Who needs to cook when Romeo's is three blocks away?"

"I'll give you that one. They do good burgers." He rocks back in his chair, throwing his hands behind his head. His arms are obscenely hot, but I'm too offended by his comment to linger on them.

"Excuse me, Romeo's does the *best* burgers."

"Hard disagree on that." He smirks. "You haven't had mine yet."

It's not the only thing I want from him that I shouldn't.

"I know exactly what you're trying to do, and that is the laziest type of reverse psychology I've ever heard."

"But is it working?"

Yes, dammit.

"All right, answer me this," Charlie says, walking around to perch on my desk again. His pants (powder blue flannel, perfectly tailored, no belt required) tighten around his thighs, completely stealing my train of thought.

I've had to restart a paragraph from scratch three times today because the man leans so attractively.

I meet his gaze. Strong, unwavering eye contact that sizzles under my skin.

Charlie has a way of looking at me as though he can read my darkest secrets.

"You liked what we did last time, even though you got frustrated."

My heart lodges itself in my throat. "Is that a question?"

He smiles, the plush curve of his wildly seductive mouth detonating a series of explosions somewhere south of my ribs. I must be spending too much time around him. His playfulness is catching.

"You enjoyed yourself, yes or no?"

"Yes."

"Good. Nothing you would have changed?"

I pretend to think about it, adding an exaggerated hum. "The ending, I think."

He arches his brow. "Is that an attitude I'm hearing, Miss Conway?"

I flush so fast I twist my face away from him, but there's nowhere to hide. It's like being sixteen again.

When I do recover and turn back to him, he's still smiling.

"So," he says. "I'm curious. What's the difference between getting yourself off while you're alone and doing it while I watch?"

Is it possible to spontaneously combust? Because my

body temperature has rocketed to such an extreme that I'm close to finding out.

"This isn't exactly appropriate for the office," I say, even though we're the only ones here.

"Come on, we can argue about work anytime. I'm interested."

"What a strange and unusual state for you to be in," I tease.

"I know you've already thought about it."

Dammit. He knows me too well. After I finished the job, so to speak, I lay awake and replayed it all, searching for a clue.

And if we're going to try again, he should know.

"I couldn't stop worrying about it. Everything felt good. The way you were touching me, and your mouth…" It was like being worshipped. "All I could think was, will it happen?" Ducking my head and focusing on the worn spots of the keyboard, I force myself to share what scared me most. "Is he going to get annoyed when it doesn't? How long until he gets bored and leaves?"

"Emma, look at me."

Without waiting for me to obey, he pulls my chair closer, between his knees, until my arm brushes his pantleg.

"If it never happens, that's okay. And I'm definitely not going to get bored. This isn't about you performing for me. I only want to make you feel good. Any man who wouldn't, doesn't deserve to be there in the first place."

I lean in to pluck a long, white hair from his jacket.

It's strange to see him even a little disheveled. "Mohair?" I ask.

"Husky." With a wry smile, he elaborates. "The shelter had an emergency visitor last night, so Reese asked me to take Dug for her. It could have gone better." He brushes a few more hairs off his arm. "When he was first brought in, he wouldn't let anyone near him, just cowered in the corner, nose down. The assholes who dropped him off hadn't fed him in god knows how long. He's healthy now, but we're trying to help him acclimate to new places. Thought it would be easier at mine because he knows me, but he woke up every hour or so just to make sure I was still there."

Oh god.

He *is* secretly a superhero who saves dogs in his spare time. The shiver that runs through me is impossible to stop.

Instantly, Charlie sheds his jacket and puts it around my shoulders. "Have you considered that you might be demisexual?"

"I have, and perhaps it's a version of that, but I experience it differently. I can be extremely sexually attracted to someone I've just met, but being physically attracted isn't enough to get me there. Even if they are doing everything right. I get all the way to the gates, but…"

"Entry denied."

My heart sinks. "Exactly."

"Interesting." He hums, surveying me like he's searching for something.

Thank god he finds this fascinating instead of the

alternative. He's like no one else I've ever met. "You're one of a kind, Charlie."

With a tip of his chin, he grins. "Right back at you, sweetheart."

I've already thanked him, but I truly don't think he realizes how much it means to me that he's willing to help. I've been wrestling with this problem for so long, I didn't know what a relief it would be to have someone stand beside me against it. A person I could confide in.

Suddenly, it's not an immutable fact, but a puzzle. A riddle with an answer.

And Charlie is here, at the ready, to help me find it.

Pulling his jacket around my shoulders, I hold in a breath, hoping he's okay with one more favor.

"Charlie?" Nerves skitter through me, all the way to the tips of my toes. "Do you own a tuxedo?"

His brows lift, and a wicked smile slowly spreads across his face. "Is this arrangement going to start dipping into role play?"

I'm no scientist, but I'm fairly sure the world just tilted sideways, sending all the blood rushing to my head. Forcing myself to breathe evenly, I quietly will my body to stop reacting to him.

If only it would listen.

I stand on shaky legs. "No, but my parents are throwing a fundraiser at their estate this weekend, and I need a date. Logan's going to be there."

The light in his eyes dims, and they grow a little harder, calculating. "You're hoping when he sees us together, it'll tip the scales."

"You don't have to say yes."

A muscle in his jaw ticks. "I'll do it."

Thank goodness, because I don't have a backup plan, and I really wasn't looking forward to disappointing my parents by showing up alone. It'll mean introducing them to Charlie, but I'll worry about that later.

CHAPTER 22
FANCY SEEING YOU HERE (WHERE I INVITED YOU)
EMMA

The secret to a great tuxedo is simple. It isn't about the price tag, believe it or not, but how well it fits. Even a rental will look phenomenal if the tailoring is done right.

And on Charlie?

The tux fits. It *really* fits. I've never seen any garment worn as well as this one.

Traffic comes to a screeching halt in my brain. All thoughts are at a bumper-to-bumper standstill under a flashing sign that reads *I want him.*

"Wow," I say instead of hello, because my brain went offline as soon as I opened the door to the world's sexiest suit.

Charlie raises his hands. "Yeah, okay. Get it out now. Make fun."

"No, you…" Where do I even start? Our status quo is one of a tentative alliance. The only reason he's here is because I want to make Logan jealous. This isn't a date.

It's not a date.

But if it was, it'd rank high.

Because Charlie is *gorgeous*.

Top shelf, top model, *top me*, gorgeous.

He raises a teasing brow. "Yes?"

I am so well and truly screwed. "You… You look good. Really good." I can do better than that. "Incredible, actually."

When he waggles his eyebrows and grins, goose bumps erupt over my skin, making it so much better and a thousand times worse.

I swear my insides are melting.

Between my legs, my pussy is constructing an ode to his mouth. I rifle through my clutch, pretending I can't find my phone when I know full well it's on the couch behind me. Anything so that I can avoid looking at him right now.

"Are you objectifying me?" Forget the North Star. The twinkle in Charlie's eye leads toward much more interesting ends. He leans in, and god, he smells incredible. "Keep going. I like it."

My breath skitters like wind chimes, and I want to press myself against every inch of his body.

I need to get a grip before I faint.

"You okay there, sweetheart? You look a little peaky."

I hate him, I remind myself.

It would be better if I could stop forgetting that part.

Because *this?* Charlie and me? Is a bad idea. We're too different. We're from completely different worlds, and more than that, we're still competing for the same promotion.

Then I catch sight of the flowers he's holding.

"What are those for?"

"Do I need an excuse to bring you flowers?" He clears his throat, the sound low and rough. "Apparently, peonies aren't in season, but the florist did me a favor."

I'm speechless. Peonies? But how did he…?

"They were right," I eke out, as I take the bouquet, my heart slamming wildly against my chest. It's beautiful—bright pink and tied with twine.

"Come in," I say, turning for the kitchen. I plug the sink and leave the flowers in fresh water. It'll have to do for now. "I'm almost ready. I just need to find my earrings."

Charlie's hand on my wrist stops me. "Quit running for a second. Let me look at you."

Breathing deep, I turn to face him and wait as he takes his fill. And does he ever. His gaze works over me like a caress, eager and insatiable. As the seconds drag on, I fight the urge to fidget.

Twenty-seven is too young to have hot flashes.

The dress is a rental. Something I considered abhorrent as a teen. But I was much sillier then. Now I'm draped in deep forest silk georgette from Givenchy. It's backless and sleeveless and beautiful, and I don't even have to worry about whether I'll wear it again.

"I'd apologize for staring, but I wouldn't mean it. I've never seen anyone so beautiful." Charlie's appreciation works wonders for my ego. "You sure you want to go to this thing? Because I can think of plenty of ways to spend the next few hours, and all of them involve a lot more than just looking at you."

His dimples are going to ruin me.

"We're going," I say, swallowing back the temptation. I'm not wasting the chance to show off that tux. I might be as tall as Charlie in these heels, but there's only one way I've ever been able to get on equal footing with him. "If, by some chance, Logan isn't thrown into a jealous rage, every woman there will be when they see your ass in that tux."

And as it turns out, leaving Charlie speechless is exactly as amazing as I imagined it would be.

———

For all that I know about clothes, I know less than nothing about cars, but even I can appreciate Charlie's black beauty. I can't help but touch the gleaming wood-grain dash.

"It's gorgeous," I say. "Is there a story behind it?"

"The guy who originally owned her lived next door. He ran a repair shop and didn't mind teaching me, then gave me a job after I'd learned enough. I helped fix her up after school and on weekends, and I kept on working for him right up until we moved here."

His voice is full of a fondness that makes my heart swell.

She is a classic, I'm informed. With a personality.

"We've been through a lot together." Charlie rests his arm along the back of my seat, teasing the bare skin of my shoulder. "I even lost my V-card in her back," he adds with a wink.

I run my hand over the smooth leather. If he's not careful, I'll show him a few more tricks back there. "Virginity isn't real, and also, I don't think your hand counts."

He throws his head back to laugh, and I grip my clutch tighter to stop myself from hauling him in by the lapels.

"But if you're going to do it anywhere, this is a good choice."

He leans in, and his lips brush against my cheek. "You'll need to stow those ideas away for later, sweetheart. As much as I want to rip that dress off you, we're running late."

I'm trembling so much I barely notice when he sits back and starts the car.

The engine growls when he accelerates. I've never heard anything quite like it. While idle, it hiccups and grumbles, more like an out of breath chainsaw than a purr. But I'll forgive a fifty-year-old antique some rough edges when it's so lovingly kept.

Charlie looks even better behind the wheel, the warm dusk light enhancing how sharply handsome he is. It makes him look dangerous.

A man on a mission.

"Lead the way," I say.

———

The (now singular) Conway residence sits on five acres outside town. Despite boasting six bedrooms and seven bathrooms, it's considered modest compared to its neighbors.

My heart bucks like a palomino as Charlie turns into the drive. Ahead of us, a steady line of cars slowly approaches the house, and attendants greet guests so they can take over and park the vehicles on the empty lot down the street.

My throat tightens.

Though I'm not ashamed—I love my parents, even though they regularly frustrate me—ostentatious displays of wealth are not my style, and now I'm terrified that when I look over, a sneer will have replaced the playful smile.

"Hey." Charlie's voice tears me out of my thoughts, and I realize we've stopped. Both doors are open, and a valet waits at the driver's side.

All of Charlie's focus is on me. It helps. Gently, he raises my hand to his lips, kissing first the inside of my wrist, then my palm.

"We've got this," he says, his breath ghosting my skin.

And as though the words are keys in a lock, I feel myself restart.

———

We're directed to the terrace, where the party is being held. I have other plans, though, and instead drag

Charlie through the house (which we've been told to stay out of) in search of a drink.

Every detail of these parties is perfectly arranged as a performance. The clothes, the speeches, the friendliness.

Here, words are weapons and destruction is a sport.

I've spent enough time around the rich to keep my guard up. Betrayal left my trust hard to win and even harder to keep, which is why it's so nerve-racking to put my trust in Charlie tonight.

"This might not even work," I say, airing out the fear that's plagued me the whole way here.

"It'll work," he says gruffly. "If he's got any brain cells at all, he'll be sick at the sight of you with anyone else."

"Let's hope," I say, not entirely convinced.

The kitchens swell and heave with catering and wait staff. Within the storm stands my mother. She's completely swallowed up as the smallest person in the room and yet still in command of it all.

Charlie gleefully swipes tiny portions of food as servers pass, enjoying the morsels with little sounds of pleasure that burrow into my mind like rabbits building a warren.

When my mom's attention lands on me, I elbow him in the ribs.

Mom sweeps me into a hug, looking lovely in a floor-length Balmain. "Darling, don't you look stunning."

"I said the same thing," Charlie says. "As do you."

Mom is looking at him the same way Charlie looks

at pie, with delight, and I'm suddenly hit by how terribly things will go when this whole charade is over and I have to witness the disappointment on her face.

Oh Em, she'll say. *This one too?*

"No one else is coming through the house, are they?" she asks me, peering around me, her forehead furrowed in worry.

"No, just us. It's okay."

"Thank goodness. I told Violet to keep it outside, but you know how nosy everyone gets."

I do. "They love a secret."

"Speaking of secrets," she says, being as subtle as a foghorn as she openly assesses my date. "You must be Charlie."

He angles in and kisses her cheek, and oh god, being jealous of my own mother might be a new low.

Mom gives me a sly look over his shoulder. "Emma's told us almost nothing about you."

Wow. Thrown under by my own family. Nepotism isn't the same as it used to be. I stifle a laugh.

"What can I say? I'm a man of mystery," Charlie says.

She raises her chin. "Hopefully not to my daughter."

When an attendant passes with a case of wine from the cellar, I sidestep out of the way, but not before swiping a bottle for myself.

"There's nothing she could ask for that I wouldn't want to give her," he says, stealing my mother's heart along with all the air in my lungs.

It's the most romantic thing I may ever hear in my life, and it's a lie.

How fitting for the fallen Conway heiress.

As another case of wine is brought in, and another, a familiar worry creeps into my gut.

"Mom, who's paying for all this?"

"Emma, you know that's impolite," she says, eyes on Charlie.

I sigh. "Mom—"

She cuts me off with a wave of her hand. "Tonight is about the foundation, and I told you, everything's covered. Now, go mingle and enjoy yourselves." Carefully, she plucks the bottle of rosé out of my hands. "You're worse than your father. You didn't come all this way to hide in the house. There are plenty of drinks being served outside with our guests."

She's one to talk, in here with her clipboard. I'm convinced she likes hosting because it gives her an excuse to escape awful conversations.

I watch forlornly as a server takes the bottle out of her hands. Then, without another word to us, my mother swans after him, orders spilling from her lips.

"Chardonnay?" another asks, appearing out of nowhere, as if Violet had the whole crew complete ninja training.

"No thanks. I've got just what we need," Charlie says, pulling a flask from the depths of his jacket. As the server departs, he looks at me, playful and wild, lighting a spark under my skin that threatens to bloom into a flame. "What do you say? Want to get a little naughty with me?"

Do I ever.

"Why am I not surprised," I tease, slipping it from

his hand as we exit the kitchen. "Next you'll be asking me to get fresh in the back seat of your car."

"It's always good to be prepared," he whispers. "Ask me what else I have on me."

The fire in my chest roars.

———

Charlie whistles low as we step out onto the terrace. "Bet this was a nice place to grow up."

Beyond the terrace are rolling hills, green as far as the eye can see. Of course, I didn't do all my growing up here. There was the beach house and the cabin upstate. The beautifully restored Tudor. All sold now.

"It was, when we stayed long enough to enjoy it."

"I get it. I moved around a lot as a kid. The novelty wears off quickly."

"Yes, it does."

We've settled at the edge of the party, by the railing that looks out over the view. It's the best vantage point to people watch.

Charlie throws me a wry smile. "No need to act coy for my benefit. I already clocked the Rubinstein. I get it. I don't get the toy box you're choosing to live in, but this?" He gestures around us. "You don't have to pretend to hate it."

My life, I'm certain, could be a production, and my role in it, at least the one I've been asked to play every time I enter my parents' world, filled by anyone. I'm dispensable, replaceable, extraneous.

A pretty extra with a welcoming smile who says little to nothing.

"I'm not acting. I promise you."

The wrinkle between his brows is pure skepticism.

Okay, let's prove it.

I gesture to Freddy Welsh, third son of a pharmaceutical CEO. "See the young guy in the gray Versace?"

"With the floppy hair and an eat-shit attitude?"

I nod. "In the last two years, his parents have paid to refit three private planes because Freddy and his friends partied so hard that the aircrafts were left soaked in booze, vomit, and smoke."

Cringing, Charlie curses.

I continue. "Over my shoulder, by the pool, there's a woman in a yellow dress. Very lithe, is probably talking a lot with zero expression."

There's no denying how beautiful Logan's mother is. Violet has done more to advertise her plastic surgeon's services than ten years of advertising could, and she looks every cent like the million dollars she's spent on it.

"I see her."

"Her father got caught stealing millions of dollars from domestic abuse charities, and instead of jail, he got off with a small fine." I finish my drink and turn my back to the crowd. "I can't tell you how many people I've overheard laughing about what they've gotten away with. How they've gutted employees' wages to double their own bonuses or hiked up the prices of luxury herbal remedies that have zero health benefits."

"Poor, unfortunate souls," Charlie bites out. "Does everyone here have skeletons in their closet?"

"Some don't. It might shock you to know that not everyone with money is a mustache-twirling villain."

"Doesn't mean you don't all benefit from the ones who are."

You, not they.

We might be friendlier, but Charlie still sees me as the enemy. Maybe he always will.

"Says the man in Armani," I say.

He doesn't answer.

I take a deep breath. We're surrounded by opulence, beauty, and a choreographed dance of happiness.

"I can't change how I grew up, Charlie. Honestly, I don't care whether you believe me or not. But I don't want to be a part of all this anymore. I like my shitty apartment," I say, even if I do actually hate that the heating doesn't work and I'm not sure the smoke alarms do either. "I like my job," I add, ignoring how I want to quit every time it's being mansplained back to me. "I won't deny I've been extremely lucky, but all this? The parties full of people who are only here to brag to each other? It isn't for me."

A breeze passes over the terrace, making me break out in goose bumps.

"This doesn't define me. I wish you could see that." I don't want to care what he thinks of me, but I do. A week ago, I was laid out in my lingerie before him, but right now, I feel more vulnerable than ever.

He shifts closer, concealing me from the wind.

"It goes both ways, you know," he says. "There's

more to me than the suits and the charm. No matter how good I make it look." He settles his hand on my lower back, the heat of his skin burning into mine, and I shiver for a completely new reason. "I know what it's like to be misjudged, and I wouldn't be here if I thought you were like them. So maybe we can both do better."

The moonlight's turned his eyes so pale they're practically transparent.

"Deal," I whisper.

He drags his gaze down to my mouth, making my pulse jump.

"Good," he says, taking a step closer. We're so close now that the word dances along my cheek. And in the next instant, his lips press to the spot.

I'm not cold anymore.

I clear my throat and step back, sipping my wine to cover my blush.

"So," Charlie asks with the same cadence as a doting grandmother. "Which of these smirking pricks is yours?"

As subtly as I can, I point to where Logan is standing. "Over there. Tall, blond, and avoiding me."

Like every man in attendance, Logan is dressed well. Notch lapel, French cuff, black and classic. The sight of him doesn't give me the same heart flutter Charlie has all night, but he still looks good.

I swear Charlie inches closer. "You can do better."

"You don't even know him."

"Yeah, but I'm getting to know you. Enough said."

———

As soon as he spots me, Dad is by my side, looking dapper. His comically large mustache is trimmed and proper, coordinating perfectly with the slightly unorthodox turtleneck he's wearing under his double-breasted jacket.

"Guess" is all he says as he places a wineglass in my hand. It's our favorite game.

Intense blackcurrant hits me immediately, typical of a Cabernet Sauvignon. He isn't even trying to make this difficult. I hold back a smile. "Bordeaux," I say, because that's the easy part.

"Oh? Why do you say that?"

I narrow my eyes at him. He knows why.

Then a subtle shift of his eyes from Charlie to me gives away the game.

Oh. He's helping.

It's so touching, my heart clenches. He's setting me up to impress Charlie, who has somehow already charmed both of my parents.

Because of course he has. The man could charm the secrets out of water.

And here is my father, trying to make me look good in front of my date. It's completely unnecessary and exceedingly sweet.

So I play. "Easy, the flavors are bold and complex. Concentrated. From the left bank. It's too focused for the right."

The closer I get to the answer, the bigger his grin gets, and it's as infectious now as it was when I was nine. By the time I've finished, I'm grinning too.

I forgot how fun this was.

"I'm going to guess Château Margaux."

"Excellent!" He claps, drawing the attention of several people mingling near us. "Charlie, isn't she amazing?"

"And more." Charlie is giving me a strange look. I'd almost call it fond, if that were ever something I could imagine him feeling toward me.

"See?" Dad continues. "This is why you'd be such an asset to the foundation. With your business acumen, you could be a titan."

"Nana did all the girlbossing this family needs, Dad."

"And she'd be as proud as I am to see how you're forging your own path. I know it hasn't been easy on you, but you've handled it with a grace and strength few could. I wish I could take credit for it, but you've always been a singularly bright star."

Speechless, I sip my wine and will myself not to cry.

This is why I do anything I can for my parents. Because they're good people, and they've always tried to be good parents.

Once, we spent a whole day setting up a train set in one of the guest rooms, goading each other to see who could make the most elaborate track. Dad won (more like cheated) when he boosted his track over mine with non-traditional parts.

Of the three of us, he's the out-of-the-box thinker.

"You continue to impress and inspire me," Dad says.

The time we spent together was priceless. Because he didn't work, he got to stay home and have fun with me.

He might be an odd duck, but I'm lucky to be his duckling.

A little nudge from Charlie alerts me that Logan is coming over. When I reach for his hand, he squeezes back, and the tight feeling in my chest loosens.

"Now, Charlie," my father says, as though they're old friends and not complete strangers. "I've noticed you don't have a drink. What can I get you?"

"I was just about to ask you the same thing. Why don't you walk me to the bar and tell me more about this wine?"

Dad's already launching into his speech before they leave.

———

Since I last saw him, I've considered that maybe I made up Logan's reaction. Let my imagination show me what I wanted to see, that he missed me, that he too wondered what could have been.

The worry followed me all the way up the drive, into the house, and onto the terrace tonight. But the moment Charlie and my father step away, Logan is slipping in to fill the gap. The air barely has time to go cold before he's stepping in closer than is polite and lingering at my side.

"You're a vision," he says.

I forgot how grandiose Logan's compliments can be. It's a skill we're taught to master early, and we're expected to always have them at the ready. If you can't be the first to fire one off, make sure to best it. I never quite got the hang of it—too honest, too concerned with saying something genuine—but Logan is a natural.

"Aren't you sweet," I say, because the only thing worse in high society than not getting a compliment is actually accepting one. "Violet's done a wonderful job with the party."

"I heard we have your mother to thank for this," he says.

A sharp spike of panic hits me, but I cover it quickly with a smile. It's just a turn of phrase. Of course Violet wouldn't openly take credit. *Relax.* I focus on how warm and steady Charlie's hand felt on my back, and it's easier to breathe.

"How—"

"Are—"

We both chuckle.

"After you," I say.

"You brought a date." It isn't a question.

On the inside, I cheer, my pulse jumping. *He noticed.*

Outwardly, I dip my chin. "You noticed."

"It's hard to miss. And I'll admit, I've been curious about him." He peers over my shoulder, where I assume Charlie is. "Now that I see him, I'm not sure I understand it."

"That's funny," I say, raising my chin. "He said the same thing about you."

His gaze snaps to mine. "Did he now?" This time when he looks me over, his eyes are hungrier. Territorial. "And yet he left you here all by yourself."

A shot of defensiveness fires through me. Not for myself, but on Charlie's behalf.

"You left me first."

When we dated, I never allowed myself to be bold. I did my best to make myself softer, quieter, sweeter. Only Ivy and Charlie have seen this side of me, and it's obvious Logan is surprised to witness it.

"You have to know I didn't want to leave, but I felt I had to, for both of us."

"I know you did. That doesn't change how hurt I was."

He reaches out, brushing his fingers against mine. "That makes two of us."

In all the time I've known Logan, it's rare to see him openly vulnerable.

"I'm sorry things ended that way," I say.

He hums and takes another step closer. "I'm sorry it ended at all."

An arm slides around my waist, the touch startling me before Charlie speaks, and relief washes over me.

"I hope you didn't miss me too much."

He presses a kiss to my cheek, making my heart jump into my throat. The brush of his lips is a little closer to my mouth than I'm expecting, but since when does Charlie do *anything* I'm expecting?

CHAPTER 23
BDE (BORING, DULL, EX)
CHARLIE

The deck is packed with wall-to-wall trust-funders, local politicians, and press. But I only care about the exquisite blonde in dark green.

I'm not the only one.

There isn't a single person in this room who hasn't admired her tonight. But I'm the lucky bastard holding her, and that's only making one rich dick green with envy right now.

My instincts are telling me it's a show, but I hope for her sake it's not.

"You must be Logan," I say, making a point not to introduce myself or offer my hand.

He smirks. "I am. Who are you?"

The guy who's gonna kick your ass if you hurt her.

"This is Charlie," Emma says, placing her hand on my chest.

By the tick in his jaw, it's obvious he got my message loud and clear.

Rent a Douche's whole attitude changed the second I slipped my arm around her waist.

"Emma! There you are." And now, suddenly, there's another player. This time it's the older woman Emma pointed out to me earlier. She tugs on Emma's hand. "There's someone who's dying to talk to you."

A tiny crease forms between her brows as she looks from the woman to Logan, then to me. "I shouldn't be long. Will you be okay?"

I nod and give her a reassuring smile.

As she walks away, Logan slips a hand into one pocket. "I heard you showed up in a pretty nice ride," he says. "A '70s Charger."

I take my time getting a look at him. Jesus. Everything about this guy is… too perfect. Lightly tanned (and he's definitely the type to fake it), stark white teeth (if they aren't veneers, I'll eat my shoes), and a practiced laugh that makes me want to scrub myself clean afterward.

He's like a Ken doll.

I nod. "That's the one."

He lets out a low whistle. "Must have set you back a bit."

It's so obviously a test. Get me to talk about money so he can prove whose dick is bigger.

But I don't need money to win that bet. So I shrug off the statement like it's not important, hoping it annoys him.

The truth is, that car all but cleared out my savings at the time, but I've made up for that now. Piecing her together with my own hands meant more than the money. I've had offers since restoring her, for two, three, *five* times what she's worth, and I've said no every time.

Some things are too valuable to give up.

There's no way a guy who walked away from Emma knows anything about that. Dude has *hit it and quit it* written all over him. But Emma said they were together for a year, so what the hell do I know?

"How long have you and Emma been seeing each other?" He looks away as he asks, pretending to be distracted, and takes a drink from a passing waiter.

I see right through him. He hasn't taken his eyes off her since she walked away.

Hasn't stopped looking at me like I'm shit he scraped off his shoe.

"Long enough."

"Well, I wish you luck," he adds, leaning in, his voice dripping with contempt. "It's a shame. She really is perfect apart from that problem of hers."

I've never wanted to deck someone so badly in my life. One punch wouldn't be so bad, would it? Just a small one. Rearrange his nose a little.

She deserves so much better than this fuck nugget.

He probably approaches sex like a truck stop bathroom—get in, touch as little as possible, and get out as soon as he's finished.

I don't need a fancy education to know that Logan is a grade-A marbled-fat asshole.

"Problem?" I ask, faking ignorance. "Oh, you mean..." I snap my fingers and grin. "That's right. She did mention she had an issue with you. Guess I'm doing something you couldn't."

Maybe I'd feel bad about throwing that in his face if he wasn't such a raging dick. I don't even have to fake my glee as his jaw twitches, his eyes narrowed on me like a bull's-eye.

Good. I hope the fucker can't sleep tonight, wondering how I succeeded where he failed.

Shit like that is a splinter under the nail of guys like him. They can't stand having their manhood questioned. As if a two-pump chump like Logan would even know the first way to please a woman, especially one of Emma's caliber.

Jesus. And she wants him back?

Reese is right. I am a glutton for punishment.

———

"Was this house designed to be a maze?" I ask as we turn down another hallway. "Are you keeping lost boys in your basement?"

The little mansion that could is huge but as empty as Logan's personality. I've got to admit, I was expecting more, and not just because of the name. Emma's mom seemed right at home in the middle of the chaos, and her dad was cool in an odd sort of way.

Reese would go apeshit over that stache.

It makes no sense that the house has no personality.

Though, as we venture deeper, there are small signs of life. A pair of reading glasses, a mug left out, something fuzzy hanging off the back of a chair.

Someone definitely lives here. They just... do it sparsely.

Maybe it's some new minimalism trend. Maybe that mug cost $150 and the blanket is Balenciaga.

Rich people are odd. What the hell else is new?

"You asked to see the wine cellar," Emma teases, shooting me a look over her shoulder. "It would have been easier to go through the kitchen, but this way is quieter. How else would I sneak around with boys without my parents finding out?"

"Naughty girl."

I fucking love the way she blushes.

"Right here," she says, and *finally*, a door and a staircase later, we're alone.

Just Emma, me, and about four hundred bottles of wine.

"Do you really think he's jealous?" she asks.

Logan is the last thing I want to talk about. I cage her gorgeous body against the shelves. "Yes. Now keep quiet."

She looks incredible. Every curve kissed in liquid green silk as deep as wet moss.

She's a fucking eyeful and lethal as anything with those gorgeous tits on display.

Dropping to my knees, I thank whoever designed this dress for the easy access slit and waste no time getting my mouth on her, tonguing through the lace of her underwear.

Fuck Logan. I'm going to obliterate every other lover from her memory.

Her hips jerk when I suck on her clit, and I skate my teeth over the sensitive spot just to hear her moan louder. It's music to my ears. She drops her hands to my shoulders, and fuck, I'm desperate to have her rake her nails across my skin. But she's holding back, her fingers flexing tentatively.

I pull off, admiring how soaked her panties are.

Fucking gorgeous.

"Touch me, Emma," I say, peering up at her. Fuck, she makes me want to live on my knees. "The way you've been eyeing me all night, you can't pretend you don't want to get your claws in."

Her chest is heaving, nipples peaked and straining against her dress. She smiles, her eyes heavy-lidded. "Anyone would think you want me to hurt you."

I lick a line up her pussy, and she moans.

"Only one way to find out."

Fuck, she tastes amazing. I've been dreaming of this since last time. The way her hips moved, how she teased and circled her clit. I copy every move with my tongue.

Her thighs quiver under my palms, but her hands still lie weak on my shoulders. So I take a chance and scrape my teeth against her.

Emma grinds against me with a sharp whine, and finally, finally, she digs her hands into my hair and grips.

"Fuck, Charlie. More. Please."

I pull off, licking my lips. We both know what she wants, and as much as I'd love to give it to her, I won't. She needs to realize that this can be just as good without a finish line. Orgasms are great, but they're not a task to tick off on a to-do list.

Getting there is the fun part. That soulless dirtbag

clearly didn't know how to show her that, but I fucking can.

The lace is soaked, completely ruined, so I rip them off her. Fuck it, I'll buy her a suitcase full of them if she wants.

She's shaved, not bare. I'll be wearing signs of the burn when we leave. Good. Let every asshole here see how well I worship her.

"Anytime now," Emma says, but the command is lost to how ruined she sounds.

"These are mine," I say, pocketing her underwear. "And you don't get to make demands right now. All you're allowed to do is stand there and enjoy this."

She shakes as I breathe hotly over her clit.

"And don't you dare come."

I lose time to the taste of her, savoring every sound she makes as I lick and suck, spreading her apart and spearing my tongue as deep as I can manage.

My pants strain against my erection, but I ignore it. I don't need anything except her writhing against my lips.

If she never breaks through her issue, we don't have to stop. I can keep her. Give me long enough, and maybe I can convince her she's not broken. Orgasm or not.

I reach up, covering her hand with mine, squeezing until she's gripping tight. It stings just this side of good.

Eyes closed, reveling in the pain, I grit out, "Fuck my tongue."

"What?"

"You heard me."

Like my perfect fucking dream, she does as she's told. I lap at her, greedy for more of her delicious pussy as she holds my head in place and grinds against my mouth. I'm panting like a madman, desperate for every whimper that pours from her lips, getting high off how wrecked she looks.

I almost come in my pants like a teenager.

She's fucking perfection. How she could let the opinion of anyone—especially that asshole—rule her life keeps me up at night.

If she never comes, I don't care.

And if she does, I'm going to make it so goddamn good that no man can ever measure up. Fucking *Logan*.

Let him try.

Actually, fuck that. I don't want him touching her again.

As soon as her thighs tense against my hands, I stop. She's lingering on the precipice, right where I want her. I wipe a hand over my mouth as I stand, congratulating myself for the beautiful flush on Emma's cheeks.

"Oh my," she pants, trailing off as she collects herself.

She looks the way I feel.

Fucking incredible.

"Give me a few minutes to picture something disgusting so we can walk out of here," I say, fixing my pants.

"You don't want to take care of it?" she asks, assessing the hard outline of my dick, which jumps like it's trying to get a gold star.

Christ, she's temptation itself.

I tip her chin back, hovering so close we're sharing the same breath. "Told you before, sometimes a little delayed gratification is better."

Her knees tremble for the first few steps beyond the wine cellar, and hell if I'm not a smug son of a bitch as I slip my arm around her waist to help her back to the car.

The fundraiser is still going, and Emma might miss the pinched smile on Logan's face as we leave, but I sure as shit don't.

The way he seethes when I wink is almost as good as the lingering taste of Emma on my tongue.

CHAPTER 24
ANOTHER RUDE INTERLUDE
CHARLIE

"You're so predictable," Reese says as I put her on speaker. "You've always had it bad for a cute blonde."

I resent that.

It's true, but Emma is a hell of a lot more.

"Reese, I'm fine."

"You're eating shredded cheese out of the bag again, aren't you?"

I still my hand in the bag. "No."

Reese laughs. "Liar."

"Whatever. Go back to torturing your Sims. This is… it's what I signed up for. She's still in love with her dick of an ex, and I'm just… offering a helping hand." And mouth.

"You're only saying that because you're jealous. It doesn't make him a bad guy."

"He dumped her because of sex. What else would he be?"

"See? This is why women are superior. Men keep finding new ways to disappoint me. He can't be all bad if she wants him back. Maybe he has hidden depths."

Doubt it. "Hell if I get it." I tip my head back and shake the last of the cheese into my mouth, then throw the bag into the trash.

"I will never understand how you eat so badly when you cook so well."

It's been a long time since I had someone to cook for. It's not the same when I'm only doing it for myself.

"Seriously, Ree, you should see this guy. It's like the bag of dicks manufacturers went back to the original formula. All the dick, none of the taste." As soon as Emma stepped away, he turned hostile. It doesn't sit right. Does he really want her back? Or is he just pissed that someone else is playing with his toys?

"First, gross. Also, she wouldn't be the first woman to fall for a bland asshole. Just tell me you didn't fight him."

"I know better than that."

She snorts. "While you're at it, why don't you just cock a leg and pee all over the tri-state area? He'll be sure to get the picture then."

"It's not like that. Emma makes her own moves. If she even thought someone was trying to own her, she'd clear them a new breathing hole with her Louboutins."

"I'll start preparing your funeral then, shall I?"

Probably for the best, honestly. I bite back a smile. "I can handle myself."

"Uh-huh."

Reese is right. This is only going to end in disaster. If I was a smart man, I'd end it.

But why bother? What's another scar? At least I'm going in with my eyes open. I'm walking a sure road to a broken heart, but I'll take the gut punch I see coming over one I can't.

CHAPTER 25
BREAKING NEWS, I WANT MORE
CHARLIE

"Hey, while you're out, can you see if they've got the will to live? I can't find mine."

I've spent the last hour arguing with a hothead in Subsea who needs seven hundred documents transmitted to a vendor but wants it done in a way so shoddy that Nixon would have given it the green light.

I'm one step away from cc'ing his boss in a reply that starts with *Go* and ends with every curse word I know, including a few in dead languages.

"I suppose you think you're cute," Emma says.

"I know I am, and more than that, I know you do too."

She smiles as she shakes her head. She does that now—smiles at me. I shouldn't get used to it; this arrangement has a shelf life. I know better than to get attached, but it doesn't stop me from wanting to collect every smile I can.

It's bad enough that every taste of Emma only

makes me hungrier. Feasting on her isn't enough. I want to know her.

Why is it her parents live in that big house while Emma's crammed into a tiny box? They clearly get along.

Why is she chasing Logan, who has as much depth as a kiddie pool, when she could run circles around him?

How long before she comes to her senses and throws me to the curb?

She shrugs, the smallest of smiles tugging at her lips. "You're kind of adorable… when you're not mouthing off."

I throw my head back with a laugh. Fuck, I love it when she lets loose. What I would give to crack her shell the rest of the way.

"Coffee?" she asks.

"Please."

This is our routine now. Smiles and coffees, early mornings and long afternoons, listening before reacting. Small steps toward understanding.

She's back in the time it takes to send my actual response to the hothead, which is so safe it could babysit a toddler. Some days I really hate my job.

"I thought we rolled out a request form to all the DC teams," Emma says, peering over my shoulder. Today she smells like dessert and luxury and midnight trysts on thousand-dollar sheets. I want to bury my nose in her neck and never leave.

I lean back in my chair, getting closer to her and that addictive scent. "Digital did. But I know these guys, and making them fill out fifteen fields on a form every time they have a request will only piss them off. So we never implemented it."

There's a long, deep breath and release. It's her go-to move when she wants to argue with me but is holding her tongue.

"Okay," she finally says, and I can practically see her mind working in real time. This is her in project mode. It's a sexy look on her. "So, you're what? Individually recording every request in the report?"

Lips pressed together, I nod. "Unless you've got a better idea?"

Of course she does. She's a fountain of good ideas.

"I might." Called it.

I can't help but grin. "You mean *you do*. Don't be afraid to own it."

A blush brightens her cheeks, and thank you, I'll take that win.

When she points to my laptop with a brow raised in question, I wave her forward. She gets to work, and I know better than to interrupt, so I simply sit back and enjoy my second favorite Emma-related activity. I watch.

"What if we automated it?" she asks, not looking away from the screen. There's a cute little crease forming between her brows.

"At least twice a day, you threaten to strangle your mouse, and yet you're always coming back to automation. When the great robot uprising happens, I can't work out whether they'll hate you or love you."

"Maybe my mouse likes to be choked," she says so seriously I stop breathing.

"I'm putting a pin in that, but you better believe we'll be circling back later," I say.

The smile that spreads across her face is so bright it lights up the whole damn floor. She's becoming seriously dangerous for my control.

I sit forward, needing to divert this back to work before I do something stupid. "Tell me what you're thinking."

Emma turns to face me, propping herself up against my desk. It wouldn't take much to pull her into my lap, and I grip the armrests to stop myself from giving into temptation.

"There's a way to run a bot over the inbox. It won't process anything, but it'll save you from having to log it yourself. It's already running over the Digital inbox, so we should be able to implement it without needing any extra budget. I'll email the team to find out."

If that's true, it'll save the team hundreds of man hours. No wonder corporate loves her.

"Have dinner with me."

"Charlie," she sighs.

"One meal. I promise to be a gentleman."

She arches a brow. "That'd be a first."

Fuck. I can't get enough of her.

"You're right. I'm lying. But can you blame me? A man's got to use everything in his arsenal when it comes to a beautiful woman."

There's no response except for a roll of her eyes, but

there's no hiding the faint blush that's spread over her cheeks. Bingo.

"I'll think about it."

Fuck. There it is.

That smile could tempt me to commit any number of sins.

———

An hour later, a guy with a floppy haircut and a dismissive attitude stares down at Emma like she just asked him to sing "Rainbow Connection" at karaoke. "You needed something?"

The way her shoulders cave makes my blood boil. Who is this guy?

"Yes," she says, her tone far more polite than I would be. "I was telling Charlie about the bot you built for the inbox—"

"And?"

Okay, fuck him.

I round the desk, holding back my frustration. "Hey, man. Charlie." I hold out a hand. "Didn't catch your name."

The moment he clocks the suit, his attitude changes, and he shakes my hand with a smile. Yeah, I definitely don't like him. "Hey. Landon. Nice to meet you. You were in Ops, right? I did a rotation there when I was a grad. Too much pressure for me."

Less than three feet away, Emma's back at work as though this clown didn't just disrespect her. As if this kind of shit happens every day.

Which.

Fuck. It probably does.

My heart cracks under the thought. It wasn't so long ago that I was giving her attitude, jabs weighted with assumptions I'd made about her, along with the baggage of my own life.

And she handled it, handled me, without backing down. Still does. I've always respected that about her. She's tougher than she looks, but she shouldn't need to be.

"So you're interested in the bot, huh?" he asks. "Our team calls him Benedict. Kind of an inside joke. But I can set something up for you. No problems."

He says it like it's a favor. Bro to bro. *No problems.*

Seems like there were plenty of problems a few seconds ago, when Emma was the one asking.

"Yeah, sounds great, thanks."

I'll smile and play nice for now, because if Emma's right about this thing, it'll save me hours of work. But I've got a long memory and a shit list, and Landon just shot up to the top ten.

———

We finally nail down a spot in Baxter's calendar. After the fourth decline, I made a personal visit to Kamile to sell her on the changes. It was clear by then that the only way we'd make this happen was with her help. It only took an hour after that for him to accept.

Now we're facing our first uphill battle.

Emma wanted more time. The Engineering VP is

notoriously stubborn, and getting an early win under our belt would make facing him a little easier, but I know people, especially the ones working under him, and once Baxter champions the cause, good luck going against him.

We get him? We've already won.

The hard part is selling him on it.

"You're proposing we remove critical engineering information from the Standard."

Beside me, Emma's knee is jumping under the table.

"I'm proposing that engineering information be housed in an engineering-specific document, one that sits underneath and is referenced by the standard but that isn't muddied with rules for Corporate documentation."

He leans back, crosses his arms. This is a man not easily persuaded. "By removing it."

Emma's expression might as well be cast in bronze. It gives nothing away. "Yes."

Once upon a time, I thought her cold, as unchanging as Baxter here. In reality, she's full of warmth. Burning with it. The ice queen act is just that. A defense. And I can't blame her for it. When she's being challenged at every step, why wouldn't she learn to give nothing away?

The fact that she lets herself be vulnerable with me is a miracle.

He checks his watch, and we're running out of time to convince him. "I fail to understand why Digital wants to create more procedural documents when we already have too many, and no one can understand half of them anyway. In addition, it sounds as though this new document will be so void of actual detail that it's largely useless."

Kamile and I share a weary look. He means well, but damn, can he be an ass about it.

"The new standard will set a precedent definition of the levels of information that are stored across the organization, regardless of source. What it will do is ensure all the relevant engineering information is in one place, without the noise of rules that only apply to Projects or Corporate."

Baxter leans forward, elbows on the table. The blue jeans and Helix branded polo he's wearing are no match for his serious tone. "Why can't we merge it all and keep it in separate sections?"

"We could," I say, because even though Emma looks calm, she hasn't taken a breath in the last twenty seconds. "But then the standard would be a hundred pages long and need to be updated with every new capital project. What happens when you need to review the contractor deliverable codes? I know for a fact that list is updated regularly, but a standard that includes Corporate rules would need to be reviewed by every major function head, and by the time it's accepted, a new change would be ready."

As expected, he hates that idea.

"Alternatively," Emma starts, her calm voice clashing with the head tilt of doom. "We follow my original suggestion."

Kamile's eyes dance, but she hides her smile well.

"Another benefit to that solution," Emma adds,

"would be a single engineering-focused procedure that can spell out contractor requirements so clearly there's no room for misinterpretation. You'd be able to mandate delivery according to each contract and track which version of the procedure a vendor is subject to."

Is it too early to pledge fealty?

Damn.

"It's a good solution," Kamile agrees. "One of our longest-standing hurdles has been fighting with Projects when they want to deviate from the process. I'm assuming this change will require them to establish their own internal procedure if they go that way."

It's a question I answered for her last week, and it's clear her butt-in is the last nail we need. "One that requires Ops and Engineering approval, yes."

Jeremy silently mulls it over, but he can take all day for all I care. It won't change anything. Emma's served up the best option, and like I knew it would, this workshop has proven that.

Beside him, Kamile nods her agreement, and then time's up.

Come on, man. Make the right decision.

"Given the points you've raised, it appears that the change you've proposed is the best way forward."

Without another word, he stands and leaves, with Kamile not far behind.

I have to contain my reaction until Emma and I are alone.

When she drops her face into her hands, I worry I've pushed her too far. Fuck. I should have listened to her, agreed to the meeting with Operations instead. That's the easiest win we've got. Rory already gets an earful of my praise for her when we catch up each week. I think he'd be happy to finally meet her.

I'm gearing up a pep talk when she squeals into her palms. It's a sound I remember all too well from the day Reese got her acceptance letter for school, and I'll be damned if I'm not a little proud right now.

Reese can never find out. There's no reason to worry that the sight of Emma's beaming smile and the relief in her eyes moves the ground under me.

Fuck.

"Did you see that?" She slaps a hand on her thighs, brimming with so much energy it's almost blinding. Yet I can't look away. "I can't believe we actually convinced him. I've never won an argument with Engineering before. Baxter's always terrified me."

"You did," I correct. I'm pretty sure there's a firework going off somewhere in my ribs right now.

"Hmm?"

"You convinced him," I repeat, leaning in, mesmerized by her smile. "I was just the pretty assistant."

Her smile is wider than I've ever seen it. "Holy shit. I did, didn't I?"

She's glowing. It's hard to look away from her on a good day, but it's downright impossible now. It's better than if I'd done it myself. Better than sex.

Witnessing her brilliance is a high I may never recover from. Because where do I go from here? The way her mind works, seeing the forest while I'm busy fielding emails from the trees, is a rush.

I'm not remotely mad that I had nothing to do with

this win, because it's so much more satisfying to add fuel to her fire.

Self-immolation never felt so good.

"Come on, this will still be here in the morning."

"What?"

"Pack up. I'm buying you dinner. Let's celebrate."

"Charlie."

"Do you need a Teams invite? Come on. I'm starving, and you're beautiful. Let's go sit near each other and eat."

"I can buy my own dinner."

"Not this time."

She looks like she wants to shove me a little, and I definitely want her to.

I guess I'm just cold-blooded, chasing the spark in her eyes as she pushes back. Anything to have her light aimed in my direction.

"This doesn't mean I like you."

"Don't lie. You think I'm adorable."

Her laughter is a balm.

CHAPTER 26
WINNER, WINNER, TAKE ME TO DINNER

EMMA

I can barely contain myself. The rush of convincing the Engineering VP—*Me; I did that*—has me near euphoria. Below the worn and sticky vinyl-topped table we're sitting at, I can't stop tapping my foot.

It's like I've had too much caffeine, or I've just taken the first sip of a perfectly light champagne. It's the rocket jump of my heart when Charlie touches me.

"God, when he called the standard useless, I almost lost it." We've been at Roger's (I don't care what Charlie says, these burgers are amazing) for the past hour, and I've been rehashing the meeting since we arrived.

Charlie settles back in the booth, his smile easy and warm. As though he's enjoying my work rant. It's so unlike the glazed-over look Logan used to get. It makes me a little giddy.

"You don't need me at all, do you?"

"Of course I do. I couldn't do this without you." *Please don't go. I like having you here. I didn't know how lonely I've been until now.*

"We both know that's a lie, but I'm happy to help."

It's a far cry from where we started. Now, the idea of not doing it together, not seeing him every day, turns my stomach over.

"You do help. More than you know." With an elbow on the table, I angle closer. "What would you be doing if you weren't here?"

"Still fixing cars. The older the better, especially if it's a restoration. There's nothing like getting your hands on a classic. Bringing it back to life."

It's impossible not to zero in on those hands as he speaks. Capable. Clever. Strong. Just like him.

I clear my throat, cool it down with a long sip of water. "Yours certainly left an impression at the party. My dad hasn't stopped asking me about it. I haven't seen him this excited since he discovered HGTV."

"He'd love the antique place I go to. Next time he's up this way, tell him to give me a shout. I can help him fill some of those blank spaces in the house."

If only he could. My father would be a kid in a candy shop, and Charlie seems genuinely interested, which twists the knife a little deeper. Because there's no way to say no without explaining why or rejecting him, and I can't bring myself to hurt him. Not anymore.

"One trip to that store, and he'd come home with replacements for all the things we just got rid of."

Charlie might play around most of the time, but he's incredibly smart, and I see the way his eyes go sharp at the word *we*.

"Bit of a sore subject, I take it?"

"That's putting it mildly."

"Does it have anything to do with why you live one step up from Fagin's lodgings and take the bus everywhere?"

See? Smart.

I trace a watermark on the table, averting my gaze. "Yes."

He hums. "Thought so. I picked up on the tension at the party."

"Let's just say my parents like change about as much as Baxter does."

"And look how well you handled that. Have you talked to them?"

"Oh, I've talked to them." I've lost my breath trying to get them to understand. "But they won't listen to me. All I want is to stop worrying. If they just moved to a smaller place, stopped with the lavish parties, lived more modestly…"

I trail off. Who am I to complain about anything after having the world at my feet?

But he asked, and I feel compelled to tell him.

I let out a slow breath, hardly knowing where to begin. Dealing with the fallout has swallowed up my whole life (and most of my wages).

"The first thing you should know is that the profits Nana made from selling the company set her up for life. She did the smart thing. She bought a house—the one you've seen—and put the rest away as a nest egg. That money was meant to provide for our family for generations. But with a safety net that big, Dad never had to work, and then he didn't want to. Our family money was always managed by a professional, and he trusted it would always be there."

"Ah," Charlie says, probably already a step ahead of me like he always is.

Maybe I should stop there, but I've never talked to anyone but Ivy about this before, and I trust Charlie. He's remarkably easy to talk to now that we've stopped taking swipes at each other. So I let the rest spill out of me.

"The thing is, in those circles, all the material things you have? They're never enough. Why have one house when you could have five? Why stop at a million? Twenty? A hundred?" Endless cash seemed like fun when I was a kid, until I learned that there was no way to have that much without taking it from others. Nothing came without a price. "Between the bad investments and the reckless spending… well. It was bad enough that it necessitated the swift liquidation of almost everything."

Including my post-college plans.

"Your parents didn't seem the type to embrace the blank-on-blank lifestyle aesthetic."

I offer him a sad smile. "No, they're not. But in the same way it caused the problem, it also solved it, because they had so much to spare."

"They weren't the only ones to clean house, though."

Why, oh, why did I ever think Charlie was ignorant?

"No," I admit, swallowing thickly. "Harvey managed it all through various contacts, some auctions, some private sales. Everything I have left is in my apartment."

Our plates get cleared away, the bill left between us with no urgency. There's a low rumble of conversation around us, no one paying us any mind, but it doesn't lessen how exposed I feel.

I couldn't talk about this with Logan without his parents finding out. Charlie is safer, but I can't stand the thought of him looking at me differently.

He shifts, leaning in, talking low.

"I've never told Reese this, but I keep two emergency funds, one for each of us. She hasn't needed my help in years, especially now that she has the shelter and Mae, but I still put a little away each month. We lived so long with nothing. I never want to go through that again. I don't think I'll ever stop worrying about her or needing to know I have the means to help if she ever needs it."

It's another glimpse of the real Charlie under all that swagger, another clue to solving the mystery of him. And it makes my heart clench tightly in my chest.

When I met him, I was blinded by the clothes, the attitude. I assumed I knew him, his type, all the while hating when others made similar assumptions about me. I hate how wrong I was, but more than that, I hate how I treated him because of it.

"Charlie—"

"I already told you: don't you dare apologize."

"I guess that means I'm always going to be right," I say dryly. He may not want to hear my apology, but he deserves to. "I shouldn't have judged you before I knew you. I never thought I'd say it, but I'm really happy Roberts forced us together."

"Me too," he says, catching my hand in his and adding a soft wink. The plush curve of his mouth detonates a series of explosions in my chest, helped by the heat of my hand in his.

Today might just be the best day of my life.

"You know," I say. "When I was nine, I decided I wanted to be the first woman to climb Everest."

He looks surprised. "But you hate the cold."

"Don't interrupt," I tease, and revel in Charlie's laugh. "Of course, I was quickly informed I was much too young, and there was also the small fact that I was too late to be the first, or even the tenth. Do you know how many women have climbed it?"

"Not a clue."

"Hundreds. Maybe thousands by now."

"I bet you'd look cute in all that gear, though. Perfectly windswept at the peak, pink parka and everything."

"Honestly," I say, thinking back, "I only said it because Amy Lynne was bragging about visiting Versailles, and I wanted to one-up her. I picked it because it was the farthest place on the earth anyone could go."

"You're really holding a grudge against Antarctica, aren't you?"

I laugh freely and, feeling bold, turn my hand and thread my fingers through his. Like a sense memory, my thumb finds the scar there, stroking softly. It's presumptuous and familiar, but Charlie doesn't stop me.

I can't remember ever holding Logan's hand, now that I think about it.

"I always wanted to go to Venice," he admits.

If I could charter a plane right now, I would. I'd give him the world. "You should. It's beautiful."

He stares intently at our linked hands. "Reese and I used to sneak magazines home anytime we were forced to go to the dentist. Didn't matter how old they were. We'd pore over them, pretend to shop the clothes, plan trips to Tahiti or Tulum, get to the out-and-about section and pretend we knew everybody. 'Oh, did you hear about Gustav? He lost his ostrich.' Shit like that."

"What a swelegant, elegant party it must have been. I'm sorry I missed it."

"If I'm Sinatra," he says, getting my reference and pleasing me far more than he should, "you know that makes you the Princess of Monaco."

Gorgeous and untouchable. Is that how he sees me?

"But the real prize," he says, "was the thick store catalogs. We'd sit for hours and shop for our someday house. Reese had one of those old-school calculators and everything. Size of a brick."

"For some reason, I'm picturing those ticker tape machines."

Charlie laughs. "You're watching too many old movies, sweetheart."

I can almost picture the two of them huddled together at the dining table, or perhaps sprawled across the floor, circling the items they wanted.

It's about as far from my own childhood as he could get.

"As someone who once got to go on those shopping sprees for real, your way sounds more fun." Maybe he can teach my parents to enjoy fantasy spending for a change.

He hums the same way he did the other night, and my blush heats up into a tingle.

"Emma," he says, and why does he have to say my name like that? Like a beloved souvenir? "I won't ever know what it's like, being rich, but I don't care about any of that. What you did today? It had nothing to do with money and everything to do with you. I've seen guys older and scruffier buckle under Baxter's scrutiny. You were hot as hell in there. You should be proud of yourself."

I'm a firm believer in not needing anyone's validation but my own. It's what made me such a terrible fit in school, what's gotten in the way of most of my relationships, what drives me to work so hard.

On my best days, I'm a phenomenon. A warrior. Every path is a catwalk, every room my stage. On my best days, I'm unstoppable.

So the wild joy that hits me under Charlie's praise is a shock.

I could face an army of Robertses right now, because the man next to me—this wisecracking, sweet-talking, larger-than-life man—believes in me.

He's a wonder, beautiful and confounding. I take a shaky breath. "Why are you helping me?"

He squeezes my hand and levels me with a serious

look. "Something you need to know about me? I don't do anything I don't want to do, and I'm never anywhere I don't want to be."

My naïve heart knocks against my ribs, ready to jump into his arms. But I don't trust it. "If this is about last year, I've already accepted your apology."

"It's got nothing to do with that."

I want to believe that more than I can say.

———

The car idles, growling in a way that's become familiar and reassuring. We arrived at my apartment five minutes ago, but haven't moved.

"Do you want to come up?" I finally ask, hands clenched in my lap.

Charlie brushes his fingers along the back of my neck and leans in close, the soapy sweetness of his after-shave surrounding me, pulling me farther under his unique spell.

"The answer to that question will always be yes, but I can't tonight. I've got a plan for the next time I get you naked, and it involves giving you some homework."

It's almost impossible, holding myself back from kissing him, with his tie loosened, voice rough, ripe for the taking. I want to curl that silk around my wrist, drag him the last few inches, bite down.

I want to pull and push and needle my way under that shirt. I want to slip under his skin until his blood is roaring in his ears and he can't think beyond the sound of my name as it leaves his lips.

But I've been told before that those aren't things I should want. I need to sit back, wait my turn, and be responsive, not aggressive.

So I tuck the urge away and say good night, waiting until I'm alone to let it out. And if I come from the memory of Charlie at my feet, hair tight in my grip, that's between me and midnight.

CHAPTER 27
LET'S TRY THIS AGAIN
EMMA

I hope there never comes a day where Charlie stops surprising me.

Tonight, I open the door and find him in a trilby and a trench coat, like he's Humphrey Bogart.

As he leans in, his dark wood and spice cologne makes my knees weak.

"Evening," he says, low and sultry. "Name's Charlie. I'll be looking after you tonight."

It's hot and ridiculous, and I have to stop myself from jumping him in the hallway. At least none of my neighbors are around.

I wave him inside, then I lock the door behind him and lean against it, tugging him in by the coat's belt loops. "Come here, Nancy Drew. Let me take your coat."

The hat goes first. As good as it looks—and it really has no right looking so good—it's a crime to cover up that hair.

Slowly, I slip the ends of the belt free, the quiet

sound mingling with our breaths. He's watching me, standing close enough to kiss, arms by his sides. His attention is like a drug, making me high, tearing away my inhibitions.

It also makes me want to curl up beside him and never let go.

I keep my attention on the buttons as I undo them, one by one. The fine make of the coat is clear as I study it. Good stitching, a little wear and tear.

Vintage. Possibly from the '60s.

Interesting.

"What is it?" Charlie asks softly.

On a hunch, I abandon the buttons and inspect the lapel, confirming it's double stitched.

"Emm—"

"Shh, I'm trying to work," I whisper, enjoying the soft feel of worn cotton and the heat radiating from his body.

In my periphery, his grin grows, and my own smile softly settles. I run my hands down his chest. Double breasted. Peak lapels. Plaid interior. The color's faded, but the coat is well looked after. I bet the label still has the original 's'.

It's definitely original. Burberry. Like everything else, it suits him.

When I look up, I realize how close we've drifted. I only need to tilt my chin up for our noses to brush.

A little closer, and I could kiss him.

Curling my fingers around his collar, I fight the urge to lean in. This was my one rule.

Clear. Concise. Smart.

"Ready, sweetheart?" His voice is dangerously soft. It sends butterflies skittering around my stomach, which is exactly why I need to get us back on track.

"Are you?" I challenge, arching a brow.

His grin grows wide. "Always."

Every step toward my bed sends my pulse higher. Along the way, Charlie loses the coat, leaving him in a black shirt and pants. The tie is already gone, his collar devilishly open, his bare skin beckoning me.

He takes his time stripping me out of my clothes and underwear, keeping his touch light. I bite back my impatience and wait for his next move.

He has a plan for tonight, and I do love a good plan.

A thrill rushes through me when he pulls fabric cuffs from his bag.

There are four, two more than I've used before, and I'm saying "please" before he can even ask.

"All of them?" he asks.

"Yes."

"Naughty girl," he teases with a wink. "Lie down."

It takes all my self-control not to scramble onto the bed, but I do as he asks.

The cuffs are infinitely soft, gliding like crushed velvet over my wrists, igniting sparks beneath my skin. He's firm and methodical as he straps me in, my arms and legs stretched out, taut but not pulled, bound to each corner of the bed frame.

It's perfect.

He stands, taking in the sight of me, growling the way his car does. "Fuck, Emma. Just look at you."

I've never been this turned on in my life.

"You should be doing more than just looking at me," I say, chest heaving with anticipation.

"Bossy. Would you like to take over?"

I almost say yes.

But I want to see what he has in store. "No, that's not… Please, Charlie."

"I'm going to take care of you. Say no anytime, and we stop."

I nod.

"I told you I had a plan, and it's this." He holds his phone in one hand and a pair of headphones in the other. "Now, you sent me a spicy little audio clip last night. Do you remember?"

My mouth runs dry. "Yes."

"You sounded so good coming for me. Do you know what I did?"

"Tell me," I plead.

"I filmed myself getting off while I listened to it."

Oh, fuck.

I squirm in pleasure, whimpering as my pussy clenches in the cool air.

"Is that something you want to hear?"

God, yes. Why haven't I ever thought of this before? "Please."

"Good, okay. I also thought we could use this." He sets the headphones on the bed, then reaches into his pocket and pulls out a silk sleep mask. My mind races two steps ahead, and my clit throbs.

"I already have blindfolds."

"Are they as nice as this?" he challenges. "Lift your head."

I do.

As he slips it over my eyes, my lips part with a gasp. The mask blocks out the light and his eyes, but his deep, seductive scent keeps me calm, even as fireworks explode in my belly. He's barely touched me, and I'm already dripping.

"How do you feel?"

So, so good.

"Gonna need a verbal, sweetheart."

I can hear him smiling, the little shit, but I'm so damn turned on it's hard to do anything but moan. "Good, Charlie. It feels really good."

His touch is still infuriatingly light as he draws his fingers along my skin, from my elbows, up my arms, brushing my neck. I stretch up, trying to get more of his touch, pulling the cuffs tight, only for him to pull away and start over.

He's taking great pleasure in drawing this out. I want to interrupt. Take over. Take charge.

I hold my tongue.

After several more seconds pass, I have to say something, have to know what is going on.

"Charlie," I whine.

"Yes?"

He's such a tease.

"I want more."

His hand stills.

There's nothing but the sound of our breaths and

the heat of him. He's close, but I can't tell where. The air between us is heavy. I'm ready to tear out of these binds, throw him down on the floor, and demand what I want. But all I can do is flex my fists and wait.

Then he's touching me again, ghosting the same soft caress between my breasts. I groan in frustration, and when Charlie chuckles in response, I scowl behind the blindfold.

I shiver as his mouth brushes my ear and he whispers, "You're not in charge right now, sweetheart."

"If I was, this would be going a lot faster," I grumble.

He hums, pleased, kissing my jaw, mouthing along my neck.

"You're being very methodical about this," I rasp, my voice catching as he sucks a bruise along my collarbone.

"Haven't you heard it's about the journey, not the destination?"

He circles his tongue around my nipple and gives it a wet kiss, then moves to the other.

I arch my back, needing more of his mouth. "Someone made that up so we'd all pretend to enjoy long, cramped plane rides. Not sex."

He chuckles, low and deep, and it rumbles through my stomach as he moves lower. When he presses his lips to the inside of my thigh, there's no stopping the whimper that escapes me. His breath ghosts hot over my aching pussy. He's so close.

Another kiss, higher this time. My pulse picks up. I

want to thrust forward into his mouth, force his lips to my clit, but I can't.

"If you're always in a rush to get to the end," he says, his voice gravel, "you miss the best part."

He's slow and tender as he teases my clit. I whimper. The shiver that passes through me is seismic, hitting at least an eight on the Richter scale, and tremors follow with every pass of his tongue.

Fuck.

I'm hungry. Starved. Eager.

And he's feeding me.

"Charlie," I whine, gripping the sheet. "Oh, fuck, your mouth."

"Good?"

I'm panting. "You know it is."

"Keep going. I like hearing you praise me."

"If you even think about stopping, praise is the last thing you'll get."

He moans low, and it's the last thing I hear before he fits the headphones over my ears.

At first, all I hear is my own breathing, heavy and slow, broken by little whimpers I swear I've never made before, and I'm suddenly glad for the mask. Heat races to my cheeks as I listen to myself, remembering the slow circles I drew around my clit last night.

Thank god I'm not a talker. Hearing my own voice played back to me might be a mood killer.

Charlie's voice, though…

"Listen to you," he purrs in my ears, clear as a bell and fucking sexy. "I bet you have no idea how many times I've gotten off to this."

I want to try something, he said. *Something I think you'll like.*

He's right.

The Charlie in my ears groans, and the sound goes straight to my clit.

The whole point of this arrangement is to focus on my pleasure. But I can't help it. I enjoy seeing my partner getting off. I love being the reason for it. The thick, hard outline of Charlie's cock straining his pants has been on my mind since I first saw it.

I've imagined him at home, pulling his cock out, coming to the memory of me. It's what I was picturing when I recorded myself.

The sound of his zipper is practically obscene. "Fuck," he says.

A moan claws its way out of me, causing my back to arch along with it, because I can hear it, the slick slide of his hand as he strokes himself.

"I love hearing you come," he says, deep and raspy, just like I knew he'd sound. I never want him to stop talking.

Fuck, I wish I could see him. I bet he's huge. Long and thick. Powerful. How wet does he get? Is he cut? Does he like a full stroke, or does he prefer it fast with a twist over the head?

I bet he has a beautiful cock.

Pretty, like the rest of him. If any man on earth could have a pretty dick, it'd be Charlie.

I want to taste it.

"Fuck," I gasp out, the sound muffled, overtaken by

the Charlie in my ears, whose strokes are getting faster now.

The slick sound of him fisting himself is loud, but it's the hitches in his breath, the whispered "ah, fuck" that sets me on fire.

Between my spread thighs, Charlie sucks on my clit.

I convulse with pleasure, pulling the restraints tight. I'm at his mercy, bared and open. He could do anything he wanted right now, and I'd be forced to take it.

He could feast on me for hours or leave me hanging, tied up and waiting, until he comes back for more.

Never letting me come.

With two fingers, he thrusts deep inside me, his tongue still circling my clit.

"Please," I beg, overwhelmed by a wave of ecstasy, desperate. "Please don't stop."

I can still picture him, on his knees, licking me open. Those cunning blue eyes looking up at me, taking in everything.

The Charlie in my ears is getting close, getting louder, his hand moving faster now, his voice rough. "I hope you're not finished yet," he goads. "I'm not nearly done with you. Maybe I'll keep you there all night, wake you with my fingers or my tongue when I need another taste. But you can't come yet. Can you do that, sweetheart? Can you hold off for me?"

Holy. Shit.

Like some sexual Uno reverse card, Charlie's order to hold back only gets me closer, turns me on more, and I'm suddenly rocketing toward the edge.

And it's so very fucking good.

"Fuck," he growls. "I wish you were here. You would look beautiful painted in my cum."

He finishes with a groan, the sound pulsating through my body over the fast slap of his hand and my own quieter orgasm playing underneath.

It's the most erotic thing I've ever heard. I'm on the edge, so close to coming. Right here, right now, with the sound of Charlie in my ears and his tongue between my legs.

But I need to see him. I need to look into his eyes when it happens.

I twist and pull at the cuffs. "Stop, Charlie. Please. I need to see you. God, please let me see you."

The headphones and mask are ripped away, and he's hovering over me. Fuck. His mouth is slick and red, his chin glistening.

"Do it," I command. "You promised me you could. So show me." With my hands and feet tied, all I can do is push my hips against him. "Make me come."

He growls again, then he's on me, licking deep into my pussy, his eyes locked on mine. That's all it takes to send me hurtling over the edge, screaming out and shaking as it finally happens.

I almost cry with relief.

My orgasm racks my body over and over and over, each new wave making me writhe and whimper uncontrollably. He doesn't stop, doesn't let up, sucking my clit between his teeth and pulling more and more pleasure from me.

It's incredible, relief and pleasure and want exploding all at once, with Charlie at the center of it all.

"Ah, fuck, fuck." My voice breaks, my heart pounding in my chest. But I'm not done. "Charlie, I swear. If you don't have your dick out in five seconds, I'm never speaking to you again."

Without even a heartbeat of hesitation, he unzips and shoves his pants down, pulling his cock out.

Finally, *finally*, I get to see him.

He's huge. Thick, uncut. Wet at the tip. And beautifully, wonderfully hard.

I was right; his cock is gorgeous.

I moan, my clit throbbing. I might come again just from looking at him.

"Is this what you wanted?" he asks, taking himself in his hand, and *yes*. It's exactly what I've wanted.

I'm transfixed. Pleasuring himself on my command. Muscle, power, strength… enough that he could take what he wants. I'm completely bound. I couldn't stop him. But instead of taking, he's giving me this.

It's better than I imagined, even though I can't touch. His face is flushed as his cock slides in and out of his fist.

Goddamn, if it isn't impossible to look away from him right now.

I can't even move, and yet I feel like the one in control. I'm giddy with it.

"I want to see you come, Charlie. All over my stomach. Give it to me."

"Fuck." He throws his head back with a groan, bucking up into his fist, the muscles in his neck straining as he spills over, onto his hand, my belly, my thigh. Like a shockwave, his pleasure washes over me, and I close my eyes, already wishing we could do it again.

Plan A was good. Now I want to see plan B. Let's see them all.

As my heart rate slows, I force my eyes open and find Charlie on the bed beside me. He releases one wrist from its cuff and rubs circles against my skin. I sink into his touch, my entire body loose, my strings cut in every sense as he removes the rest.

My mind is hazy, floating in the fading cloud of lust, and I reach out for him, needing more. But instead of skin, he's zipped up.

Job done. Ready to leave.

"Good plan?" he whispers, brushing my hair back.

I can't help myself. Things will change tomorrow, but it's not tomorrow yet. Maybe I can keep being a little selfish.

He lets me pull him closer. If I had any energy left, I think I'd kiss him.

"Great plan," I say. "Exceeded," and sleep is already starting to take me, "all of my expectations."

CHAPTER 28
I'M NOT READY TO LET GO (TELL ME SOMETHING I DON'T KNOW)

CHARLIE

Things I didn't know about Emma before this morning:

She sleeps on her back, legs thrown out like a chalk outline.

Her fridge is barer than a frat house.

She looks even more perfect in the morning.

I shouldn't have stayed last night. It isn't what we do. But then we did a lot of things we don't do last night.

All I can think about is the way she came undone. How deliciously she let go. Shameless, moaning as she listened to us together. It was easy to get off while she watched, hungry for every drop. Like I imagined she would be.

I almost left. After I cleaned us both up, the plan was to take my stuff and go, but then she blinked up at me and asked me to stay.

And what the hell was I supposed to do?

I said yes. I'll always say yes to her.

Carefully, I slide out of her bed and already miss holding her. Waking up with her in my arms will go down as one of the best moments of my life, but I can't let myself get attached.

Don't forget she hates you.

She's so beautiful, it hurts. Hair fanned out across the pillow, lips parted. I allow myself one touch, stroking her cheek softly, just to prove she's here, that I'm not dreaming.

The coffee table is littered with notes, and familiar clothes hang on a small rack in the corner. It's a carefully curated selection of items, but no more.

As if I can talk.

Everything I care about can be summed up in a few words: Reese and my car. Everything else is dressing.

The sheets rustle, catching my attention.

"Good morning," she says, blinking awake. It's just past eight, and I need to shower and eat, but I don't want to miss a second of her like this.

"Morning, sunshine."

There's no hesitation in her smile, no guard up. Just a softness that reaches into my chest and squeezes my heart.

Doesn't she know what she's doing to me?

She sits and pulls an oversized T-shirt over her head while I mourn the loss of her bare skin.

"So," she says, nervously tugging at the hem.

Ah, I know where this is leading. My gut sinks, but I remain silent, waiting for the inevitable.

She clears her throat. "Thank you. For last night. And for agreeing to this whole thing in the first place.

I…" She pulls her lip between her teeth, thinking. "I know it was an unusual favor to ask, especially since we're only coworkers, but it means a lot to me."

Only coworkers? Fuck. I swallow past the lump in my throat and force a smile. Because I'm just the guy she fooled around with. I'm not the one. "Hey, it was my pleasure."

"Literally," she teases with a smile so sweet it twists the knife deeper.

"Yeah," I grit out. I should never have stayed. "So… Job done, huh?"

"I guess." She nods. "You passed with flying colors."

"I think that's my line, sweetheart," I say, my heart tied in knots.

I always knew it wouldn't last. But I hoped I'd get more time with her. "So, what about the other half of this deal? Any other shindigs I need to get the monkey suit out for?"

There's something pained in her smile before she clears it away. "Not if I can help it."

That's right, hotshot. Don't forget this is temporary.

"Okay, so where else will we find him? I can't hold up my end of the bargain very well if he's not around. Unless you plan on keeping me till Christmas?"

She flushes. "He'll probably be at that new beach restaurant, the Seaside. He loves that place. If he's out right now, that's where we'll find him."

I lean in, pleased when her eyelashes flutter. "I guess that only leaves us one option."

"What's that?" she whispers.

"I'm taking you to breakfast."

Emma said this place was stuffy. Talk about an understatement. I know white torture is a thing, but I had no idea the rich were so invested in it.

There isn't a single comfortable surface in the entire place.

Even the staff look starched and pressed into shape.

I let Emma take the lead, drinking in the sweet smell of her shampoo, dropping my hand to her back in case Logan is here. It's an excuse to touch her, and I'll take every single one I get.

My ass hasn't even hit the seat before we're being greeted.

"Good morning. Apologies for the interruption. Can I get you any drinks to start? Tea? Coffee? Mimosas, maybe?"

Maybe if Logan shows up. "Double espresso for her and a hazelnut latte for me."

"Yes, sir. I'll get those started for you." He bustles away, back ramrod straight, chin high, never dropping the act.

"Do you think I could get him to bark like a dog?"

Emma's calm facade cracks so minutely anyone else would have missed it. But I've studied her face too closely to not notice the quirk of her lips, the mischievous sparkle in her eye.

She taps her fingers, and I'd bet money she's imagining raking those nails across my skin. I know I am.

"Probably, but I'd rather you didn't."

There's an entire table between us, which is a crime. If we were dating for real, I'd be much closer. Fuck it. I slide my chair around until I'm next to her and angle in to press a kiss to her cheek, stealing as much of her as she'll allow.

You know, in case Logan is here.

Emma leans into it, sweet and precious. Under the table, she lays a claiming hand on my thigh, higher than I anticipate, and squeezes, filling my head with a thousand dirty thoughts I can't act on.

"Tell me about this," I say, teasing the soft skin around her watch.

"It was my grandmother's." She slips it off, passes it to me.

I rub a thumb over it, soaking in the warmth of her that lingers, and turn it over. The engraving says *you can, you will.*

"It was the first thing she bought when she sold the company. She walked by it every day on her way to work, but Nana said the staff always gave her the eye if she went in. She took great joy in standing there while they engraved it."

It must be nice to have tangible proof of your own history. I've never inherited anything other than a blood type. "I've already decided that when Reese finally has kids, the car will go to them."

"Not your own?"

"I wasn't planning on having any, to be honest."

There's a reassuring squeeze of my thigh. "Something else we have in common."

Another reason I should walk away. No matter how

perfect we are on paper, it'll only end badly. Everything does.

"I've been sure for a little while," she says. "But I've been too scared to tell anyone. As modern as the world is, it's still seen as cruel or selfish for a woman to not want children. As though I'm betraying my own biology by choosing a different life. And it's hard, because there are so many people in this world who want kids but can't have them."

"It's your life and your body. Biology can jump in a lake."

"Yes, well, not everyone agrees."

"Trust me, there are way too many abandoned kids around for a world that claims it gives a shit about protecting them. Reese and I are proof of that, and I've met enough bad parents to say I'd rather be a selfish person who doesn't have kids than one who does."

Emma slips her hand in mine, a silent show of support.

I have to ask. "Logan doesn't want a litter of Logan Juniors?"

She shrugs. "I'm not sure. We never got around to talking about the future. He accepted that I worked, but I'm not sure he'd understand my reasons for not wanting children. We were usually too busy talking about our sex life."

I get close, brushing my lips against her ear, because I need her to hear this. "Do you see it now? You don't need fixing. You never did. Anyone who thinks otherwise can go fuck themselves, because they definitely haven't earned the right to fuck you. Sex is about more than coming, and if you're having it, the least it should fucking be is enjoyable." Heat is rolling off her in waves, tangled up in her green eyes, and Christ, I wish I could kiss her. "I meant what I said. You're sexy when you're turned on, whether you come or not."

Emma has a habit of closing her eyes when her reactions might give too much away. Like she can only react to them in secret because no one else will understand.

So the fact I've been allowed to see her at her most vulnerable is a gift I won't waste.

"Watching you last night..." she whispers. "It might be the hottest thing I've ever seen. Better than I imagined when I recorded myself."

It takes a few slow breaths to collect myself, and luckily, our drinks arrive, because I don't even know where to start with that. Preferably by getting her back in bed, but that option's gone now.

———

I'm inside paying the bill when he arrives.

Even though I knew he'd be here, even though I was the one to suggest coming, my blood still boils when Logan strolls over to where Emma's sitting alone. I'm stuck standing at the register watching as the asshole takes my seat, kissing her hand and making her smile.

If he touches her again, I'm gonna rip his fingers off one by one and stuff them so far up his ass he won't be able to sneeze without giving himself a prostate exam.

I always wondered how Superman never had to cover his eyes while Cyclops did, but I get it now.

Because if I had laser vision, Logan would be a pile of ash.

As soon as I can, I make my way back, but he must sense it, because he's up and gone before I can get to him, smirking at me and begging to be taken down a peg.

"That looked cozy," I say when he's out of earshot, hating that the chair is still warm from him. Hating that Emma is avoiding my eye right now. "What did he want?"

"To be presumptuous," she says, her expression impossible to read. "He asked me if I was free next weekend."

Right. I should be happy for her. I wish I could be.

"And?"

She shrugs. "I said I'd think about it."

The first time I got my nose broken hurt less than hearing that.

"What's there to think about? I thought that's what you wanted?"

Emma finally looks at me. In fact, she stares at me for so long, her eyes so conflicted, that I give her the out she so clearly needs. "If you're worried about me, don't bother. This was always going to be temporary."

If anyone's to blame for stepping on my feelings, it's me and me alone.

She holds my gaze. "Where does that leave us?"

I shouldn't push my luck.

We were barely even coworkers before this, and once the procedure is done, Emma will wash her hands of me.

But I'm a selfish man, and when it comes to her, I'll always want to take the mile.

"Friends," I say, as if it wasn't in question. And fuck me, if the smile that lights her face doesn't damn near squeeze my heart right out of my chest.

"Good," she says. "I'm glad that's settled."

There's no good reason to stick around, but walking away from her is becoming impossible.

"What now?" I ask.

"I was actually hoping you'd show me the rescue shelter."

Our arms brush as I lean in closer than I should, but it's worth it to see her eyes flutter. "If you think you can handle it."

Emma goes so deliciously pink when I tease her, I never want to stop.

"I'm not worried." She smiles. "I'll have you there to help me."

CHAPTER 29
OH. (IN ITALICS)
EMMA

When I tell Ivy I want to skip Pilates in favor of spending more time with Charlie, she laughs so loudly that I have to pull the phone away from my ear or risk rupturing an eardrum. Even he can't help but chuckle.

I get my revenge by lightly scraping my nails along the sensitive spot at the back of his neck, turning his laugh into a groan that goes straight between my thighs.

Then I remember myself and pull my hand back.

Because what happens now? What would a friendship with Charlie even look like, especially after last night? I can't stand the thought of us going back to being nothing to each other.

I want to know everything there is to know about him. I want to replace every wrong assumption I've had about him with the truth. Because he might not know it, but he unlocked something for me last night.

He gave me back a key that had long ago gone missing. Opened my eyes to all the reasons I enjoyed sex in the first place. And he's right. It wasn't about the finish line, but every step leading to it.

And he did it without asking for anything in return.

I'm tempted to press my burning cheek into the car window. Every time I think of last night, my pulse trips over itself. The sight of Charlie, wild, ravaged, undone, is forever seared into my memory, better than all the art money can buy.

It's a shame I'll never see it again.

———

The shelter is smaller than I pictured. Compact but using every inch of space efficiently.

It's been a while since I've been this nervous to meet someone. Everything Charlie's told me about Reese (which is more than I've dragged out of him about himself) assures me she's friendly, but nothing prepares me for the blur of red hair that launches itself at me as soon as we walk in.

"Please, please, please tell me you're Emma. I've got a bet to win."

"That depends," I say. "Do I get a cut of the winnings?"

Reese beams at her brother. "Oh, you are totally screwed." Before I can even turn to gauge his reaction, Reese pulls me out of the foyer and into the back. At the end of the short hallway is a doctor's room—vet room, I suppose—and to the left, where we end up, are the kennels. "Welcome to the circus," she says. "I sure hope you like animals."

Although her tone is light and playful, there's no doubt this is an interview. It's flattering that she wants to make sure I'm good enough for her brother. It's obvious they care fiercely about each other. I'm over-whelmingly jealous, which is new.

"I do."

"Good." Reese crosses her arms over her Led Zeppelin shirt. It suits her. So do the well-loved leather boots, the wallet chain, the twenty-sided die pendant around her neck. "What was the length of your longest relationship?"

"A year."

Her eyes are as shrewd as her brother's. "With the ex that Charlie is helping you get back?"

Ah. So he's told her about that.

"Yes."

On the wall is a poster loudly proclaiming *Happy Rex Manning Day!* I'll have to ask Charlie about the reference later.

"Drugs?" she asks.

"Caffeine, aspirin, wine."

"Red or white?"

"Yes."

Reese's eyes light up. "Heads or tails?"

Keeping people on their toes runs in the family, I see. "Tails," I say.

She nods slowly. This must be what it's like to stand trial. "Why?"

"Tails don't lie."

"No, they don't," she crows. If her smile gets any wider, I'm worried she'll burst, and then I'll really be in trouble. "History or geography? We're having a quiz night next week, and we need to round out the team."

"Then you're in luck, because I aced geography." In all of five minutes, I know everything I need to know about Reese. She's interesting and caring and is deeply protective of her brother.

I really don't blame her.

"Now I have a question for you," I say. "How long would you last in a zombie apocalypse?"

Reese gasps, and I'm tangled up in her arms again. "Charlie," she calls out. "She's the one."

He appears as Reese and I are swapping numbers, but she quickly dismisses him with a task list.

"I didn't come here to be bossed around, you know," he says as a massive fluffball named Zeus tugs on the leash, dragging him toward the door.

"But you take orders so well," I tease.

Reese chokes on a laugh, her eyes shining with glee, while Charlie trips over his own feet.

"Christ," he murmurs, and then he's gone, the back of his neck flushed pink.

"Ready to get to work?" Reese asks as she passes me a bag of dry cat food almost as big as I am.

I almost topple over adjusting it in my arms. Damn, I'm going to feel this tomorrow. So this is how Charlie burns off all that pie.

"Why do I get the feeling I'm still being tested?"

Reese smiles. "Don't question the process, young grasshopper."

While we work, I meet her partner, Mae, and they fill me in on how they came to open the shelter, newly graduated and hopeful. How community donations help them stay open. When they debate the most effective way to increase funds so they aren't playing catch-up every month, I can't help but interrupt.

"Feel free to say no," I hedge. "But my mom has been hosting fundraisers my whole life. I'm sure she'd love to give you some advice, and probably some contacts." Just as long as she keeps the checkbook at home.

"Holy shit, Emma. Yes. Are you serious?"

"Of course." And maybe I'm hoping giving Mom something to do in the city will sell the idea of moving.

"Okay, I gotta ask. Have you ever gone swimming in money? Because I used to dream about dive-bombing a pool of coins, McDuck style."

I know then and there that I like Reese. How could I not? Her no-nonsense approach is so similar to Ivy's. "No, but I have gotten a twenty-four-carat facial and been massaged with crushed diamonds."

"Fuck." Reese sighs. "Being rich sounds amazing."

"If it makes you feel better, I had a terrible eczema flare-up from it. I spent the next week hiding indoors and trying not to scratch."

"That does make me feel better," she says so genuinely I have to laugh.

"So Emma," Mae starts, "know any bachelors that would pass inspection from a sixty-two-year-old lit professor, by chance?"

"Um…" I stall.

Reese, thankfully, saves me from having to answer. "Your cousin specifically asked us to stop setting her up."

Mae frowns. "You already tried to set her up with Charlie!"

"That was before I knew how ridiculous he was about Emma," Reese argues, pointing to me. The instant the words are out of her mouth, they both go wide-eyed and silent.

Awkward.

Reese winces and turns to me. "Please don't tell him I said that."

"It's okay." It's not like it's the truth. She's just being nice.

Mae gets called back to the front, and while Reese and I finish up, she introduces me to every single animal, backstory and all. I can see why Charlie spends so much time here. There's so much love, I feel like I have a contact high.

"Sorry about the interrogation, but we've been wanting to meet you for weeks. Charlie's never brought anyone here before."

My heart jumps. It's such a silly thing, but I can't help it. I'm special, in this at least. If nothing else happens between us, I'll remain selfishly happy that I got to be the first. The only.

"Why did you want to become a vet?"

"All the coolest characters are cats and dogs, you know? Plus, as a kid, I thought having a pet was the thing all families did. We never had one ourselves, but once I set my mind to something," Reese says. "I almost turned down my scholarship because it meant moving out here by myself. I just couldn't stomach it. But then Charlie quit his job and packed up the car, and we drove for three days to get here."

Another slice of Charlie clicks into place. There's grit in him, a hearty surface shielding a soft, endearing center.

For so long, I saw Charlie as nothing but a smile in a suit, a climb-into-your-grave-while-it's-still-hot kind of guy, not an ounce of care for anyone but himself. I've never been so glad to be wrong.

"I almost studied zoology," Reese says. "But then I volunteered at a rescue center back home and immediately knew I wanted to open this place one day. It felt important."

"Plus you're great at it," Charlie adds, flushed and a little out of breath as Zeus pulls him back inside. The whole room brightens when he's in it, or maybe it's me he's lighting up.

I think I could always be happy just being near him.

"That too." Reese beams.

Growing up, everything was easy.

Plans could be made at the drop of a hat. New phone announced? Buy it. Front row at a concert? Easy. Clothes, meals, trips? I never thought about the cost. Price tags meant nothing to a limitless budget.

What I don't miss is the attitude. The elitism. The competition. I've seen grown men buy businesses and send them to ruin simply because someone else wanted them. Time and again, sons—and daughters—get away with illegal deals simply to impress their fathers.

The worst ones get defensive, but the best ones know how lucky we are, privileged to start life as close to the top as it is to get. Even if we work hard, there's no denying how much shorter the journey is for us.

But. The perks.

Champagne on take-off (even at five a.m.).

Champagne while shopping at Celine in Zurich.

Champagne at… well, there's a lot of champagne.

There are also beautiful clothes and private tours and exclusive parties.

But it never once felt as real or honest or lovely as watching Charlie play fetch with a Saint Bernard. I always thought him most in his element in the office, suited up and holding court with ease. That is, until I saw him like this.

Happy and unburdened. It's breathtaking.

"You're welcome, by the way," I say, and Charlie looks up. "I think I saved you from a blind date."

"They're still on that? Ever since Lucy…" He shakes his head. "Anyway. I'm glad you came today. Reese was sure that this whole thing," he gestures between us, "would blow up in my face."

"Let me guess. You once broke a sorority queen's heart, and your sister has been worried ever since."

I'm eager to hear about Charlie's prior love life. I could pretend it is harmless curiosity, but I know myself better than that.

Even worse, I'm jealous of the other me—the me Reese believes is dating her brother.

"Sorry to disappoint you," he says, giving me a crooked grin.

"No? Just the rest of campus, then? The heartbroken women left in your wake must have started a club."

"Actually," he says, the tension in his voice catching my attention, "I never went to college," he says.

My train of thought crashes. Charlie is one of the smartest people I've ever worked with, quick and clever on his feet, reactive in a way my brain can't fathom.

"Whatever joke you want to make," he says, his voice tight, "do it now, but I promise you, I've heard them all."

My heart aches for him. "I don't want to joke about it."

He raises a skeptical brow. "You'd be the first."

I don't know what to tell him. That people are awful? Clearly, he's aware. That he's expecting me to use this against him proves that I have failed the both of us.

What happened last year is still a sore spot, but it's healing slowly, and I would like to believe that we're more than strangers. Charlie has given me the space to be vulnerable, and he deserves better than he's gotten in the past.

The pain he buries under his smiles crushes me. I want to erase every trace, rewrite every wrong he's lived through. Show him just how *good* he really is.

I stride over and place a gentle kiss on his cheek. "You're worth so much more than what can be presented on a piece of paper, Charlie. Everyone in the company knows that."

I'm only sorry it took me so long to see it.

It's easy to lose track of time here. Whether it's helping Reese hand feed a week-old Bengal or debating with Mae over which version of *Sabrina* is better (the costumes in the 1954 version are phenomenal, as is Audrey Hepburn; but the 1995 remake is eminently charming).

I don't want the day to end, and I can't take my eyes off him as he drives me home. He's gorgeous, but he's also so much more.

My heart knocks against my chest in deep, echoing thumps.

Charlie sees problems in a way I can't and can ask me a question I've never considered and open my eyes to something new. He'll clear the weeds away so I can find the answer and then look at me as though I'm brilliant for discovering it.

Sex might be off the table, but I can't lose his friendship. I don't want to give up his teasing smiles or clever quips.

I can't lose the time we get every day in his car. Even when we don't talk, it's enough to simply know he's there. Every time I sink into the worn leather, I get the urge to tell him to forget the office and suggest we take a new road and keep going. It wouldn't matter where.

Ever since my life changed course, I've wondered what my future could look like.

When I look at Charlie now, I finally see that future looking back.

CHAPTER 30
KARMA WITH A KO
CHARLIE

Another day, another crisis. Maybe I should find a desk for Drue upstairs so that I don't have to travel so far every time he has a problem.

Few people would guess where I've come from. I've made sure of it. Not because of shame, not because I give a greasy rat's ass about what some suit thinks of me, but because I'm more than a made-up birth certificate and a history of juvenile delinquency.

Being underestimated isn't new.

But I used it to my advantage. Got under people's skin, never backed down from a fight, worked my ass off so they never had anything to use against me. It wasn't easy, but I fucking did it. Spent junior year waking up every morning at the ball sack of dawn, mowing the lawns of the monstrous houses on the hill while they were still shrouded in mist.

I hated a lot of my guardians, but Jude and Dana are good people. Better than most. Then, Reese arrived. There was no way I was going to spit in the face of that.

So I stayed. Said yes when they wanted to make it official. And planned to make a better life for myself.

I started by taking notes on how the assholes of the world did things.

Lessons in the shape of other kids' fists with the scars to match. I taught a number of those classes myself. They're probably the only tests I ever passed with flying colors.

Eventually, I learned to beat them using their own tricks.

With words.

It turned out a bit of charm went a long way. And a turned-out three-piece doesn't hurt.

Now look where I am. Earning more in a year than my parents combined and in line for a promotion—all before my thirtieth birthday.

I'm steps away from Drue's desk when a strong hand comes down on my shoulder.

"Charlie, just the man I'm looking for. I hear I have you to thank for a six-figure saving on this year's budget. Excellent job on the automation idea."

Jesus fucking Christ.

Of all people, chief operations officer Greg Bailey has found me. Behind him, Drue mouths *sorry*. Fuck. So this is the real reason I was summoned.

"It's this sort of proactive thinking that makes you a shoo-in for management. You can be sure I'll be having a word to Emmanuel about this."

My gut sinks like a lead shoe. He's giving me the win, if I want it. The golden ticket, the parking space, all of it, just like Roberts said. But I can't take it like this.

Brilliant, frustrating, gorgeous Emma is so far beyond my league, I shouldn't even be allowed in the building. In the same area code. Not only did her tip about the damn bot work out, but her whole idea has landed me another fucking commendation from the COO.

One I didn't even earn.

Karma sure has a twisted sense of humor.

"While I'd love to take the credit, you'll need to thank Emma Conway, as it was her idea."

He raises a brow. "Well, it's about time Digital made a positive change."

A few months ago, I would have agreed with him. And I would have been just as wrong. It shouldn't have taken me this long to open my eyes. Shouldn't have taken being forced to work with Emma and not against her to realize how badly I fucked up before.

"Actually, sir, you'll find she's responsible for a lot of good around here."

CHAPTER 31
AND SO IT GOES...
EMMA

Ivy takes one look at me and freezes in place. I don't blame her. "You look flustered. What happened?"

We're the only ones in the cafeteria, but I still lower my voice. "Nothing."

She drops into the seat across from me and smirks. "Make sure to say hi to nothing for me."

"Ivy, this is serious," I hiss. "I *like* Charlie." Fuck. Who authorized this?

"Let's pretend that wasn't completely obvious. When did you realize?"

My stomach knotting, I bury my face in my hands. "After the incredible orgasm, but before the puppies."

She tosses her long hair over her shoulder. "What about Logan?"

I lift my head and sigh. "Logan who?" I finally got what I'd wanted—namely, Logan asking me out—and I didn't say yes. Instead, I wanted more time with Charlie. I still want more of him.

Ivy rocks back, her lips parted. "Oh, wow."

"I know."

Oh god. I like Charlie.

I like how he rolls up his sleeves when he needs to concentrate. How he'll release a long sigh when he's annoyed but he wants to keep his thoughts to himself. I like that I can tell when he's joking to tease me or joking to deflect. The way he melts when I scratch the back of his neck.

"I haven't forgotten what happened last year," I say. "But since we've been working together, he's had multiple opportunities to take credit, and not only has he not taken them, but he's stood up for me. Charlie is not who I thought he was. I'm not excusing what he did, but he apologized, and I accepted it. And now I know him better, and…"

"And?" she asks, grinning like she already knows exactly what I'm about to say.

"And I like him."

I should have expected the "I told you."

———

Change isn't anything like herding cats, no matter how many middle-aged white men say it is. The motto fed to us might be to *do what's right, not what's easy*, but apparently, it's only applicable for making us accept unpaid overtime.

Not only does Roberts try to rewrite the procedure every time I have my back turned, but he's promised Contracts an automated confidentiality policy that we have no way of implementing.

And now this.

"You can't remove a security level without warning," Melissa from Legal argues. At least she looks apologetic about it. "Privacy regulations demand we have a separate label to ensure that employees' data will remain private and confidential."

"I know," I say, keeping my frustration to myself.

Roberts deleted the label after his morning run because of a Tech podcast he listens to. Not that I'll tell her that. Nor will I tell her that I've already had this argument with him. I spent an hour working to convince him, only to be told that it wasn't my decision. That the only way he'd be convinced would be with a written rejection from Legal.

Hence, this meeting.

"If you wouldn't mind putting your objections in writing, I'd be happy to—"

"I shouldn't need to explain in writing that this company is required to follow the law," Melissa says.

She's right. It's common sense. But try explaining that to Roberts. "I understand."

I want nothing more than to throw my boss under the bus, tell her no one hates this more than I do. This meeting shouldn't have even been an email. It should have been a brain fart quickly passed when no one was around to hear it.

I almost cry when I return to my desk to find Charlie shaking his head. So I guess his meeting didn't go well.

I sag into my seat. "Do I want to know?"

"Not at all."

Great. "Think we should keep going, Thelma?"

He stretches a long leg under our desks to tap his foot against mine. "Anytime you want to run away together, sweetheart, just say the word."

The idea is heavenly—just us and the open road. No emails to answer, no destination in mind. Only the bone-deep safety of having Charlie by my side to face it all.

Please.

But I only want it if I can have all of him. It's all I've been able to think about.

How much would it take to break him? Tease him until he pushes me against the wall and kisses me like he did at my doorstep months ago?

"Let's make it plan B," I say.

"Emma." Roberts appears, looming over my shoulder, the final sign that today has gone to hell. "I need to talk to you in my office. Now."

No *please*. No attempt at polite imposition.

There's no way this won't be painful for me.

Even Charlie's reassuring look isn't enough to stop the swirling pit of concern that's picked up in my stomach. I touch two fingers to Nana's watch and take a deep breath. I am strong. I am smart. And I'm afraid of worse things than my pedantic boss.

I can, I will.

———

Never again will I doubt my intuition.

Hell is an apt descriptor, maybe even a little generous, given that when I walk into Roberts's office, he isn't alone. Standing in the corner—looming is the only way to phrase it—is Helix's CIO, Emmanuel Fletcher, and both men are wearing dissatisfied frowns.

If they think their stony expressions are going to unnerve me, I'll be glad to disabuse them of that idea.

Disappointment is a look I've learned to weather well.

Get in line, gentlemen.

If anyone has earned the right to be frustrated, I can guarantee it's me.

"Take a seat," Roberts commands.

The last time I was in a room with Emmanuel Fletcher, Charlie was being lauded to the entire company for my work. At the time, I was a little distracted by the blood rushing in my ears to pay him any mind.

Not unlike how I feel now.

I sit as instructed, but when it becomes obvious that Roberts isn't going to introduce me, I take matters into my own hands. "Good to meet you, Mr. Fletcher."

"Emmanuel, please, and the pleasure is all mine, Emma. The digital signatures initiative you pioneered has saved me a lot of frustration."

The recognition is a refreshing surprise. The project was presented as a growth opportunity, and I naively thought it would be an easy sell. Who would argue against increased efficiency?

As it turns out, a lot of people.

"I'm glad to hear it."

"Emmanuel is here to get an update on the procedure," Roberts intones in a way that sounds very similar to a threat.

"In that case, I think Charlie should be here." I'm not letting Roberts push him out. It wasn't that long ago that they were peas in a pod.

"That won't be necessary," he says, and yes, that's definitely a threat.

Heart lurching, I straighten.

"Based on the document logs," he says, "the only changes made to the Procedure in the last month have been from your account. In fact, I had to have the Tech Bar unlock the document for me, because I couldn't access it. The best they could tell, that was because you changed the security on it."

No shit. It was locked because he kept rewriting it. And the only changes are mine because I type faster than Charlie, and we work better when I take the lead while he keeps Operations happy.

But as I open my mouth, Roberts continues, like he was waiting to cut me off. "When I presented this opportunity to you both, I asked if you'd be able to work together. You assured me you could. Then I asked if there was any tension between you, and you promised things were fine. I'm sure you can understand why I'm having trouble believing that now, given the evidence."

Again, he pauses, and again, just as I open my mouth, he speaks.

He's baiting me, but I keep my expression calm, digging my toes into the ground while I wait him out.

"Because based on what I'm seeing and the email

Emmanuel and I received this morning from Legal, it's become clear you aren't ready for this promotion."

Are you done? I want to scream. Instead, I pointedly let the silence extend. *Go on, interrupt me again. Make it obvious.*

But Roberts seems to be done. Or maybe having his boss in the room is enough to rein in his worst instincts.

I always suspected this was coming.

I dig deep, searching for the fierce energy Charlie inspires within me, the badass office assassin who's capable of anything. But all I feel is white-hot blinding rage and the added sting of embarrassment. This is not how I wanted my first meeting with Emmanuel to go. This man will be the deciding factor on the lead team, and it'll be difficult to impress him after this charade.

If I was a sensible person, I'd offer an apology and quietly accept defeat.

But Conways are not sensible people.

"Respectfully," and it pains me to say the word, "I disagree. Charlie and I have been working well together. Rather than continue to cross our wires, we decided to pool our efforts into a single version of the document. Locking it down made that easier, and," I bite out, "you've been able to provide your feedback in every review, as requested."

I chance a look at Emmanuel, and though it's clear he's paying very close attention, his expression is unreadable. Roberts, on the other hand, has turned red and blotchy, clearly livid.

"I'm pleased with the progress we've made," I say, struggling to keep my tone clear, "despite the issue I discussed with Legal this morning. In fact, Engineering and Operations have already signed off on the changes—"

"Yes," Roberts interrupts. "I was disappointed to hear that I was not invited to either of those discussions."

I'm at a loss. There's a tremor under my skin, my composure slipping, so I clasp my hands tightly in my lap and hold on for dear life.

"I'm not sure what you want me to say," I finish. Because there clearly isn't anything I could say.

Finally, Emmanuel steps in. "I'll admit, I wasn't able to read the document itself prior to this meeting, but I will rectify that today. I'll also follow up with those areas you mentioned before we move forward. No matter the outcome, I'd like to thank you and Charlie for the hard work you've done so far."

My voice is smaller than I like when I say, "Thank you," but I can read between the lines.

Emmanuel isn't here by accident.

Charlie wasn't excluded by accident.

My head is clearly on the chopping block, and Roberts is holding it there.

Last year, when he pushed for minimum viable product during the system upgrade, I suffered through it.

Most Digital initiatives go this way. A grand idea in the beginning, passed down with the authority of a testament. No instructions on how we would deliver it, only a deadline and the understanding that failure isn't an option.

The real secret of tech in big business? Sunk cost fallacy is real. They'd rather spend millions of dollars to deliver a bad program and replace it later than accept defeat.

Especially if they have a fall guy.

Shit, I wish Charlie was here.

The truth is, confidence wanes. Like the tide or the moon, I'll be on top of the world one day, then suddenly so riddled with impostor syndrome that I might as well be an NFT for how little value I have.

Right now, the tide is slowly rising, and I'm desperate to hear his voice. For him to tell me it'll be all right. I need his steadiness, the way he looks a problem in the eye and cracks a joke.

Roberts stands, ending the conversation, and without even the lie of a thank you, he opens his office door and lifts his chin, silently signaling that it's time for me to leave.

It's a dismissal, swift and silent, and I bite back the curse that rises up.

———

Charlie is up and out of his seat as soon as Roberts closes the door behind me.

Anger storms between my ribs and batters against my shutters, ready to spill out at the first crack in my armor. I resist it, clenching and shoving it back.

It won't hold forever, but I only need it to last a little longer.

Charlie watches me with wide eyes as I stride back

to my desk and silently begin packing my bag. There's still an hour of the workday left, but I don't have a single care about leaving early.

Let Roberts see.

It would be all the reason I need to finally quit.

When I look up, I find Charlie packed up and at my side. Ready to follow me, with or without an explanation. I waver, the anger and hurt ready to break open within the safety of his arms.

"I can't," I choke out, the words catching in my throat.

I can't think. Can't talk. Can't hold myself together much longer. I grab Charlie's forearm, needing a life raft. "Can we leave? I need you."

With a nod, he leads me out, his hand an anchor on my back, strong as steel.

I don't care where he takes me. I just want to fall apart. I can do that if he's there, holding me, keeping me safe.

I've always been too scared to show anyone this side of myself—the raw, exposed nerve of fear, anxiety, and rage that pulses underneath my careful facade.

But it's different with Charlie.

From the beginning, he found his way under my skin, under my armor, and it never turned him off. Even when we argue, he keeps up, keeps digging deeper.

With every layer he uncovers, he leaves a mark. Time and time again, he proves with his hands and his mouth and his attention that every part of me is worth seeing.

Even the parts I hide are valuable.

CHAPTER 32
I'M A THIEF, SWEETHEART
CHARLIE

I've worked my ass off to get an address on Park Blvd. Four hundred square feet overlooking an alleyway might not impress anyone else, but it's more than I've ever had. And—and this is the real kicker—I can afford it.

Never in a million years did I expect to have more than two dollars to scrape together, and here I am, with actual savings, a closet full of labels, and a fridge full of food.

I still don't know where I'm going, but it's better than where I've been.

Emma was so worked up after meeting with Roberts that I did the only thing I could. I kept her close and brought her home.

I get it now, how she felt when I saw her place for the first time. Opening herself up to scrutiny. Allowing me into the inner sanctum.

I don't feel like boasting much now.

After what feels like an eternity, she turns back to

me, a question in her eyes. "I'm not sure if you remember, but my apartment is on the other side of town."

"Your point?" It's a tease, a gamble, to lighten the darkness she's drowning in. I'm not about to trivialize her anger—she's earned it—but I want to make it clear that I'm offering her a lifeline.

The smile she gifts me is small but powerful. It lights up the dark corners of my heart in the way only Emma can.

"You're a good man, Charlie."

I've been called worse things, much truer things, but she can call me anything she wants if it makes her smile.

Because it's so goddamn beautiful.

And I hate myself, because I'm about to make it disappear.

"I have to tell you something."

I don't know what happened in Roberts's office today, but I can take a pretty good guess. And now I owe her the truth.

Emma is quiet while I lay it all out—how Roberts has been working against her, every ugly detail I remember.

I expect her to blow up. I'd deserve it. So would he. By my own hand, we've come full circle—her slighted, me to blame. She should be raging.

I want her to.

She doesn't. Worse, she apologizes, sorry that I got pulled into a scheme neither of us could have seen coming or had any control over.

It's a testament to how incredible she is.

What a fucking joke.

No, not a joke. Jokes are funny. Even clever.

This is bullshit. Plain and simple.

"That's why you were so adamant we work together," she says.

I nod. "He's set against you for some reason. So I wanted to make it as difficult as possible for him to pin any win we had on me."

"Why didn't you just take it?" she asks. Before I can reiterate *because fuck him*, she adds, "Not because of Roberts, but because you've earned it."

"I've had to fight for a lot in my life, but I've never stolen anything, and I'm not about to start now."

"I should have expected this," she says with a defeated scoff. "My last boss, Mason, warned me when he left to be wary of Roberts, but I thought I had it under control."

My gut twists. I've seen firsthand how low people can sink, but somehow, they keep going lower.

"Don't you dare." I run a hand through my hair. "You've done everything right. He's the asshole. And so am I."

"Charlie, no."

"I should have told you earlier."

"It wouldn't have changed anything."

Yeah, but she wouldn't have been blindsided.

Dammit.

She covers my hand with hers and gives it a light squeeze. "Thank you for telling me."

It's a solid hit, enough to put me on my back if I

wasn't sitting. There is absolutely no reason she should be thanking me, but that's Emma. Beautiful, generous Emma.

She leans back, looking at the ceiling, and lets out a long breath. "This is worse than the time Jesse Olsen tried to cheat on me with my best friend and then stole our ride back to the hotel." A broken huff of a laugh escapes her. "Good thing he'd forgotten to close out his tab. Once we realized he'd taken off, we enjoyed a very lovely bottle of 2008 Cristal on his dime."

Her voice is too quiet. She's trying so damn hard to stay composed, but I don't need her to be calm for me. I like her fire and brimstone. There's a fighter in her, and it kills me to see her throw the match.

"I should quit," she says.

Every fiber of my being revolts at the idea. "Absolutely not."

She lets her head loll against the back of the couch so she's facing me. "Why would I stay? You said it yourself; Roberts has it out for me. Whether I get this promotion or not, he'll find some new way to make my life as difficult as possible."

For me. Stay for me.

I should know better than to wish for things like that.

"Sometimes I think I'm still there out of spite," I admit. "Just to prove I could stick it out."

"And now?" she asks, her brows pinched. "You're exceptional at your job. There's no doubt in my mind that you could keep going if you wanted to. But is it what you want? Not because you need to prove something, but for yourself."

"Not everyone has the luxury of choice."

She hums, thoughtful. "That's true. Which is why it's important to not waste it if you do."

I've never let myself think about it for too long, because once I have an answer, I won't be able to forget.

I'm not going to lie; I like the lifestyle. Wearing clothes that aren't secondhand. Slipping on an oxford and a silk tie, walking into the world knowing I look damn good. Powerful. Persuasive.

But we aren't meant to be talking about me.

"Hold up," I say, rerouting the conversation. "I already know how good I am. I want to know why it sounds like you're rolling over right now." I refuse to let her dim herself for that asshole. "Let me ask you this: if Roberts hadn't played this bullshit game with us, and the lead team pulled you into a room and said 'tell us who should get this role,' what would you say?"

Without answering, she lowers her head, brushes an invisible spot from her pants.

"I get it. You think I'm the best. Honestly, who could blame you?"

It's not quite a smile, but the curl of her lip sends a wave of relief through me, and I finally unclench my jaw. Now we're getting somewhere.

"But put all of that aside. Day one, you had no problem telling me you'd earned that job. What's so different now?"

She sighs, keeping her gaze averted. "I appreciate

your faith in me, but this isn't a self-esteem issue. I should have done more, fought harder, pushed more."

Shifting in my seat, I angle in closer. "Don't beat yourself up."

"Why not?" she asks.

Fuck. I hate seeing her like this. Hate that I feel so useless.

"You shouldn't want the approval of a dickwad like that."

"I don't want it," she says. "But I won't get anywhere without it."

She's stronger than me, able to put herself aside for those she loves. What Emma needs is someone to be selfless for her.

"I'm in awe of you," she says, because the world makes no sense, and Emma will never cease to amaze me. "You learned to play the game, but it's more than that." She turns to me, and every word makes me fall faster. "You have a natural talent for people. The kind of skill that other people pay thousands of dollars to learn. None of them make it look as good as you. It's no wonder they want you."

Honestly, the longer this project goes on, the less I want it. I wanted to earn the role, not feel like I was ripping my own heart out and sticking it into a hydraulic press.

"They want me because they think I'm one of them. Thanks, but no thanks." I shake my head and shudder. "And do you really want to play who is better? Because I'm good, but I've got nothing on you, sweetheart."

She looks away. It's physically painful not to wrap

my arms around her, show her how much she means to me. "We're smart. We can figure this out."

"How?" Her eyes swim with doubt. "Nothing we do will matter if Roberts isn't going to back us up."

My heart aches at the defeat in her voice. "I'll fix it." I'll do whatever it takes.

So softly her words are hard to make out, she says, "I'm not sure you can."

"Then we'll face it together."

If she needs help breaking down barriers, I'll ask her to point and be her wrecking ball. If she wants to go high, I'll give her a boost. If she wants to go low, I'll grab a shovel and start digging. There's nowhere I won't follow. No corner I won't have her back in.

"Okay, that's it." I stand before I do something stupid like kiss her or drown us both in my weak, mortal feelings.

"You want to know my secret? Well, here it is." I hold out a hand, and when she slides her palm along mine, I pull her up. "Stand tall, shoulders back, chin up. Make them look up at you."

Her lips curl into a smile. "It's like being back at school."

"Are you going to call me sir?" I waggle my brows, lust stirring under my skin.

She tugs on my tie, her attention slipping to my mouth. "Only if you're good."

Christ.

My pulse kicks up, and want roars in my ears. Damn if I don't love a woman who takes control, enjoys the blood-pumping back-and-forth of taking and giving ground. And in all my life, no one has matched me like Emma does.

"Yes, ma'am."

I'm playing with fire, waving a flare at a T-Rex and hoping I don't get eaten. But I can't stop.

She wants it, that's obvious. Her pulse flutters at the base of her throat, and she's practically vibrating. I keep waiting, fucking ready to let her devour me. Desperate to know if she'll follow through.

What she'll do.

"What next?" she whispers.

I've known hunger before, but never like this.

"Use silence to your advantage. Make them wait, and they'll fill it for you. They'll show their hand before they're ready."

I lick my lips, heart pounding in my chest as she drops her gaze and copies me. I swallow past the tightness in my throat.

"Another trick is to know when to give them no other options, even when there's an alternative. If you know the best way, and we both know you usually do, present that and that alone. If they don't like it? Make *them* explain why. Put them in the hot seat. It's a great way to see their true intentions. Don't be afraid to push back."

How the hell does she not see just how powerful she is?

Emma doesn't simply solve problems, she vaporizes them.

"Don't shrink yourself for anyone," I say, crowding in, dizzy with the heat pouring off her. "You're damn good at what you do, and when you stop forgetting that, you'll be fucking unstoppable."

No wonder Roberts is scared of her. The entire world should cower at her feet.

If management knew what they had, he'd be reporting to her.

I run my fingers along her jaw. "With your words and my charm, we can do anything."

There's wonder in the look she's giving me. Want and awe and all of it is dangerous to my resolve. When she licks her lips, I stop breathing.

If we don't do something else, and soon, I'm going to mess up this friendship.

I step back. "Hey, do you want a beer?"

Her lips part, and her cheeks are a deep red. "I'd love one."

"Good. I know just the place."

CHAPTER 33
LET'S PLAY
CHARLIE

Reese discovered Rocky's minutes after we moved here. What can I say? She's got excellent radar for good music and cheap drinks. It's served us well.

The story goes—at least, if you believe a word out of the man's mouth—that the bar used to be called Rick's, but the original owner lost a bet, and bam, Rocky's was born. Apparently, when Rick retired, he signed the bar over to him "as was my birthright."

Needless to say, Rocky's tales are as long as his hair.

But the man serves a mean beer and never gave one shit when I hustled the occasional jackass for a few weeks' rent.

In all the years I've been coming here, it hasn't changed. It still smells like weed, still has the same jukebox with "old man music"—

"Hey," I say. I will put up with a lot of things, but disrespecting Robert Plant is not one of them. "Watch your tone. These are classics."

"I'm learning so much about you tonight," Emma says, her smile the ultimate weapon to my state of mind.

—and it's still run by Rocky himself. These days, he's a lot quieter. He speaks almost exclusively in grunts, but he throws me a friendly nod and a couple of cold ones when we approach the bar.

With our beers in hand, I guide Emma to the pool table in the back. We're not the only ones here tonight, but it's quiet enough to make our little corner feel intimate.

I pass Emma a cue. "Do you know how to play?"

"I know enough."

If I had to guess by the glint in her eye, that's a lie, but I let it slide for now. I want to see her moves before I show off.

"All right," I set up. "Let's see what you've got."

She breaks, and it's not bad. It's also not great.

"Little rusty?" I ask.

She flushes, the color deep and dark, like a secret I want to keep.

Fuck, she's gorgeous.

I take a long pull of my beer and rein in the urge to push her up against the wall and have my way with her in the shadows. With nothing sunk yet, I take the easy shot, pocketing the fourteen in the top right. I follow it up with the ten. I check myself before I run a trick shot on the nine, pulling my stroke just enough that it's not obvious I'm holding back.

"You're good at this." Emma hovers over the table,

stalling before taking her shot. She hits the two, but it catches on the pocket and doesn't fall.

"I've had a lot of practice. Reese went to vet school one block over." I sink the nine but purposefully miss the next shot. "During those years, there wasn't a week we weren't here. She and Mae hooked up in that bathroom," I say, pointing to the door with my cue. "About time too. They circled each other for a year before finally admitting they liked each other."

Emma lines up a shot directly in front of me. The way she leans over the table pulls her trousers tight against her ass. If it's a trap to destroy my concentration in this game, then I might as well hand her the win now.

I take a long drink to distract myself.

She then skips the cue ball off the edge like a leapfrog.

Oh, come on. It's not possible to be accidentally this bad.

"Give it up." I huff, stepping up beside her. "I've watched you destroy a decade's worth of procedure in ten minutes. You can stop playing."

"I *am* playing," she teases, smiling around her beer.

I tear my gaze away from her lips, willing my heart not to take off at a breakneck speed. "You know what I mean."

The laugh she lets out goes straight through me, slipping through the cracks of my beaten-up heart.

"This place feels like a time capsule. My mom would love it." She props her cue against her hip.

"Before I was born, one of her hobbies was following bands on tour."

Ah. The walls here are plastered in band posters, not a spare inch in sight. They spill out into the hallway, the bathrooms… "As far as I can tell," I say, "he doesn't take the old ones down before he puts new ones up. Scrape back far enough, and you could probably find out how old Rocky is."

"Like tree rings," she says.

A smile splits my face as I survey the space. I like it here with its don't-give-a-fuck attitude. It's open late, only faintly smells of spilled beer, and right now is giving me something to do with my hands that won't get me in trouble.

When she fumbles another easy shot, I have to call bullshit, saving the black from a premature death. One look at the mischief in her eyes tells me she knows she's been caught. She's beaming with joy, which, fuck, only makes me like her more.

I reset the table. "All right, enough with the games. Let's really play. And this time I'm not gonna go easy on you."

Emma steps in close, sultry. "Bold of you to assume you have a shot at winning."

My heart trips over itself. She's right. When it comes to her, I lost a long time ago.

She leans the cue against the table, rolls up the sleeves of her pale blue shirt past her elbows, loosens a button at her collar.

She's never been sexier.

"You like it?" she asks, brow raised as she fingers the neck of her shirt. "I learned this trick from you."

This time she breaks on the second ball, shot as sharp as she gets when she's breaking a problem down.

Damn. This is my kind of foreplay.

"I knew you were holding back," I say.

"If only outmaneuvering Roberts was as simple as this."

"We'll think of something, I promise."

She straightens, takes a drink. I try not to stare at the long stretch of her neck but fail miserably.

"It's so nice to talk to someone who sees how awful he is. Logan hated when I talked about the office."

And the asshole tally goes up.

"My ex was the same," I admit. "She always complained. Said I cared about work more than anything else."

"That's not true," Emma says, brow furrowed in offense. "You work harder than almost everyone else there, but I don't doubt for a second you'd quit if it was the right thing to do. I don't want to make aspersions against a stranger, but this woman didn't know you very well if she couldn't see you put family before anything else."

With a knot rising in my throat, I step around the table to sink the twelve and get a little room to breathe.

"Is that why you broke up?" Emma asks.

"Lucy didn't think I was capable of loving anyone." That single sentence sinks the mood like a slab of concrete in a swimming pool.

"What do you think?"

"I think there are much more interesting things we can talk about."

"I disagree." She steps back from the table, leaning the cue against her hip. "Your sister is happy that you've moved on."

Getting over Lucy wasn't easy, but I bet it'll be a joyride compared to Emma.

I rub my jaw. "Reese seems to think I've been crying myself to sleep every night for the past two years."

"It wouldn't be a failing if you were. Breakups hurt. She's worried about you."

With a scoff, I chalk my cue. "I don't know why. I've got everything I need, plus some shit I don't. Heartbreak is for people who take love too seriously."

People fall in love too easily, throwing themselves at it in blind faith, romanticizing the fall and being shocked when the landing hurts like hell.

I don't want love to be easy. I want it hardened, fortified, absolute. What use do I have for feelings that come and go as quickly as mile markers on the highway?

"You can't believe that," Emma says. "Love is one of the most beautiful things we can experience. It's more than heartbreak. The right person will make life sweeter. It takes work, but it's all the more rewarding for the effort."

"Speaking from experience?" I ask.

"No," she says, ducking her head. "Hope, actually."

I can't fault that. I'm glad she still has hope.

I lost mine a long time ago.

"The last time I got stood up," I admit, finishing my

beer and signaling for two more, "I was sitting at the bar talking to Rocky. This older couple arrives, and they take the seats next to me. They're laughing, talking, so Rocky asks them what they're celebrating. You know what they said? Their divorce."

Emma's jaw goes slack with surprise.

I nod. Pretty sure my reaction at the time looked exactly like that. "I've seen newlyweds more miserable than these two. I finally asked them about it, and they said they weren't about to throw away twenty years of friendship just because the sex was terrible. I knew then that's what I wanted."

"Terrible sex?" she teases.

I smile, hoping it doesn't look as sad as it feels. "Funny, but no. What I want is a partner."

I've spent my life sure of one thing: the less I have to lose, the better.

But that doesn't mean I want it. Every day, I witness what Reese and Mae have. I envy it.

There are no half measures for me. When I make a decision, there's no time for second guessing, and love is no different.

I don't want to fall. I want to stand firm beside a person worth fighting for. Someone who'll stand and fight for me.

"Now, are you going to take this shot, or do I have to take it for you?"

———

Those pants must be working, because Emma is kicking my ass.

"And then we took a two-hour detour so Reese could see the world's largest rocking chair."

"I'm jealous. The coolest thing I've seen is the Alps."

"How awful," I tease. "It was surprisingly fun. Growing up, long trips always meant starting over. I never knew if it would work out, so the drive was one long walk to the gallows. I hated passing through places like they didn't exist. Like we didn't exist. So I made sure we made memories on the way, even if they were ridiculous."

"It sounds like you're ready to make some more."

My lungs get tight at the thought. "I've been telling myself the same thing for the last few years."

"What are you waiting for?"

I shrug.

I never planned to stay forever. But somewhere along the way, I stopped thinking about moving on and fell into the cycle of "maybe next year," growing more cynical with each corporate announcement.

"Getting hired at Helix was a big deal. I worked my ass off to prove myself, and I used what I saved to help Reese open the shelter."

Now, eight years have gone by, and I'm not sure what the future holds.

Lips pressed together, I scan the mostly empty bar. "Honestly, I'm not sure why I'm still there."

"For what it's worth," she says, taking a step closer, "I'm glad you stayed."

A lightness I've never experienced blooms in my chest. "I bet you never thought you'd say that."

She laughs. "I wanted to strangle you when Roberts announced we'd be working together."

"There's still time," I say with a wink.

She rolls her eyes as predicted. "Do you ever think about doing something else? Working on cars again or maybe becoming a suit model?"

"I'm starting to think you like my wardrobe more than me."

She tips her head back and finishes her beer. When she sets it on the table, she eyes me. "It's fifty-fifty."

The cold bottle in my hand does nothing to cool me down.

The truth is, I haven't thought about it, but already, it's tempting. I have a lot of experience starting over, but as Emma takes her next shot, I know I'm not going anywhere soon.

"By the way," I say, "Reese and Mae loved your mom's suggestions. Said to pass on their thanks."

"It's me who should be saying thank you. I haven't seen her that excited since I got my first paycheck. I'm going to need to carry smelling salts if I ever get engaged. She's been worried I'd never settle down."

It takes work to swallow down the jealousy bubbling up inside me. It's violent enough that I miss my next shot, and the ball rolls off the short rail, away from the pocket.

Jaw tense, I force out, "They've got to be happy about Logan, then."

Focus fixed on the pool table, she makes a noncommittal sound. Honestly, before I met them, I expected her parents to be assholes. More money than sense types. And maybe they are. Or maybe they used to be. But I've also seen firsthand what bad parents look like, and no one who adores their kid the way her parents do can be all bad.

Don't ask. It'll only hurt. But I'm a glutton for punishment.

"Have you answered him yet?"

Why the fuck do I even want to know? For proof, I guess. Anything that will kill the hope I've got for a future I can't have.

Abandoning her shot, she faces me, eyes earnest and vulnerable. "No."

Good. I still have a shot at this.

"Hold up." I slot in behind her, and her breath stutters. "Take your time," I guide softly, nudging her right foot in line with the shot. "Better."

She tilts her head just an inch my way. "I thought you wanted to win."

Angling closer, I brush my lips against her ear. "Who says I'm not?"

Her breath leaves her in a rush, her hips pushing back into mine.

Christ.

I step back.

You're only friends, asshole.

Emma glares at the table. She's already circled it twice,

searching for a shot and scowling adorably. It probably doesn't help that I've blocked her shot.

"Want to move some of your balls out of my way?"

"Oh, sorry, am I making it too hard for you to win?"

"That yellow is taunting me." Then she rolls the cue ball in a fantastic kick shot that sinks it. Damn, she's good.

It's been too long since I've had this much fun in a game. Reese isn't a bad player, but she prefers to limit her competitiveness to *Mario Kart*.

"How'd you learn to play? Don't tell me they taught billiards in private school."

Emma peers up at me from where she's leaned over the long rail, inspiring a thousand filthy thoughts. I'm ten seconds away from getting us kicked out of here.

"Oh, of course. Right after pickleball. No, Dad had a table, and I had a lot of time on my hands."

Without taking her eyes off me, she shoots, sinking the black like a pro, winning the game.

I might be in love.

———

Emma asks to come back home with me, as if the answer is ever going to be no. I find her a pair of sweats and a T-shirt to change into and settle in for a movie. I'm not going to think about what this all means or how soon it'll be over.

I get it. When it feels like everything is slipping through your fingers, you need something to hold on to.

Right now, I'm a convenient buoy in a chaotic ocean, and if she needs my help to stay afloat, I'll be that for her.

Ten minutes in, and she's asleep on my shoulder, soft hair falling out of place. If I could believe she'd stay here forever, I'd give her anything she asked for, including me.

Because I might not be capable of loving someone, but if I was, I'd want it to be her.

CHAPTER 34
I SEE YOU IN MY NIGHTMARES

EMMA

I t's still dark, but I know immediately I'm not in my own bed. I can't hear the upstairs pipes groaning, and everything smells like Charlie, deep and cool.

I blink my eyes open and instantly know what woke me.

"Charlie?"

He's sitting up, intensity rolling off him in waves. Even his breathing is loud and fast.

"I'm here, okay?" I soothe, sitting up. "You're safe."

He blinks in the dark, his eyes unfocused, as if he's not quite here.

My heart rate picks up as I watch him. Shit. What does he need? I think back, remembering the weight of Charlie's hand on my chest, of being covered and kept. It's worth a try. So I wrap my arms around him and blanket his back, leaning into him. Willing the burden to let him go, hoping to drain it out with my touch.

The moment stretches out as he takes a long slow

breath, then another. The rhythm is oddly grounding. So soothing I find myself matching him. In, out. In, out.

His breathing slows.

"That's it," I say. "You're okay. It'll be okay."

Bit by bit, the tension leaks out of him, until he's reaching up, covering my hand with his own, our palms slotted neatly over his heart.

"Didn't mean to wake you," he says, his voice as ragged as shattered glass.

"I don't care about that."

His eyes are clearer, the fogginess lifted for now. How often are his dreams haunted?

Heart aching for him, I ask, "Do you want me to go?"

"No." It's quick. Certain. "Stay," he adds, softer.

"Reese told me some stories at the shelter. Of what it was like for her." I leave the blanks for him to fill.

"She's always been braver than me. Always found it easier to talk about it."

"We don't have to talk about it. You don't owe me anything." I only want what he's willing to give. "We can go back to sleep."

"It's not like that. I mean, some of it was. But it wasn't all bad..." He takes another long, slow breath. "Some just kept to themselves. Treated me like a tenant. Only one or two were the kind of bad you're thinking of."

He doesn't elaborate, and I don't press. Just the idea of what he's been through makes that ache more acute. But his scars are enough to tell me it's better left unsaid tonight.

"I got lucky with Mom and Dad. Luckier than a lot of other kids get. Reese was what saved me, though."

Squeezing a little tighter, I ask, "What was the dream about?"

"The usual shit. Someone's in trouble, and I can't get to them."

"Reese?"

"Usually," he says, locking eyes with me. "Not tonight."

Instantly, my heart trips over itself. I'm eager for every crumb of his attention. Every place we're touching heats up, a stark contrast to the cold night.

"I'm not going anywhere," I whisper.

It's not just about the way my body lights up when he touches me, the way my mind comes to life when he challenges me, or how every little piece of information I learn about him makes my chest swell and ache.

I used to avoid Charlie at all costs, and now I can't get enough.

I keep waiting to reach the end of it, this thirst for his opinion, a smile or a joke, the frustrated sighs from behind my screen that tell me Ops is being needy again.

But the end is nowhere in sight. And I don't think I'll ever find it.

There's a treasure trove underneath the suit and tie, and I want it all.

It's hard to remember that he's the same man who cornered me once, fire in his eyes and an insult at the ready. Like this, he's soft, a relaxed curve of heat and muscle, a safe harbor. Protection. His hair is mussed, lips as pink as ever. Gorgeous doesn't even begin to describe him.

I can't hold back from stroking his hair. After a silent moment, I lower my hands and shift until I'm sitting next to him, staring down at my knees.

Slowly, he reaches for my hand. He turns it over and slips his fingers between mine. His grip is sure, his palm soft and warm. It's not until he gives me a gentle squeeze that I look away, choking on the weight of his tenderness.

"Thanks," he rasps. "I guess I haven't grown out of the habit of worrying about people."

"But who worries about you?" I ask, that ache returning. He's always using his endless fucking care for everyone but himself.

I inch closer so we're pressed together from hip to shoulder. "Maybe we both need someone to look out for us." Softly, I kiss his shoulder. "Maybe we can look after each other."

He turns his head toward me, eyes dark and intense, never leaving mine as he cups my cheek. He's so silent, holds so much inside, keeping it safe. As though he could save the world simply by taking its pain as his own.

And in that moment, I want him to know I see him too, that I don't just want the pretty packaging, but everything underneath, even the shadows.

Even the scars.

In this moment, in the dark, as the moonlight shrouds Charlie in silence, I close the distance between us and kiss him.

CHAPTER 35
IT'S US AGAINST THE WORLD
CHARLIE

"**A**re you sure about this?" Emma asks, heel tapping on the floor.

If we weren't in an elevator, she'd be pacing, I'm sure of it.

"Are you kidding me? He's been against you from the start. We're not going to make anything up. This isn't about forcing him out, even if I wish I could. I just want to see if there's anything to find."

"And if there isn't?"

Fuck, I hate how discouraged she sounds.

"Then we'll think of something else. But he can't just fucking get away with this," I say. "Haven't you ever wanted to give a bad guy his just deserts?"

She says nothing, but there's no hiding the twinkle in her eyes.

I grin at her. "You have."

"Of course I have," she says, and I want to kiss the pout off her lips. "But that doesn't mean I feel comfortable hacking into his computer."

"All right, Neo, let's not get ahead of ourselves. All I'm proposing is that we visit a friend of mine over in security. Manish's a good guy. I wouldn't ask him to do anything that would risk his ass or ours."

"You promise?" she asks.

I brush my thumb across her cheek, needing the touch too much to care that we're in the office. "Don't you trust me?"

"Of course I do," she says, delivered so genuinely I'm knocked off my axis for a full minute.

"Okay," I say, when I can think again. We haven't talked about the kiss, but I can't stop thinking about it. Emma, though, hasn't made a move to repeat it, and for the first time in my life, I'm thinking *before* I do something reckless.

Reese would be so proud of me.

Manish has us meet him in the blue room, which is a secure meeting space that is, *surprise, surprise*, painted blue.

The creativity here is off the charts.

"So, who's the dude?" he asks.

I tell him.

"Oh, you mean the screamer?"

Hold up. Brows raised, I lean in. "Karl's the screamer? Karl Roberts. Our boss. That Karl?"

"Oh yeah," he says, gleeful as a golden retriever at the beach.

Emma's gaze ping-pongs between us. "What are you talking about?"

Manish fills her in while he types. His fingers move so fast my thumbs ache in solidarity. "Two years ago, at the Christmas party, I was red-cupping the security desk while everyone partied—"

"Manning it solo," I explain to Emma.

"I didn't expect anything interesting, but around ten p.m., there's a notification that someone's trying to enter the underground garage. Now, usually, it's twenty-four-hour entry if you have an after-hours pass, but we turn it off during the Christmas party."

"Because of the zero-tolerance policy," she finishes.

He nods without looking away from the screen. "So I go down there to tell whoever it is to get a cab, and he starts screaming in my face. 'Don't you know who I am? I'm going to get you fired. You're going to be living off breadcrumbs when I'm done with you.'"

"How do you know it was Roberts?" I ask.

"It's protocol to take the pass before we kick them off site. He had to retake his drug and alcohol screening and attend mandatory compliance training to get it back."

Jesus. "He's an even bigger asshole than I thought."

Manish chuckles. "Right? So what do you need?"

I hoped we'd find enough in the logs to back up our claim that Roberts has been tampering with the procedure.

But *this*?

Emma's eyes are wide and unblinking. I'm not even sure she's breathing. "I miss the person I was thirty seconds ago," she says, her voice rough.

That's... yeah. Me too.

All I can think is *thank fuck I hate using chat.*

"I'll say this," Manish says, zipping the files up. The plan is to report it through the usual channels as a random check so that it can't be traced back to us. "He's been careful. The language he uses is enough to be suggestive without pinging any of our radars."

There are a dozen, maybe more, messages flagged on-screen. Comments to or about coworkers that don't just cross the line; they slingshot themselves over it.

But the ones about Emma are the worst.

If this doesn't get him, I'm done.

Before we leave, I check one last name. "Landon Kent?" Manish asks with a sardonic chuckle. "Yeah, I know the little shit. Walks around like he's god's gift to IT. He threw a tantrum last year when the redundancies happened and they wanted to move him out of automation and into the SharePoint support team. Brought out the waterworks and everything."

"Someone missed nap time," I say.

Manish breaks into a smile like he already knows what I'm going to ask him. "I bet management is dying for a reason to boot him. After a stunt like that? It wouldn't take much."

I love this guy. "What's it going to cost me?"

He glances at Emma, then turns back to me with a brow raised meaningfully. Nothing gets past him. "Don't worry 'bout it. I never get to do anything fun anymore." But I hear the truth as if I'd said it myself. Ambitious assholes who don't have an ethical bone in their body are everywhere. Getting to stick it to a couple of them without stooping to their level won't change the system, but it'll feel damn good.

An hour later, I get a text from Manish that makes my day: *Keystroke recordings caught our buddy faking it while working from home. Already sent the report. Cheers, M.*

I tap Emma on the shoulder.

"Report's been sent. Now we wait."

"You know," she says, her voice soft, her tone far too reserved for my liking, "it might not be enough. Guys get away with this all the time."

I move in close. Too close to be appropriate for the office. She's wearing a baby blue sweater and a frown, and I want to rid her of both. "It's not like you to play devil's advocate."

It wins me a small smile. "I don't usually need to. You advocate for yourself just fine."

CHAPTER 36
MY ONE RULE (IS YOURS TO BREAK)
EMMA

Three months into my job, I discovered that what is simple in theory can easily become a *spontaneous chop because I destroyed my hair with bleach* in practice.

It's also been true in other areas of my life.

In theory, I enjoyed sex. In practice? Well…

Except it turns out, I was wrong about that.

I like foreplay and teasing, through words and flirting and touches. I like taking my time, enjoying the anticipation. I really like toys.

In the past, I've focused on making it good for my partner, too busy with their pleasure to enjoy my own.

It turns out that I simply wasn't having sex with people who wanted to make it good for me too.

Until Charlie.

And I really need him to feel the same, because it's high time I made it good for him.

Come Saturday morning, Charlie answers his door in sweatpants and a Queen T-shirt. Holy shit. I didn't think he could make anything look sexier than a tuxedo, but dammit, he does.

I've rubbed shoulders with actors and greeted congressmen. I've shaken hands with multimillionaires. But Charlie Walker bends gravity by simply walking into a room.

The laws of physics don't apply when he's near. How could they when his smile stops time and his hands reshape my pleasure into all-consuming need?

"Hey," he says, his voice thick with sleep. "Miss me already?"

"I did," I admit. It's a loose thread that's been bothering me, the sharp end of a stitch that keeps snagging on my skin.

I've been wanting to kiss him for weeks, kicking myself for my own rules. I buried the urge as best I could until the other night, and now, in the kissless days since, it's all I can think about.

He wants it too. That much has been so obvious I'm shocked HR hasn't already sent us a cease and desist.

But he's held off.

Because I asked him to.

God, he's good to me.

But I'm done holding back.

I close the distance between us. I want him. No agreement, no faking. Just the heat of his skin as I slip my hand around his neck and pull.

The short hairs there are whisper soft. I've never considered myself a tactile person, but I'm kind of addicted to the brush of them against my fingertips. Maybe it's the heat of his skin. Maybe it's how the catch of my nails against his scalp always pulls a low, hot rumble from his throat.

When he meets me in the middle, I'm hit with a wave of relief so strong my knees go weak. Our lips find each other as though they never left, or maybe are always destined to return.

He moves easily when I push forward, over the threshold. I'm eager, hungry, biting down. The way he groans makes me grip tighter, kiss harder.

In theory, it's as simple as wanting him.

In practice, it's so much more delicious.

His skin is scorching under his shirt. "Is this okay?" I ask.

Charlie sweeps his tongue against mine. "I've already told you." His hands find my waist, and I rock against him. "There's nothing you've got that I don't want."

"Good," and I push him against the closed door and *take*.

CHAPTER 37
EVERYTHING AND MORE
CHARLIE

I might still be dreaming.

How else can I explain Emma showing up at my door, looking sexier than ever, and kissing me?

Christ, the way I've dreamed of this mouth.

Her hands are everywhere, pulling at my clothes, greedy for skin, like she can't get enough.

Thank God for the door at my back. I don't want to think of anything except finally getting my mouth back on hers. Emma is frantic, but I need to savor this, so I frame her face in my hands, pull back enough to slow it down. Sweeping her mouth with my tongue, until she's soft, and pliant, and whimpering with each kiss.

"Hi," I whisper.

"Hi," she breathes, her fingers digging into my hips.

I don't stop. I just keep claiming her mouth, long and slow, inhaling her every exhale, taking as much of her as I can get.

"I thought we weren't doing this anymore," I say, dragging my lips along her jaw.

"I want you, Charlie. Not because of an arrangement, but because of you."

I pull back and drink her in. Her pupils are blown wide with lust, her lips red and delicious. Fuck, she's gorgeous. I could gorge on her for a lifetime and never be satisfied.

I'm so fucking ruined.

Tilting her head back, I mouth at her neck. "Then have me."

She does.

This is a dangerous game to play. I want so much more than sex, but I'll take what I can get from her. And honestly? I've got more practice with casual.

No doubt I'd fuck up the other stuff if I had it.

So I curl my hand around her neck and grab a fistful of hair and take as good as I get.

Fuck, she's handsy. Now that she's given herself permission, she's relentless, clawing at my clothes, devouring my mouth. She runs her hands over my ribs, down my back, grabs my ass. I love it.

Every other time she's been reserved or tied up or too fucking far away. She said she wanted it, but this is proof.

It's real and it's raw and it's so good, nothing will ever match it.

I pull her sweater out from her pants, slide my hands up, and just about pass out. She's not wearing a fucking bra. All I find are her fantastic tits, full and round and a perfect fit in my hands.

I don't realize we're moving until there's a crash.

I can't stop kissing her long enough to care.

"Charlie," Emma says, panting.

My fucking name sounds so good in her mouth. I growl, sucking a bruise into her neck. Fuck, she smells good. "I'll buy a new one."

Whatever it is, it's replaceable.

She isn't.

I keep walking her back until her knees hit the bed.

"Off, take this off." She tugs at the hem of my shirt.

Gladly.

I whip it over my head, and then she's pulling my sweats off and pushing me onto the bed, staring down at me like she's going to eat me alive.

Slowly, I slide my hand down my stomach to my cock, which is lying thick and hard and up for everything she wants to do. Emma stares as I wrap my hand loosely around myself and stroke nice and slow.

A bead of precum wets the tip, and I circle my thumb in it, damn near vibrating out my skin. She's too fucking far away. I need to touch her, need to be inside her.

She licks her lips, and a groan claws its way out of my chest. Fuck, I can't help but imagine them stretched over my dick.

"See something you like?"

"Yes." Emma rips her own clothes off so fast I'm shocked she doesn't pull a muscle.

I'm so fucking turned on, I can't help but tease her. "A little impatient there?"

She straddles me, pulling my hand off my cock, and presses both my wrists into the mattress. "My turn."

Holy fucking fuck. She's going to kill me.

With a hum, she grasps my dick. Her grip is perfect—not too tight, squeezing with each stroke. When she teases my foreskin back to thumb at the head, I can't stop my hips from thrusting up, trying to get closer.

She watches as another bead of precum pools at the tip, then leans down to taste. The moment her tongue touches my cock, I groan.

"Oh, fuck."

I've wanted her to touch me for weeks. Months. Since the day we met.

And from the hunger in her eyes, the way she can't keep her hands off me, like she can't decide where to start, it's obvious she's been wanting this too.

She licks a line down my cock, moaning as she goes. It's wet, and messy, and I swear to god, I'm close to coming already.

"Condoms?" she asks, sitting up, her mouth glistening.

"Top drawer."

As she tilts to one side, searching, I drag my hands along her thighs, skin to skin, needing to touch her.

"Interesting collection of items you have here," she says, with a mix of desire and humor.

With one hand on her hip to hold her steady, I lever myself up on the opposite elbow to see what's got her attention.

In her hand is a condom and a rabbit vibrator. Still stowed in the drawer: additional condoms, a variety of clit vibrators, cuffs, cock ring, a cage. What can I say? I like to be prepared for anything.

I squeeze her hip, relishing the way my fingers sink into her flesh. "Hatching a plan?"

She drops the toy back into the drawer with a smile and rips open the packet. "Maybe. It's nice to keep a backup nearby. Unless you're scared of a little competition…"

Her eyes are sparkling, her smile the cheekiest I've ever seen it.

It's almost impossible to keep my hips from fucking into her hand as she rolls the condom on. Her grip is tight, just shy of painful, and very much on purpose.

I pull her down to kiss her, again and again. I can't stop. "Say the word, and I'll fuck you however you want. But I think you want my cock too much to need anything else right now."

She moves easily as I grind her hips down on me, coating my cock in her wetness, her head thrown back. Every exhale she releases is a whimper, and she writhes freely, wild and loose and so fucking beautiful I lose my breath.

"I'm right, aren't I?" I ask, voice thick and rough with need for this woman.

"Yes," she breathes.

I move my hands up, thumbs on the inside of her thighs, pulling a gasp from her when I reach her pussy. She's already so wet, and I coat my fingers, teasing her clit. "What was that?"

There's fire in her eyes when she opens them. She grabs my hands, forces them back down. "Hands to yourself. I'll tell you when it's your turn."

I smile up at her.

"Can't help it; you feel too good." It's true, but what I really like is how her eyes flare bright and hot, the way they always do when I challenge her. When she wants to teach me a lesson. "I've gotten a taste for your sin, and now I'm addicted. Your pussy misses me too. It's practically sobbing." I lick my lips. "Let me help with that."

Sure enough, her hand finds its way to my throat, pressing just enough to show me who's boss.

"Do I need to remind you to be good?" she asks.

If I say no, she'll back off. But that's the last thing I want. I want—no, I need—her closer.

"I thought you'd never ask." I tilt my head back, baring my neck to her, pressing my hips up. We both groan. "You want to control me, sweetheart? Use my cock as your own personal toy? Go right ahead. Take what you need."

I'm big. It's a fact more than a boast.

And despite what the media says, not every woman is a fan.

But she takes me beautifully, sinking down slowly. The bite of her nails as they dig into my shoulders is the perfect distraction from how fucking good she feels. How hot and wet and mine she is.

Emma looks down from where she's seated above me, riding me at a torturously slow pace. "Charlie," she whimpers. "Fuck, you feel… amazing. I can't believe we waited this long. I don't ever want to stop."

"Then don't." Shit. My heart pounds against my chest. "Keep going. Do you have any, oh, any fucking idea how incredible you look right now?"

"I could say the same thing about you. Do you know how many times I've made myself come thinking about this?"

I growl, throwing my head back against the pillow. Fuck. This queen, this *goddess*, could demand anything she wants, and I'd give it to her. Rip my very soul from its roots and set it at her feet.

Anything to see her like this.

"I kept thinking about your cock," she continues. Her chest heaves, her breaths coming short and fast. "Imagining you at work, the way you sit in your chair, legs wide. Thinking about what it would be like if I climbed on top of you right there in the office. If I pulled you out and made you come all over your nice, clean suit."

Jesus fucking Christ.

She doesn't stop rolling her hips as she talks. "Or maybe I'd wait until we were in a meeting room. Wait until you're mouthing off. Push you up against the table or onto your knees, shut you up by fucking your tongue."

I'm gripping the sheets so tightly I swear they're gonna rip. Sweat beads at my temples, and my body is on fire, blazing for her.

"Fuck. Let me touch you."

I want to drive into her, pull every sound I can from those gorgeous lips. I want to get my hands on her, play with those incredible tits, rub her clit, feel how wet she is for me.

I need to make her come undone.

Emma seats herself as deep as she can go and

clenches around me with long, drawn-out pulses of her pussy. But it's the wild mischief in her eyes that unravels me.

"Who's impatient now?" she says, smiling wickedly.

That's it. My control snaps. Grabbing her, I flip us until she's on her back. I tug her shirt off and fling it into a corner.

Emma wraps her legs tight around me, her heels at my back, and I growl into her mouth, kissing her filthy and deep.

"Fuck me, please," she pants.

At her plea, my dick throbs inside her. I'll give it to her. I'll give her everything. I lean down, nip at her shoulder.

"It's just… I might not come," she breathes, a flash of fear in her eyes. "In case you were expecting—"

"Hey, it's all right. I've got you." I slow and press a soft kiss to her lips, then another, and a third, because I can't get enough. "I don't care. It might not always happen, and it doesn't need to. You can enjoy the rest. It can still be good. The best, even."

"I doubt this is the best sex you've ever had."

I kiss her hard. "That's a bet you'd lose, sweetheart." With that promise, I drive into her, over and over, filling her.

"Oh," she moans. "Fuck, you're serious."

"You want me to hold back? I won't come if you don't want me to." I can wait for her.

With a shake of her head, she moves her hips, meeting my every thrust. "No, I want it. Want to feel you come inside me."

I groan. "Fuck, I can feel how much you need it. Your tight pussy is choking on my cock. Can you feel that? Can you feel how much you need my cum?"

Her whine pierces the loud slap of our bodies as I fuck into her, digging my knees into the mattress with every hard thrust. Emma's thighs shake when I drag my thumb in circles around her clit.

It doesn't matter if she comes. I'm going to make this so good for her, she won't be able to touch herself without thinking of me.

"No one's ever given it to you right, have they? Not like I can. And no one ever will."

"Yes, yes, more."

Weeks of pent-up energy is exploding in my veins, lighting my blood on fire. I knew from the second she kissed me back I would never be satisfied with less than everything.

She's under my fucking skin, in my bones. I want to fuse us together.

My legs strain with the effort of fucking her. She's so tight, so fucking perfect around my cock, like a part of me has been missing.

It won't be the only part of me she'll take when this is over, but I can't think about that right now. Nothing matters except the slick slide of my cock and her needy moans as she clenches around me.

My balls ache with the need to fill her.

"Harder, Charlie. *Please.*"

She opens her legs wider, inviting me deeper, and I accept, pushing fast and rough into her wet heat.

Gone is the cold wall she used to keep the world

out. There's nothing holding her back now, every sound, every ounce of pleasure on display.

Which only makes me greedy for more.

"I've got you, sweetheart. I'll give this sweet pussy everything it needs." The bed shakes with every thrust, my muscles reaching the point of strain. But Emma takes it all so beautifully.

Any chance I had of protecting my heart died the second she kissed me back, and I've been handing over pieces of myself every day since.

It was easier before, to remember my place in her life. To touch her, taste her, make her come, but never let her close enough to hurt me.

Now she's shattering the last stronghold I had, and I'll never be the same.

"That's it, you're taking it so well. Fuck, Emma, you're perfect. Always so wet for me, just begging for my mouth. But this is what you really wanted." I slam back into her again. "You've been dreaming about this, haven't you? Fucking your fingers and wishing it was my cock instead."

"Yes, oh, fuck." She moans, then surprises me by curling her hand around my throat like she did before, her pupils blown dark.

I'm so fucking close.

She squeezes. "Fuck, Charlie. *Do it*. Come on. I need you to fill me up."

Fuck.

My hips stutter and restart, pounding into her as I come. It's not just her dirty, delicious mouth that takes me over the edge. It's her wide eyes, pleading and pulling me under, and the last of my resolve crumbles.

Honestly, I never stood a chance.

Completely spent, I catch myself above her on a shaky elbow and hide my warring emotions in her neck.

I scrape the sensitive skin with my teeth, soothe it with my tongue. I want evidence this happened. The marks she's left on me are invisible, buried deep in my mind, my muscles, my heart.

I'm only asking for one small mark in return.

It might be all I get.

It's definitely more than I deserve.

CHAPTER 38
TAKE A PICTURE, I WANT THIS TO LAST LONGER
EMMA

Charlie pants beside me, one hand lazily stroking my hip. He's so wiped out, I'm not even sure he knows he's doing it, but I'm not about to tell him to stop.

There's a pleasant ache in my thighs, left over from clenching around his waist, and a slow throb in my clit. Sweat is cooling on my skin, and everything smells like Charlie. Damn, I can't remember the last time I enjoyed sex this much.

Before him, I skipped ahead to the destination, asking "are we there yet?" so frequently my body got fed up and turned the car around.

Now, I'm enjoying the ride. Windows down, sound up, screaming at the top of my lungs. I'll be happy anywhere and everywhere with him beside me.

"Give me a minute." He turns his head and drags a kiss over my shoulder. "And I can finish what I started."

I turn to face him. His hair is dark and damp as I

push it off his forehead. My heart skips a beat when he sighs and leans into the touch.

"Actually, I want to stay like this for a little while."

I don't sleep, but it's close. I can't remember the last time I felt this relaxed.

Later, I slip from Charlie's bed without waking him and pull on my underwear but forgo my clothes in favor of his faded T-shirt. It's softer than silk, and I hope he's not going to miss it, because I'm never taking it off.

His apartment is at least three times the size of mine, and I can tell we share the same soft spot for the essentials—that monstrosity of a television for Charlie, my beautiful couch. Charlie's made an effort to combat the gray floors and walls with splashes of color, most of it in the form of animal toys.

There's a dog bed on one side of the television and a cat tree on the other. Food and water bowls sit drying on a rack over the sink, and colorful toys are scattered through the apartment like the pet version of an Easter egg hunt.

There are easily more animal items than human ones. Besides a coffee machine, the kitchen counter is bare, and the same goes for the living room.

My heart aches. I'm tired of seeing empty spaces, and Charlie is too full of life to live within a blank slate.

In a hopeful moment, I sit cross-legged on the floor, batting away the robot vacuum that is dutifully clearing away stray cat hairs, and open the TV cabinet.

I've lost count now of the movies Charlie and I have watched together, passing comments through text and, more and more frequently, a phone call. He never complains when I talk over the movie to point out a detail my Nana passed on. I pretend not to love his commentary, even as I laugh. So, I'm curious to see how many of his favorites he owns. But inside the cupboard, instead of a row of DVDs, I'm met with a series of Polaroids and a small box of childhood collectibles.

With my hand on the lid, I debate whether to open it but stop when my phone buzzes.

It takes thirty seconds to locate it—dropped and kicked under the couch during our mutual strip earlier. On the screen is a text from my mother.

A blush rises all the way from my chest. Semi naked is no state to be talking to my parents in.

"Morning, sunshine," comes from the bedroom.

Charlie is standing in the doorway, smiling. Sunlight creates a halo around him, his hair out of control. My fingers curl with the urge to run through it.

"Technically, it's noon," I tease.

"Only if you want to be specific." He makes his way straight to the coffee machine. "Something important?" he asks, nodding at my phone.

I send off a quick "call you later" response and join him in the kitchen. He's pulled on the sweats he was wearing when I arrived, but he hasn't bothered with a shirt, a decision I'm fully onboard with. I'd be okay if he never wore a shirt again.

I slip my arms around his waist and bury my nose in his neck. His skin is warm, and he smells like sex and sleep. I never want to be anywhere else.

"My birthday is next week, and Mom is trying to

convince me to let the foundation throw a luncheon for it, but it's the last thing I want."

"Then don't do it," he says, pressing a button on the coffee maker. "Do what you want to. Although if you say you want to work, I'm withholding sex."

"I'd like to see you try."

Tugging me closer, he grabs my ass and squeezes. "I'll take that bet."

As penance, I scratch my nails lightly across his skin, just enough to tingle.

His breath stutters. When he opens his eyes, his expression is serious. "You seemed to enjoy being in the driver's seat earlier. Have you ever tried that before?"

I almost want to laugh. It sometimes feels as though my entire life has been an endless search for control. "No. I've thought about it, but no one's ever been interested before."

"I am. You're sexy when you're in control."

My heart pounds out a happy rhythm. "So are you." It's true. When I asked Charlie to take over, to help me let go, he did it wonderfully.

All while making sure I still felt powerful.

"That's why management likes you. You're decisive."

He shrugs. "I'd rather say sorry than please."

I can't help but laugh. That explains a lot.

But damn, it's a delicious picture. Charlie asking, begging. The fantasy sears every other thought from my mind. "Would you say please if I asked you to?"

He's thinking of it too, I can tell. The hitch in his breathing, the open hunger in his eyes.

"Sure you don't want to ask for something bigger?"

Being with him is like the swoop of turbulence. Something altogether scary and exciting. Unpredictable. And I can't get enough.

I kiss him instead of answering.

"Do you enjoy it more one way or the other?" I ask. I want to make it good for him.

"I like both," he says. "Depends on the day, how I'm feeling, who I'm sleeping with. I don't have a problem with switching it up. Life throws enough shit at us to not find all the pleasure we can."

"I think it's time you showed me your list," I tease.

He ducks his head, kisses and tugs on the tender part of my ear. Goose bumps flood my skin. "I'll show you anything you want, sweetheart. Just know my list begins and ends with you."

When the coffee is done, he fills two mugs without moving out of my reach. The coffee is good. But truly, I'm so blissed out he could hand me a cup of burnt tar, and it would taste like ambrosia.

"What would you do?" I eventually ask. "If you could do anything for your birthday?"

"I've heard Napa is wonderful this time of year," he says, mimicking Logan's voice.

I playfully nip at his collarbone. Getting a serious answer out of him is almost impossible.

With a chuckle, he relents. "I'm the wrong person to ask. Somewhere along the way, my paperwork got lost. Had to get a new birth certificate made up, and I mean *made up*. The records at the hospital were so bad, they couldn't find my actual birth date, so they just put one in. I have no idea whether it's right."

My heart aches for him.

"So," he continues, very carefully not meeting my eyes. "I decided to make every day count. Hell, today could be my birthday. It might be the best one I've ever had."

I know what you mean. Time with you feels like a gift.

Before I can blurt out something ridiculous, I kiss him.

"I think," I start, the wish slipping out soft and low, "I could be happy doing anything or nothing at all, as long as you were there."

He presses a kiss to my temple. "In that case, leave it up to me."

I don't think I could hold back my smile if you paid me to. "I'm in your capable hands."

———

"You realize your phone takes photos too, right?" I tease when I ask about the Polaroid later.

Charlie appears at my back, kissing my neck and sending a thrill down my spine, and takes the camera from me.

"These are special. You get one shot, so you have to make it special. Have to make sure you only capture the really important stuff."

With that, he steps around me, holds it up, and clicks.

It's a few breaths before my heart remembers how to beat again.

"What's this?" I turn to him, distracting myself with a worn red toy that looks like a child's binoculars.

"You're kidding," Charlie pouts.

"What?" I huff a laugh. "I've never seen one before."

It's another sign of how differently we were raised.

"It's a View-Master," he says. "Go ahead. It won't bite you."

I bring it up to my face, and pull the lever, watching the slides change. It's fascinating.

"Was it yours?" I hold it out to him.

He nods, his expression solemn, and takes it. "I didn't keep much from the years before Reese. I never wanted to have more than I could take with me or less than I was willing to lose."

He shakes himself out of his melancholy and dips in for a kiss.

"Since your birthday is coming up," he says, holding the toy out to me again, "let me be the first to give you your present."

My heart lodges itself in my throat. "I can't take this. It's yours."

He presses it into my hands. "Yes, and I want to give it to you."

"Charlie…" That's all I manage against the rising swell in my chest.

"Emma," he commands, playfulness dancing in his eyes. His tone is deep and so damn sexy it makes my body flush. "Let me give you the damn toy."

There are a few things I'm certain of. Cold pizza

tastes amazing. There's nothing sexier than a man rolling up his cuffs. And Charlie is secretly the most thoughtful man I've ever met.

I nod and try not to be completely infatuated by him. I do a poor job.

How is it that this four-dollar piece of plastic has my stomach fluttering? No one's ever given me a memento like this before. Small and ridiculous as it may be, it fills me with an explosion of glee I haven't felt in… maybe ever.

Oh, if only eight-year-old Emma could see me now.

"Thank you," I say. "Is there something I can get you?"

His gaze is unwavering, blue eyes warm and full of affection. "I've got everything I need right now."

I've often wondered how my father—a gentle, quiet giant—came from my Nana. What she lacked in stature, she made up for with an enormity of presence. A direct opposite to my dad.

I inherited his height, and though I didn't get much time with her, he's assured me that I have her spirit. Growing up, it always sounded like a pretty lie, the kind parents start out telling their kids. Who we are by way of who we resemble.

I've never outright questioned it. To be honest, I'm flattered. Even if it isn't true, it gives me a goal to aspire to. I've been attempting to emulate her ever since.

But maybe her watch isn't all I have of her.

I couldn't see it before, but the way Charlie looks at me, as though maybe I, too, have the power to shift the universe, makes me want to believe.

CHAPTER 39
IF YOU'RE THE FOREST, I'M THE TREES

EMMA

When I said I'd be happy doing anything, this was not what I pictured. But here we are, sitting on the hood of his classic car, at a park on the hill like a couple of wayward teens while the streetlamps cast a yellow glow across Charlie's cheekbones.

The heat of him holds the chill of the night at bay, and I sink deeper into his arms. With every inhale, I drink more of him in, letting his warm, wild scent envelop me. If he asked me again to run away together, I'd say yes.

If he asked me to stay with him forever, I wouldn't even hesitate.

It's like no other birthday I've ever had.

It's perfect.

I'm feeling so good that I answer my cell without checking the caller ID. At the sound of Harvey's voice, my smile disappears. He wouldn't call me this late on a weeknight unless there was an issue.

"Evening, Emma. My apologies for calling at this

hour, but it's important we meet to discuss your parents. There's been a development."

My blood runs cold. No, no, no. Not again. They promised.

They *promised.*

"When?"

"As soon as possible."

Fuck. That's bad. That's really, really bad.

"Now?"

"If you can come to my office, I'll let my secretary know to expect you."

My heart's beating a mile a minute. Either it'll jackhammer its way out of my chest or overwork itself into burnout, and right now, I'd welcome either.

I cannot believe they did this.

"Whoa there." Charlie's suddenly in front of me, running calming hands over my shoulders. "Breathe."

It's all too easy to step into his arms. His heartbeat is strong and steady, same as his breathing. "I have to go. It's my parents."

"Everything okay?"

"No" is all I can manage.

He squeezes me a little tighter. "Do you need backup?"

Of course he'd ask.

I press closer, holding tight, trying to absorb a little of his strength. Last time this happened, I faced it alone. I was angry and lost and faced with the reality that my social circle came with a buy-in cost. One I couldn't afford anymore.

So his presence, his willingness to face it with me? It's priceless.

I rest my chin on his chest. "A ride would be nice."

Leading me to the passenger door, he pulls his keys from his pocket. "What the lady wants, she gets."

God, he's so good. Ready to help at the drop of a hat. It knocks something loose between my ribs. Four letters, starts with *L*, difficult to say.

When we arrive at Harvey's office, I convince Charlie to stay in the car. I'm not sure I'm ready to reveal the full scale of catastrophe that is my family's financial situation. I'm sure he has his suspicions. How could he not? He's incredibly smart, and I've dropped enough details for him to put it together.

I can't pinpoint the moment having Charlie by my side changed from frustrating to comforting, but knowing he's waiting for me is half the reason I'm walking steady right now.

Harvey's office is quiet at this late hour, only adding to my growing dread. I thought we were finally out of the woods. The last time we slipped into the red was awful, and I'm praying this isn't as bad.

It can't be, right? Surely they wouldn't be that cruel.

"How bad is it?" I ask as I enter Harvey's office. The space is surprisingly modest, considering his rates, but I suspect that's on purpose. No distractions. For someone as straightforward and formidable as Harvey is, it makes sense. His office doesn't need to be intimidating. He fills that role himself.

When I met him, I genuinely thought my parents had hired private security. And while he's a few inches shorter than me, I have no doubt he could easily destroy me in a fight. Honestly? He would probably best Charlie, and that's saying something.

Harvey stands until I've taken a seat, as polite as ever. "Not as bad as last time, but it's not good."

Happy birthday to me.

With a long breath in, he slides his glasses on and reaches for a folder.

Oh god. My heart jerks painfully in my chest. The problem's big enough that *staples* are involved. Any receipt longer than a single page is bad news. That's at least an extra zero more than we can afford.

Wordlessly, he passes it to me. There's probably nothing he can say that will prepare me.

When Logan would take me to dinner, he'd make a show of sliding his black card into the bill without even looking at the figure. What I'd give to be able to take care of this in the same way. But I need to know the damage. Ignoring it will only make things worse.

One look at the total, and I can't decide whether I want to scream or cry. Bar staff, florist, catering… the whole fucking fundraiser.

I blow out a hot breath and slam the folder closed. "I thought Violet was paying for everything." If my mother lied straight to my face, I'm not sure what I'll do.

"They were sneaky about it," Harvey says, his mouth turned down in frustration. I know how he feels. "Mrs. Williamson Cross organized all services on behalf of the foundation. Everything, down to the silverware, was booked under her name, but the bill came back to your parents. I'm sorry, Emma. I should have caught this sooner."

"There are only two people to blame for this, and neither of them is in this room."

Most people get it wrong. The full quote is "The love of money is the root of all evil." Money alone has no ill will. It can be used for good just as easily as bad. But the love of it, a life spent in a constant need for more and more, until the value of it and the reality of what was done to gain it, loses all meaning. That's what's dangerous.

"What should I do?" I ask.

"There's no choice now. They'll have to sell. I've spoken to the event planners, and they've agreed to a delayed payment schedule as long as we can settle half of it by the end of the month."

My heart sinks. That's only two weeks away.

Harvey offers me a sad smile. He genuinely looks like he wishes he could fix this.

"Okay," I say. "Let's find the money, then." I don't have many options, but I have no choice.

———

Charlie is waiting exactly where I left him, and the sight of him is a relief. While everything is falling apart within me, he's more solid than ever.

I always expected love to hit fast, like being thrown off a horse. One minute, all is right, and the next, the world is turned upside down.

In reality, it's been slow. A gentle walk down a long

path so smooth I didn't notice how far I'd gone until I stopped and looked back.

It's hard to pinpoint when I started loving Charlie. I only know that I do, and that it's far from gentle. A part of it is soft and vulnerable, to be treated with care. But the rest?

Oh, it's a force of nature.

Fierce and wondrous, deep and natural. Fighting it would be futile.

There's a soft ache under my ribs, a muscle long unstretched, now unfurled between us.

Never could I have imagined it would feel so... endless. So energizing.

Never could I imagine I was capable of a love like this.

I'm happy to be surprised.

Charlie is playful and at times cocky, but he's also quick-witted and more observant than he pretends to be.

He cares about Reese so much he loses sleep over it, but he would never burden her by saying anything. There are more dog toys than appliances in his apartment, a wardrobe James Bond would covet, and a box of mementos that makes my heart ache for him.

He's a good man convinced he's the muscle rather than the hero. Who quips and flirts and pretends he's fine when, in reality, his feelings run rich.

And I know true wealth when I see it.

CHAPTER 40
UNITED, WE'RE UNSTOPPABLE
CHARLIE

The story unfolds as I drive home.

"You should know," I say, "I called in rein-forcements. They're going to meet us at my place, but if you don't want to see anyone right now—"

"I'd rather not be alone." She grabs my hand, holding tight. "You didn't have to do that, though."

"Yes, I did. You don't have to face this by yourself."

As expected, Reese has already let herself and Ivy into my apartment using her spare key. When we enter, Ivy is up and hugging Emma before I can blink.

"How bad is it? On a scale of the world's smallest instruments, do I have to get a ukulele?"

"It's a violin at most," Emma says. "If it ever gets ukulele bad, I'll be moving to a deserted island."

"Have you spoken to them yet? I'll come with you if you need me to, and before you say no, I'll remind you that I played Madame Thénardier in school, so I can be menacing when I want to be."

It's not hard to imagine. Ivy might barely come up

to Emma's shoulders, but she's surprisingly jacked, and anyone who's cycled into Ops from her area, Developments, always speaks of her in awed tones.

"Not yet, and thank you, but I think it's best I go by myself."

"If you need someone to practice on, I'm here," Ivy says, releasing Emma. "And in the meantime, this"—she scoops up her bag and pulls a bottle of bubbly out of her tote—"will help."

Emma practically sags with relief. "Have I told you lately that I love you?"

At those three words, it's like an invisible hand has reached into my chest and decided to use my heart as a stress toy. I busy myself with shucking my jacket and emptying my pockets while doing my best to ignore it.

"I'm assuming no introductions are necessary, since you've already helped yourself to my stash," I say, waving toward the opened bag of M&M's on the counter.

"We were hungry," Reese says, lifting her chin, clearly unremorseful. "And you know peanut is my favorite."

Of course I do. I keep a bag of them around just for her. I don't even like peanuts.

"With that out of the way, how about we get to work? Ivy, glasses are in the top left cupboard. Reese, you're on food. Emma's going to change into something more comfortable."

Using the excuse of lending her clothes, I follow Emma into my room, only for Reese to call out, "Let's keep it family friendly, you two."

Nose pinched, I shut the bedroom door behind me. "Inviting them was a terrible idea."

Emma closes the gap between us and rests her hands on my chest.

Pulling her closer is as natural as breathing.

"No," she whispers, "it's perfect. Thank you."

I tilt my head, pressing a kiss to her temple. "Nothing to thank me for. Now, get changed while I sort these two out."

Horrifyingly, I find Reese standing in front of the stove, attempting… who knows what. "What do you think you're doing?"

"You told me to take care of dinner."

"Reese, you burn water."

Turning, she points a spatula at me. "That was one time."

Only because our parents didn't want to have to call the fire department more than once. Since then, Reese is forbidden from cooking. "What's our last meal going to be anyway? Since whatever you make will likely kill us."

"It's a surprise."

I sidle up beside her and turn the burner off.

"Phone. Pizza. Now."

"Fine," she groans. "I'm on it."

Ivy passes us each a glass. "Charlie, you should catch up with my younger sister some time. You could pass notes on sibling authority."

"Don't mind him," Reese says. "We're only legally related."

Head tossed back, Ivy laughs, her necklaces

jangling. Great, now there's two of them. "That explains why you're so much cooler."

My heart twists a little more.

It's a good thing they get along. At this rate, I'll bet Reese has already roped Ivy into a game night. Emma adores Reese already, and the idea of them being friends makes me happy.

So there's no reason for me to get worked up about it.

When Ivy leaves to take Emma a glass of wine, Reese wraps me in a tight hug. "You're doing a good thing. Emma's lucky to have you."

I hug her back, even as I shake my head. She always does this when she thinks I'm secretly sulking.

"Don't start," I warn her. "I don't even know what we are to each other right now."

"Then you need to get your head out of your ass. That woman is head over heels for you. And don't even think about telling me you don't feel the same way."

I pull back. "Stop meddling. And don't forget the pepperoni."

"No, no, no, no, no. Even mortal, Andromache would beat Black Window," I say.

We're sprawled across the living room, drinks in hand, waiting on food. The television is on, but we've muted it so we can argue about which characters would win in a fight.

Reese shakes her head so fast I get dizzy. "No way. Natasha is the best Red Room had to offer."

"Andromache is six thousand years old," I argue. "Natasha—and this is if we're going by the comics, not the movies—is barely a hundred. No way she's kicking an immortal's ass."

"But she's so hot."

"You're always using that excuse."

Reese groans. "And you're a bad loser. This is just like the time you ran off Rainbow Road and blamed me."

"I'm sorry, who ran me off the road?"

Reese only laughs.

"Remind me to never play Ticket To Ride with you two," Ivy says, holding her wineglass aloft.

When the food arrives, I run downstairs, a strange feeling churning in my gut. I'm worried for Emma and angry at her parents for not appreciating how good they have it without wanting more, but it's more than that.

It's having her here. It's spending time together that isn't about work or sex or Logan. It's getting a glimpse at a future I already know is going to fucking hurt not to have.

When I get back, I find Reese and Ivy debating which Beatles song they'd sing if they were stranded on an island, and I leave them to it.

The only right answer is "Get Back," anyway.

"Thank you," Emma whispers to me. She's slotted next to me on the couch, legs curled up, eating with one hand while teasing the back of my neck with the other.

I've been trying to hide the effect it's having on me, but from the look Reese has been giving me, I'm failing.

"This is much better than wallowing on my own."

"I'll never let you do that. Just say the word, and I'll do everything I can to help."

I've never been much good at comfort; my usual strategy is to barrel right on through any problem ahead of me. I'm not sure that'll work here.

I don't have the first clue how to solve this problem for her, but damn if I don't want to.

"You don't know how much that means, Charlie."

Though her tone is sad, the words are laced with a warmth that still takes me aback.

Shifting so I can look at her full-on, I ask, "Can I say something?"

"Could I stop you?" She smiles.

"You're the only one who could," I whisper, enjoying the way her eyes darken at the suggestion.

"Then I guess I'll let you."

"Your parents are assholes."

She lets out a short laugh, then hurries to compose herself. "That's not very nice."

"Neither is the position they've put you in." I run a hand down my face. "Maybe you can forgive them easily, but it sounds like you've done everything you can to help them, and they're not only ignoring it, but they're acting like consequences don't matter, then leaving you to clean up."

"I know, and I *am* angry at them, but... I still love them."

Ivy stretches across the gap between the armchair

and squeezes Emma's shoulder gently. "You're allowed to be both. But consider this: you're their kid, not their minder. Even if you can forgive them for the last time, that should have been enough to stop them from mistake number two."

"They promised me," Emma says softly. With those three words, her walls crumble. Her eyes get watery, and her shoulders curl in. "I don't mind supporting them, but I want the chance to have my own life first. I don't want to spend all my time worrying about them. Do you know what I hate?" She wipes under one eye, then the other. "I hate that, for most people, living comfortably is *aspirational*. I hate that I'm familiar with the kind of assholes who would rather keep wealth for themselves than ensure everyone can afford essentials like health care or education. I hate that Roberts never took me seriously, that he saw how much I wanted to prove myself and used that against me. But most of all, I hate that I feel like I always have to be calm and polite about it and not fucking angry, which I am," she finishes, her breath labored.

Ivy toasts the air. "Damn, is it a bad time for a slow clap?"

Emma is no less beautiful like this, full of as much bite and bark as I've ever known her to be. It probably wouldn't turn a better man on, but I'm no better man.

As much as I want to fix this for her, this isn't about me, and also, *read the room, jackass*. Instead, I make do with brushing her hair off her face and ghosting my fingers along her neck. Emma's lashes flutter under the touch. I leave my hand on her shoulder, trying desperately to offer some help. It's not until she breathes out and relaxes under my hold that I start to feel the knot in my ribs unravel.

"For the record," I say. "All of that is worth being angry about."

———

"Why not let them wear it?" Reese asks. "Wouldn't it be on the foundation, rather than your parents?"

Emma shakes her head. "This is less about the debt and more about reputation. If the foundation gets sued, then other organizations won't work with them, and a lot of the sponsors will pull out to distance themselves."

"Don't you think they deserve a little embarrassment after this?" Ivy asks.

"Yes," she says, clasping her hands in her lap and studying them. "And if that was the only consequence, I would let them lie in the bed they've made. But ultimately, my parents mistake will cost the charities they're trying to help."

"So, what can we do?" I can't just sit around and not get involved while she struggles to clean up the mess.

Emma turns to me, lips pressed together. "I can't ask you to do anything,"

My heart cracks in half at the defeat in her tone. "You're not asking. We're going to help you whether you like it or not."

"What he said," Ivy adds.

"I appreciate that. Really, I do. But I think it's high time my parents bear the brunt of my frustrations."

Except as she lifts a hand to tuck a lock of hair behind her ear, I get a glimpse of her wrist—which is unusually bare—it's obvious she's already had to pay the price.

I only hope her parents will recognize what she's doing for them. If they don't, then I'll find a way to correct that for them.

Ivy refills our glasses as the tension disappears, and Reese tilts her head to say, "Okay. Okoye versus Catwoman."

"Pfeiffer or Kravitz?" I ask.

"Excuse me," Ivy interrupts. "Are we not even going to consider Halle Berry? Or Anne Hathaway?"

"No" is the chorus answer.

CHAPTER 41
YOU WANNA BE ON TOP?
EMMA

When we arrive at the office on Monday morning, I find a meeting invitation from none other than Emmanuel Fletcher.

I knew it was coming, especially after Charlie and I made that visit to security, but what's surprising is who isn't invited.

Karl Roberts.

In fact, as the day progresses, Roberts doesn't appear in the office at all.

His absence makes me nervous, and not in a fun way.

Charlie notices, of course, checking on me throughout the day, a worried crease between his brows. And in the minutes before I set off for my meeting, he pulls me aside to give me a pep talk. It's so sweet, all I want to do is kiss him.

I've always hated the idea of being owed benefits simply *because*, but that isn't the case here. I've worked hard for this. Earning it matters to me.

"Sweetheart, no one in this company has earned it more than you, including the top dog."

I battle the heated blush that bubbles under my skin. My foundation has never had to work so hard. It's the Charlie Walker effect.

"You're right." It feels wildly good to admit, and I let the adrenaline fuel me as I go.

———

Maybe the game is rigged.

Maybe the real win would be living a life I choose instead of working myself to the bone for a goal that might always be held out of my reach.

But if the life I want includes working hard for the simple joy of knowing exactly how incredible I can be, then what?

Who am I really working for?

Myself?

The elusive *them*?

Organizations so rarely care about their workforce beyond productivity and reputation, so it stands to reason that I shouldn't care about my job as much as I do. There's a damn good chance that all my efforts will be in vain.

I've sat beside Ivy at a HR meeting where she reported a coworker for making repeatedly creepy comments. HR's response? Handle it yourself.

I've been punished for finding problems and offering solutions. For working harder than my boss does.

I've been told to stop being combative when I speak up in meetings, and to stop being quiet when I don't.

To say yes to more while also being told to stop overloading myself.

Where does it stop?

There is a vast world of measures a woman is expected to live up to yet can never meet. I'm sick of holding my tongue, of being told to accept it because it's "how it's always been." Of being told that holding on to anger is a problem.

I want to make my own mark, as small as it might be. Carve out my own space. One I can look at and say "I did that." I made a positive impact, even if it was only for one person.

This job hasn't turned out how I hoped it would when I started. Doing work I'm proud of has given me a stake to hold on to, a tangible piece of my identity.

It's small, but it's mine, and it's real.

It's in the *thank you*s and the *much appreciated*s. The *good morning*s, the nodded smiles, the *Can you help me?*

I don't want to leave. If I do, I fear I'll go back to being everything Charlie once accused me of. The bored little rich girl playing dress-up while the world burns.

Despite appearances, I've never been in less control than I am right now. Unlike Charlie, who is the master of his own destiny, I've always been expected— rewarded, even—when I fall in line.

And for fuck's sake, if it's frustrating for me—a woman who grew up with money and attended private school, with a name whose reputation preceded me— how cruel and dangerous must the world be to those who are actively oppressed through every rule and judgment and perception?

Even at my lowest, I have access others don't. It's like Charlie said—for every sand trap he faces, he still starts with a lower handicap. I hate him for teaching me anything about golf.

I also hate how right he is.

———

Emmanuel smiles as I enter his office, and my nerves stretch tighter.

"Thank you for meeting with me. I know it's short notice and a little mysterious, but I'll clear everything up in a few minutes," he says once I'm seated in the visitor chair opposite him. "I had hoped we'd have this conversation under better circumstances, but there's nothing to be done about that, so I'll get right to it."

"Okay." I leave it at that, using the silence like Charlie said to keep from giving anything away.

It works.

"The first thing you should know is that Karl Roberts no longer works here."

My mind trips over itself, and every direction I imagined this going instantly reroutes. "Did he quit?"

"I can't get into the details, but Karl was let go over the weekend. Security will be through today to clear out his office." He laces his fingers on top of his desk. "As you can appreciate, we can't let him back into the building without risking him accessing valuable business information."

"Of course."

I keep my voice level, but I'm still trying to make sense of it. Is this because of what Charlie and I found?

"Second, I want to apologize. I've believed a number of things Karl has told me in the past, namely in regard to your work and performance. I took him at his word, and that is my failure. Now that I've taken the time to speak with others and learned of his undermining of your efforts, I know how far astray he led me."

There's a glass of water in front of me on the table, one I suspect Emmanuel put there in anticipation that I'd need it, but my hand is shaking so much I don't want to risk reaching for it.

"Emma," he says with a sigh.

He runs a hand along his jaw, and it's then that I notice how rough he looks. There's a weight in his eyes, his face, his shoulders. He is genuinely sorry. I honestly don't know what to do with that after all of Roberts's torment.

"I've read over the work you and Charlie have done, and I'm impressed with it. I'm not the only one either. Jeremy Baxter had only good things to say about how you handled yourself when presenting it to him."

My breath catches. This cannot be real. I'm dreaming.

If I could move, I would pinch myself.

"I'm inclined to postpone the appointment of the lead role. We'll need time to fill Karl's position, which leaves things very awkwardly in the air. But before I make that decision, I want to ask you, why do you want this role? What does it mean to you?"

Shaking be damned, I reach for the glass. Despite how it feels like my insides are about to spill out of me, I manage to take a couple of calm sips without spilling a drop.

"For the last five years," I say, setting the glass on the desk again, "I've done little more than dedicate myself to this job. I've completed more in that time than any one of my peers. I've consistently brought solutions to light. Solutions I have vetted and tested as best as I can, and I have been willing to take on new projects any time they were presented to me." Presented… ordered… same, same. "I could sit here and list every project I've completed and how much time or money or frustration it's saved this company, but it's a long list, and I'm sure your wife would prefer you make it home for dinner at a decent hour."

Emmanuel smiles, as I'd hoped he would, and it's what I need to keep going.

"I want this role not only because I've earned it, but because I'm the best person for it. I care about our procedures, and I care about making sure they're fit for the people using them. That our processes make sense and aren't cumbersome. That they aren't so convoluted you need to speak three languages to untangle what button to press. That our information is secure in a system that supports and even assists us in the work we're all being paid to do."

I clasp my hands in my lap. Emmanuel doesn't speak. He continues to watch me with interest.

"To be honest," I say, pulling my shoulders back, "I want this role because of the work, not the company, and not the title. It doesn't matter to me if I'm doing it here or somewhere else. I want to make a difference, and I want to put my energy into something I care about. Right now, that is this job. That's what this role means to me."

When I'm finished, he gives me a single nod I don't know how to interpret.

"You're a very attractive candidate, Emma. You're proficient in project management and reporting, and your results speak for themselves. But it's your double degree that most benefits you. It's archaic, but at these levels, a piece of paper can go a long way. With that said, I consider this an even opportunity." He clasps his hands together, elbows on the table. "Unless there's something you think I should know about Charlie that would tip the scales?"

Does he know? Or is this a test? Giving up Charlie's secret would sway the race in my favor immediately, and once upon a time, I would have considered it. Back when Charlie was nothing but a backstabbing opportunist to me, rather than the warm, silly, big-hearted powerhouse I've come to know.

If I say nothing, there's a likelihood he'll get the promotion. No matter how good my work has been, the collective memory of the lead team will have a hard time seeing anything beyond the glowing recommendation of the COO. And if there's one thing my upbringing taught me, it's that getting your name in people's mouths is a priceless commodity.

This could be my only shot. Charlie did say I needed to be more ruthless. Play the game, demand what I want. Only I never thought taking it would feel like this.

"No, there's nothing. Charlie is an exceptional worker. You'd be lucky to have him in the lead role."

Emmanuel's face lights up. "That's interesting. Because when I pulled him aside earlier, he said the same thing about you."

Of fucking course he did.

CHAPTER 42
DON'T YOU KNOW, I WAS ALWAYS GOING TO FUCK IT UP

CHARLIE

Trouble's never had to look too far to find me. By now, we're old friends.

First girl I ever kissed caught me writing her name in the back of a book. Next thing I know, kids are calling me Charlene, asking aloud if I needed a tampon. Fucking assholes. They were just angry because Charlene could still kick their asses.

Painting my nails before I broke Aaron's nose made the moment that much sweeter.

When I was twenty, I fell hard for Bess. Stunning woman, a little older than me, knew what she wanted when she wanted it and didn't want to mess around with the rest. I thought it was the perfect deal. Didn't count on my heart wanting a piece of the action.

Bess shut things down fast. "Things aren't ever going to be like that between us." It was a blessing in disguise.

By the time I met Lucy, I thought I knew what I was

doing. Figured being with someone I liked, but who didn't drive me to distraction, was a good thing.

Reese called it settling, I called it survival.

And that's what I've been doing. Surviving.

Until now.

———

I'm proud of her, over the fucking moon, that she stood up to Emmanuel like I knew she could. That role is hers. That much was clear when he spoke with me.

I'm well-practiced in the art of "you're a good kid, but this isn't the right place for you."

And I'm happy for her.

But I know this part. It's the awkward pause before the bad news. Where my heart goes into hiding, protecting itself against the inevitable.

Tonight started off the best it could, on Emma's couch, a movie playing on the TV. I couldn't tell you which one. I'm too wrapped up in her, how good she feels in my arms.

How perfectly she fits in my life.

Then Logan calls.

His name flashes on her phone like a neon sign, a glaring reminder that we still haven't talked about what this is between us. Am I still simply a stand-in, a place-holder? A temporary distraction used to fill in the time?

Emma sends the call to voicemail.

"Aren't you going to answer that?" I ask. "Could be important."

Brows furrowed, she scrutinizes me. "There's nothing he could be calling for that's important."

I've always hated the limbo of *not knowing*. If bad news is coming, I want that Band-Aid ripped right off. No waiting. No hesitation.

I twist to face her, my arm slipping from her shoulders. Immediately, I want to move back, but touching her will only make this more difficult. Already, my heart is packing its bags. Fortifying the doors and windows.

"What's going on with you and him?" I have to know. Need to.

Her lips tug down in a confused frown. "Nothing is going on. I thought you knew that. He asked me out, and I told him—"

"You'd think about it." I remember.

Her frown melts into something so soft and fond it actually makes me ache. "Yes. I did think about it. And I don't want to be with him."

"Does he know that?" I wave at her phone, which is now showing a voicemail notification.

"Yes," she says, her tone firm. "He does. I don't know why he's calling, Charlie, but I'm not interested." She closes the gap, her fingers finding their way into my hair. "I'm exactly where I want to be."

"And where's that?"

Emma's smile falters. "Here. With you."

For how long? I want to ask, but I don't think I can handle the answer.

"Not saying it's not nice to have you here, but what

happened to the arrangement? You said it yourself: I'm just a means to an end."

Sometimes I think fighting's all I'm good for.

"You know you're more than that, Charlie."

"Do I?"

Was I supposed to simply guess at what this was? When it started as bad blood and got tangled up with sex? She didn't have a problem saying she hated me when she could get something out of me.

So how can I be sure of her feelings now?

"Okay, that's fair. I should have made it more obvious. I'm sorry. I… I know I wasn't kind to you in the beginning, and I regret that."

"I told you back then—I knew what I was getting into."

Everything soft in her hardens, her eyes, her jaw, her posture. "Good to know I've been a burden to you."

"Don't put words in my mouth." Heart thundering, I turn out of her grip.

"I kind of have to, Charlie. You keep talking around whatever you're avoiding, so I'm stuck filling in the gaps and trying to make sense of it." She places her hand over mine and squeezes. "You need to tell me what you want, because I can't make heads or tails of it."

My needs.

My needs are already taken care of. I have Reese, a roof over my head, a little money saved. It's not much, but it's more than I thought I'd get. The rest is nice, but if it went away tomorrow, I'd be okay.

I'd have to be.

"I want to trust that this isn't just a whim," I admit. "Can you really promise me that you won't wake up and change your mind? Decide you don't want to slum it anymore? That you really do want Logan?"

She straightens, voice hard. "You don't get to tell me what I want."

"You're right. But if I'd known a couple of orgasms were going to make you catch feelings for me, I might not have said yes."

She rears back like I've slapped her. Fuck. "You don't mean that."

My heart cracks right in half, but I ignore it. It's only ever gotten me in trouble. "How do you know this isn't just because of sex? I'm serious. You came to me, telling me you hated me but you wanted my help. Did my feelings even factor in back then?"

Her gaze drops away from mine.

I ball my hands into fists to stop them from shaking. "I'm not saying I don't have feelings for you, but—"

"Then what are you saying?" she asks, her voice so thick with pain I have to steel myself against it by digging my fingers into the meat of my palm.

It isn't the first time I wanted everything I can't have. And Emma is the only thing I want. The last want I'll ever have. But I can't keep her. She's too good, too pure to be dirtied up by a beat-up mess like me. Though that's never stopped me from taking more than I deserved.

"I don't want to lie to you. But it's hard for me to trust this. I wish I had the luxury of blind optimism like you, but I don't. I have to believe what's here today is only temporary."

"It's only temporary because you're pushing me away. Charlie, I've fallen in—"

I put my hand up to stop her.

"One piece of advice? Don't say that to someone who isn't going to say it back."

"Oh." She goes unnaturally still. "Right. Good… good advice."

I want to say it, more than anything, but I don't trust that this is real yet. That it won't disappear the moment those words leave my lips.

Though a lead weight sinks in my gut, I clear my throat and force out the next words. "It was never meant to be anything more than sex."

"You're right, it wasn't, but then it became more." She stands. "At least for me. But fine. Push me away because you're scared of what we have. Just don't pretend it's for my benefit. I care about you, and I want to be together."

Regardless of what she thinks, we were never going to get enough time. Because we were over before we began.

"Don't worry," I sneer, my heart crumbling. "You'll go back to hating me soon enough."

"Don't flatter yourself." She steps close, dragging her hands across my chest, shoulders, cupping my face.

My throat grows thick, twisted.

"You have the biggest heart I've ever seen, but you've walled yourself off. You've locked your feelings away and trapped yourself and call it protection.

Nothing in, nothing out. You might be safe that way, but you're miserable. I hate whoever made you feel like you don't deserve happiness, Charlie, because you do. I can prove it to you if you give this a chance."

"I know you think that—"

"I know it," she whispers. "Don't you believe me?"

I want to. I've never wanted anything as much as I want this.

But life doesn't become what we want it because we wish for it. "Nothing good in my life has ever lasted except for Reese. I know I'm being an asshole right now, but I haven't had everything handed to me, all right? I've only ever had it ripped away. You're asking me to, what? Just trust in this lasting forever because you said so? That's not how the world works."

"I'm asking you to be vulnerable with me. To give us a chance."

"I don't know if I'm ready to do that."

She's nodding erratically, like she doesn't know what to do. That makes two of us.

"So," she says, her voice shaking in a way that shatters my soul. "This is it? We go back to hating each other?"

I press a palm to her damp cheek. "Sweetheart, I never hated you."

Her eyes slip shut as I kiss her cheek.

My heart might be breaking in two, but I'm going to lock that shit up and not let her see. She doesn't deserve me adding to her distress.

"Then why?"

Because I love you.

I can't say it. It's the last defense I have. Once I've said it, exposed my underbelly for her, there's no going back.

I can see her perfect life taking shape—the job she earned, the man she loves, all the good things she deserves. It's better without me there messing up the details, adding complications or whatever.

"Because it's better for both of us."

"That's bullshit and you know it. I love you," she says, as beautifully defiant as ever.

My heart roars in my chest, desperate to return the words, but my throat closes up tight.

"I know you don't want to hear it, but it's the truth. It's raw, and it's real, and it's not going anywhere." She swallows audibly, her eyes glassy. "But it doesn't matter, because you've already made your mind up about us."

The pain on her face makes me want to punch myself.

"I'm not going to bend over backward to try and convince you," she says. "I deserve better than that. I wish you believed in us as much as I do. And as for this being a whim? You're wrong. It's the furthest thing from it. If you need time to work that out for yourself, then I'll give that to you. And when you've gotten your head out of your ass, you can find me and apologize."

I swallow, locking down the twisted mess of pain squeezing my chest. Becoming the cold, unfeeling villain I used to accuse her of. This is the worst version of myself.

"You're right," I admit. "You deserve better than me."

Emma puts distance between us, the drawbridge rising. "Despite what you think," she says, a hard edge to her voice, "I don't fall in love with every man lucky enough to sleep with me. I don't want you to misunderstand me, so I'll say this clearly. I love you, not Logan. And you're wrong. You know how to love, but you won't let yourself." She's flushed and gorgeous. Completely out of my reach. "When you're ready to stop standing in your own way, you know where I am. And Charlie?"

I meet her gaze, pulse thudding in my ears.

"You better make it good."

I don't want to leave, but it'll hurt a thousand times worse if I hang on. If my heart is gonna be ripped from my chest, I'd rather be the one to do it. I can't do that to either of us. I don't have it in me to hate her.

So I walk away.

Because Emma should be happy.

Even if it leaves my world darker.

This is what's best for her. If I don't cut this off—cleave it at the root—neither of us will be free.

It's a good thing I'm an asshole. Let her hate me for this. At least she won't be holding on. The least I can do is give her a clean break. No regrets. At least for one of us.

CHAPTER 43
OOPS, YOU RAISED A BAMF
EMMA

My parents started the Conway foundation before I was born. The way they tell it, when Mom found out she was pregnant, they decided they wanted something to hand down to me. The logic of it escapes me, but then, so do a lot of my parents' decisions.

In fairness to them, the charitable organization—which funds medical research for children—has done a lot of good. They hired a strong team of people with extensive backgrounds in philanthropy, and they've at least been smart enough to know that their own strength lies in bringing in donors, rather than handling the finances themselves (something I am eternally grateful for).

Which is why I'm so furious at them.

Together, they have one job—even calling it a job is generous—and now their reckless addiction to money has put the reputation of the foundation at risk.

I find them mid-meal on the terrace.

"Mom, Dad."

The legs of the chair squeal as I pull it out and sit.

I don't bother to cover the pregnant silence, and neither do they, although Mom is close. She's folded her napkin three times now. Dad's grip tightens on his coffee, but he says nothing.

Well, I'm glad they're uncomfortable. They should be.

"I had an interesting conversation with Harvey the other day. My birthday, as it happens, which was nice timing. The conversation was equally pleasant."

They share a guilty look. Mom's eyes are rimmed with red, and Dad's mouth is tugged down. At least they know why I'm here. Surely they saw this coming.

"Is this an intervention?" my dad asks, straightening. "Honestly, Emma—"

"Dad, I'm sorry, but I'm going to need you to be quiet and listen for a change."

His mouth clicks shut.

I work hard to balance the benefits I've been given. I started in a position higher than most get to. Now I want to make sure I live a life worthy of what we were given for free.

And I'm going to start by ripping away the rose-colored glasses from my parents' eyes.

"You're selling the house."

"I don't think—" Dad starts, but I raise my hand to stop him.

"I'm done asking. Harvey has already found a realtor he trusts, and I won't leave until you've signed the paperwork. You should have done this five years ago. I did everything I could to make sure you could stay because you promised you'd be more careful, but you broke that promise. Now you don't have a choice."

I'm angry. Furious. At them, at Roberts, at Charlie. I'll be setting all those issues to rights, but first things first. "I can't believe you lied to me. After everything we went through last time."

"But—" Mom starts.

"No. No more buts. No more excuses. Don't tell me it's just one party. You know it's more than that. It's trips to wineries. It's paying for lunches with your friends. The tennis club you never visit and high-risk investments you can't afford."

Dad frowns. "I never invest anything without Harvey's go-ahead."

"Yes, because I asked him to do that. Someone needs to make sure you don't bankrupt yourselves."

"Emma, please. We're trying."

They are. It's what makes this so frustrating. "I know you are, but it's not enough."

"It's not easy to adjust after a lifetime of living a certain way. It's been hard enough confining ourselves to this house, hardly ever going out or seeing friends. So many rooms are bare. It feels like we're living with ghosts."

"And I'm sorry about that. I can imagine it's difficult. I hate seeing this house so empty. I miss it just as much as you do. I love this house. It's why Harvey and I have been working so hard to keep it."

Suddenly, Dad's hand is on mine. "Your watch is gone."

I blink back the tears. They know how much it meant to me. What it means that I'm not wearing it.

Eyes wide, he leans back in his chair and blows out a shaky breath. "Darling, you shouldn't have done that."

I swallow past the lump in my throat. "You didn't really give me a choice. If I didn't, the hire company would have sued the foundation for lack of payment."

"I'm going to wring Vi's neck," Mom says.

It takes more energy than I'd like to admit to keep my voice even. "Violet isn't the problem."

Mom raises her brow, and for a moment, it's so like the way Charlie challenges me that I have to look away.

"I'll rephrase," I say. "Violet isn't blameless, and frankly, I'd be happy to listen to you berate her. But the real issue is that you agreed to the party in the first place. That you're both still acting as though you have an endless supply of money when we all know that isn't true. It's gone, and it's past time to stop pretending otherwise."

"You're right," she says, lowering her head and wiping at her eyes. "Oh, honey. I wish you'd come here before you'd given up your nana's watch."

In my darkest moments, I sour with the urge to punish them, become the reflection of their treatment toward me, and maybe it's earned.

But I'm not interested in being the arbitrator of their comeuppance.

"It's fine." It's not, but it'll pass.

"No, Emma," Dad says. "I'll call Harvey and sort this out like we should have in the first place. Christ, we're your parents. We should be taking care of your crises, not the other way around."

"We're family. We look out for each other."

He clasps his hands on the table. "It seems to me that we need to balance that scale."

"Dad, I'm not keeping score." I give him a small smile. "I love you. I want to make sure you're both okay."

"And I adore you for that, but we're old enough to take responsibility, and we've been doing a poor job of that so far." Shifting in his chair, he regards me with misty eyes. "I'm sorry that we didn't hear you before. I know it's coming too late."

My chest aches at the sincerity in his voice. "It's not."

"Come here." He stands and holds out his arms, and I rush into them, transported back to the young girl whose father conjured magic to make her smile. So much time has passed, but I still want to believe. "You mean everything to us. I hope you know that. None of this comes close to being as important as you." He kisses my forehead. "It's going to require some work on our part, but it's about time for us to learn some new skills, don't you think, love?" he asks my mother.

"Absolutely." She smiles and stands too, and we pull her in.

"It's time we got Harvey on the phone. With any luck, we can have the house on the market by the end of the week."

They sort the money stuff out. Dad makes the call to Harvey to sell the house, and Mom calls Violet to tell her they're stepping down, insisting that as a parting gift, the foundation will throw them a farewell party. "And you're going to pay for it," she states.

I'm so proud.

It's only made better when my father holds up a hand to high-five her. The worst isn't over. In fact, we're far from it. Now that they won't have the foundation, they'll be more bored than ever, and we'll have to have several more conversations in order for them to really curb their spending habits. But finally, it feels like they've heard me.

CHAPTER 44
MISTAKES WERE MADE (HONESTLY I BROUGHT THIS ON MYSELF)
CHARLIE

I miss her. Every breath, every blink. Every damn day. There's not a thought I don't want to share with her, a second I don't want to touch her, taste her, hold her.

But it's done. Over. Finished.

I thought I knew heartbreak when Lucy left, but that was a pleasure cruise next to this.

I just need time.

There's no scrubbing away the memory of her or the time we had together. She can erase me from her life in every other way, would be right to, but nothing will take her from me. I'll die clasping on to it.

Because that's all we have now. The memories. The past. Our friendship—what's left of it—sputtering along on fumes, barely a shadow of what it was. A greeting here, a smile there.

It helps that Ops agreed to have me back at my old desk on twelve. Not seeing her every day, having the temptation in front of me, is necessary.

———

I've lost count of the number of families I was sent to before I landed with the Walkers. I'm not as close to them as I am with Reese, but I'm grateful for them all the same.

They might have taken me in, but Reese was the first family I ever had.

Some ties are stronger than blood.

Like me, she was moved around a lot, but she's much stronger than I am. Where I fought back, Reese lifted her head high and kept walking. I don't know how she does it.

My whole life, I've been biding my time, preparing for the worst. Waiting to be disappointed.

"What the hell happened?" Reese asks after I let her in.

"I fucked it up. We both knew I was going to."

I shouldn't make room for sentimentality. I still have a go-bag packed in my closet. In case of a fire, I told Reese when she found it.

It's better to not need anything, but I've always found it hard to let go. Found myself wanting to keep more and more. Of course, I still want more of Emma. When it comes to her, there's no such thing as enough.

I've been greedy my whole life.

"Do you think I'm a good person?" I ask, heart in my throat.

Reese gapes at me, blinking, as if I've told her water is too wet. "What are you talking about? Of course you are."

Yeah, I'm not sure about that. "Don't you think I'm a hypocrite? That I've become what we always hated? An asshole working my life away, strutting around in thousand-dollar clothes?" I crash onto the couch, drop my head in my hands. "Eight years ago, I had a goal. I'd work and save. Help with the shelter. Then I'd leave before it changed me. I never thought about what came after. I spent so long trying to get somewhere, but I never had a clue where I was going. Now look at me." I gesture around the apartment. "Just one more soulless suit."

Reese punches me in the shoulder, sending me reeling back.

"Ow, what the hell?"

"Keep talking about my brother like that and see what it gets you."

I sulk, rubbing the spot. Damn. I'm starting to regret teaching her that move.

She sighs, long and deep. "Do you remember my twelfth birthday?"

Weird sidebar, but okay. "Yeah, you disappeared after school and scared the shit out of me."

"I didn't think anyone would notice. No one had before."

"I noticed."

Lips pressed together, she dips her chin. "You did, and you covered for me."

"Yeah, well, I didn't know Mom and Dad were cool yet."

It's been sixteen years, and I still have to remind myself not to call them Stacy and Dave. Too many years of new guardians. New "siblings." New schools. After a while, it's hard not to feel like a broken toy, donated and recycled. Rinse and repeat.

"You had my back from the beginning, even though you barely talked. No matter how much I asked about that scar on your hand, you never told me where you got it. You could be bleeding and half-broken, but I could always count on you."

I open my mouth, but she doesn't let me speak.

"I'd never had anyone looking out for me before," she says, "but there you were, staying up with me when I couldn't sleep, teaching that little shit Jimmy Wallace a lesson when he called me a bitch, letting me beat you at *Mario Kart*."

"You cheated in *Mario Kart*. Letting you win was easier."

"Mom told me, you know. How you begged her to let you bake every one of my birthday cakes."

My neck goes hot. "I don't beg."

She rolls her eyes. "But you did make them all."

I don't know what she wants me to say. Of course I did. I'm her brother. I look after her. That's what I do. I don't know why we have to sit here and rehash it all.

"Fifteen years, you've been looking after me. I love you for that. And I'm going to need you to remember you love me too when I say this. I need you to start looking after yourself." She grasps my arm. "You're not soulless. Sure, you might live more comfortably now, but you're still the same Charlie, still looking after the people you care about. If you don't like where you are, then change it. Stop fighting and let yourself be happy."

Stomach twisting, I lower my focus to the coffee table. "What if I don't deserve it?"

It's my greatest fear.

I've done some good, but I'm not without my flaws. Why should I get to have this when so few things have gone right for me in the past?

Why should I get to have Emma when I've hurt her so badly?

"Then earn it," Reese says, and an echo of the old me roars in my chest.

CHAPTER 45
SOMEONE OLD, SOMETHING NEW

EMMA

I have to hand it to my mother.

She demanded Violet's apology in the form of a very generous donation and send-off, and she didn't back down an inch.

To my everlasting relief, it's only a small affair. Harvey has shown me the account receipts proving that the costs have already been paid by Logan's parents. It's being billed as a "generous thank-you" for all of my parents' contributions over the years. Honestly, I don't care what they call it, as long as it doesn't cost my parents a cent. The champagne is decent, though.

The sun's turned out in all its glory, as though personally invited. As I soak up every hill and valley, it takes everything in me not to get emotional. The terrace is dressed beautifully, adorned for the last time. Come tomorrow, the house will be under new ownership.

I flag down a fresh glass of Cristal and blink back the tears.

"Heads up," Ivy whispers behind her glass. "Ex at three o'clock."

My heart skips a beat, and I don't even pretend to be subtle about looking. But in the next second, my stomach sinks. It's not Charlie.

Ivy winces. "Sorry, I should have said it was the other one."

Logan lifts his chin, trying to catch my eye, but I turn back to the view. It's all too reminiscent of the last time I was standing here. Of the man who was standing beside me.

This time, instead of Charlie, I have Ivy, and she's giving me her patented "You know what you want; what are you going to do about it?" look.

"We're not broken up," I repeat for the third time. "Charlie's just being…" Infuriating. Ridiculous. Scared.

"Have you seen him this week?" she asks.

My shoulders fall. "Not even his shadow." For so long, I couldn't escape him. But ever since he moved back to Operations, he's been a ghost.

She squeezes my hand. "He'll come to his senses. I'm sure of it. You didn't see the way he looked at you."

But I did see it. Which is what makes it hurt so much.

I want to call him, ask him how his day went, ask about Reese. I want to storm over to his apartment and lock us inside until he comes to his senses.

Hell, I'd settle for him telling me to go fuck myself if it meant hearing his voice.

Morning, sunshine.

I miss it. I miss him. I kind of want to punch him.

How is it even possible to be this mad at a person I love so much?

Work is awful without him. I can't even enjoy the peace of Roberts's absence, because every time I look up, I expect to see Charlie's sparkling blue eyes, only to find an empty space.

I've drafted an email to HR asking for a desk change, but I haven't sent it. I have no idea how to phrase "I get sad every time I see the desk of the guy I was sleeping with, and oops, we were meant to disclose that but didn't, sorry."

"Where did your parents disappear to?" Ivy asks.

Oh god, for a blissful few minutes, I'd actually forgotten why I came out here. "They are presently saying goodbye to their bedroom. Biblically."

Ivy's jaw drops, looking scandalized, which is exactly what I was fifteen minutes ago when I went looking for them. At least she didn't have to hear it.

"Tell me they're not."

I tip back the last mouthful of champagne in my glass, but unfortunately, the bubbles don't erase my memory. "They are."

She covers her mouth and shakes with giggles. "Oh my god. Cheers to Mr. and Mrs. Conway."

It's so ridiculous I can't help but smile. This is why Ivy is one of my favorite people. "I'm so glad you're here."

She sets her empty glass down. "Not as glad as I am. Ciara hasn't stopped calling me since Mom moved in to help with the baby, like she didn't ask her to. If only we could harness our parents' powers for good, we could solve anything, or at least exhaust whoever opposes us until they give up."

I chuckle. "Remember that when it's your turn."

"I'm warning you now, if I ever get married, I plan on eloping. In the middle of the night. In another country."

It's so her I can't picture it happening any other way. "As long as you're prepared to be called on as a witness when my parents find out I don't want children."

"To frustrating our parents," she toasts with a laugh.

"If you're conspiring," says a familiar British accent from behind me, "I'd like to offer my services."

Well, well, well. Here's a face I haven't seen in a while. "Lincoln Bartholomew Reeves, how did you get past security?"

With a laugh, he wraps me up in a tight hug. "That might be your worst guess yet." In the years since I last saw him, he's grown his hair out and gained a tan. Probably skippering a boat around the isles, knowing Lincoln. "As if I was going to miss your parents' last hoorah."

I turn to Ivy. "Lincoln's the closest thing to a brother I have. His family owns the estate next door, but he's been MIA for the last few years."

"More like an older cousin you still talk to," he says, all his attention on Ivy as he holds a hand out to her. "And the pleasure is all mine."

"We'll see" is all Ivy says. She slips her hand into his, but she doesn't give her name. She's regarding Lincoln like he's an abstract painting and she's trying to work out whether he's been hung upside down.

I file that away for later.

————

It takes Logan another hour, where he does little else except watch us, before he extricates himself and walks over. Whatever game he's playing, it makes no difference to me. The result is the same.

I've moved on.

I give Ivy the okay, and she heads off in search of another drink.

"I believe a happy birthday is in order," he says as he passes me a glass of red wine. I make a mental note to throw it into the planter beside me when he's distracted.

"How are you?" The shorter this exchange is, the better.

"Honestly, I've been feeling a little neglected," he pouts. "You're a hard person to get a hold of lately."

"I've already told you multiple times; I'm not interested."

Logan is the same as he's ever been. Still charming, rich, personable.

But he's not who I want anymore.

He doesn't make me laugh the way Charlie does, doesn't challenge me, or debate with me about the moral implications of eating an animal cookie head first.

He never loved me the way Charlie does.

"You have," he says, "but I think you should reconsider."

I'm head over heels for Charlie, even if the short-sighted asshole would rather bury his head in the sand than touch an emotion.

But all problems have solutions, right? And Charlie's always telling me what a great problem-solver I am.

"Logan," I sigh.

I've tried letting him down gently. I expected it to be quick, the same as when he dumped me. Instead, he keeps trying to debate it, as if he can bargain his way back into a relationship with me.

Without asking, he clasps my elbow and steers me through the crowd into the house. "I think it's better if we have this conversation in private."

It won't matter where we have it, but I can appreciate him not wanting an audience.

He doesn't stop walking until we reach the wine cellar. As we descend the steps, I'm struck with déjà vu. But I push it out of my mind.

"All right," I say, keeping a few feet of distance between us. "You've gotten me here, so say what you came here to say, and let's put this to rest."

"You can't deny we make sense on paper, Emma. I like that you're different from the other girls my parents set me up with. I'm not ready to settle down, and you're still preoccupied with your career, so it's ideal. I can wait out your little hobby, and when I'm ready, you can step away from your job. You can't honestly say you'd rather be with that loser you brought last time, and you're not exactly in a financial position to be turning me down."

I'm five seconds away from putting my heel through his liver.

Logan has the audacity to stroke my cheek. "I know I had a problem with it before, but I'm willing to accept you even if you're broken."

Heart lurching, I pull away.

I have no interest in a man who wants to break me in, overpower me, or make me his prize.

I need a partner who will stand by my side. Equal. Who recognizes my worth and my power and celebrates it.

Who holds his own just as well during a storm as while it's calm.

Who reflects the breadth of my love in equal measure.

Logan isn't that man.

He lives to be heard. The right answer is always his, even if it's fed to him.

There's a platinum card where his heart should be.

But Charlie…

He raises the bar for me. He's never asked me to lower myself, and he isn't afraid to push me either.

I stare at Logan, seeing the truth now. How he preferred his place to mine, how I made *him* feel inadequate. "I'll never be able to be less than perfect with you."

"That's ridiculous. You're hardly perfect," he says. Instantly, his eyes go wide, and he backtracks. "You know what I mean."

I bite back a scoff. Does he really expect this to win me over?

"Work isn't a phase, Logan. It's not temporary, and it's not a silly little hobby I'm keeping up for fun. Even if I didn't need the money, I enjoy it. My parents understand that; why can't you?"

"What will happen when you have kids? You can't expect to do both."

"You're right. I don't expect to do both." I do a mental recap of our relationship using this new insight, and I'm left with more questions. "I thought you liked that I had a job."

"Please," he taunts, and I guess we've reached the mask-off portion of the evening. "I only entertained this charade because it meant I was off the hook to propose for a few years. All my other girlfriends have been obsessed with the ring, but not you. You were too distracted playing assistant. I know you like feeling important, but it's degrading. We both knew you'd end up back here."

"I should throw this in your face," I grit out, anger flooding me, "but I don't want to waste top-shelf wine on a bottom-shelf man." Within the confines of my heart, the piece of him I've been holding on to falls away, leaving me lighter. The shackles of promises made, the fantasy I held of our future, all of it, gone. "You lied to me."

"I softened the truth."

Footsteps descend the stairs. Probably a server looking for more wine. Good. I'm ready to be done with both this conversation and the man in front of me.

"I care for you, Emma. I always have."

CHAPTER 46
LAYING IT ALL AT YOUR FEET
CHARLIE

For me, dreams have never been happy. When I fall asleep, I'm getting turned down, dumped, fired, or worse. I've watched Reese fall down a flight of stairs so many times I have to stand in front of her on an escalator.

Where other people get their wildest wishes granted, I'm waiting in lines or trying to jump high enough to get off the ground.

Fact is, my subconscious knows the truth. If I'm not careful, I'll fuck up a good thing.

I already have.

But Emma is right. It's time I stopped getting in the way of my future.

I refuse to let this good thing get away from me.

Ivy looks ready to throw me over the balcony when I arrive, and when she tells me Emma went off with Logan, it almost destroys me.

But I have to believe it isn't too late.

By the time I get to the wine cellar, I'm taking the

stairs two at a time. Just as I make it to the landing, Logan steps in close to Emma and says, "I care for you. I always have."

My fist aches to connect with his face, because *fuck that guy,* but I ignore it. Emma looks more beautiful than I remember, or maybe it's that I've been so sick without her that just being in the same room with her is bringing me back to life.

"I have something for you," I say, pulling the delicate gold watch from my pocket.

Her eyes go wide with recognition and surprise. "Charlie," she says, like it's punched out of her. "What? How did you…?"

Gently, I slide it back onto her wrist. "I called Harvey. Bought it back. Made a deal to cover a portion of what's owed in exchange for it."

Emma opens her mouth to protest, but I shake my head.

"Then your dad found out, and he wouldn't take no for an answer, so we're all squared up now."

I close the clasp and steal an extra moment, just to hold her hand, before I step back.

Emma's owed an apology, and I'm going to make it count.

"You're the best thing that's happened in this whole shitty year." I pull in a deep breath and run a hand through my hair. "I'm trying, Emma. I'll do everything I can to not fuck this up again. You're too good for me, but I'm a selfish asshole who doesn't want to lose you."

I only have one heart. Fuck knows what's even pumping blood through my body right now because I handed that part of myself over to her the minute she kissed me.

"I've been running on empty my whole life. All I ever cared about was my sister and making sure we had enough. And when you walked into my life, I spent every second afraid of crashing, because that's what I do."

There are so many things I need to tell her, all of them clawing to get out of me. If I could simply crack my ribs open, let each confession pour out into the open, she could see how marked I am by her. There isn't a single part of me that doesn't love her.

That is equally afraid of losing her.

"I know we started off wrong, and that's on me. I should have said it when you asked me to help you, but I was too busy being selfish. I wish I'd been strong enough to tell you how I felt any of the million times I had the chance to."

Emma crosses her arms over her chest, nods. Uses the silence like I taught her too.

Swallowing, I continue. "Thinking of you with anyone else makes me want to tear this house down, brick by brick. If you don't want anything to do with me, I understand, but I'm not leaving until I tell you what I want."

My mouth is dry. I don't care.

"I want Reese to live in a big house with fur babies and a life-sized Darth Vader and Mae, who reminds her every day how amazing she is. I want my parents to live peaceful lives and not go before I'm ready to say goodbye to them. I want people to stop destroying each other over money or hatred. I want to stop looking for the exit every time something good happens. I want to spend every second of the rest of my life finding new ways to make you happy, because nothing has ever felt so permanent as the way I love you."

Emma's eyes are misty, but I can't stop. I won't let her get a word in, not yet, because for fuck's sake, I've only got one shot at this, and I'm shit at words and feelings. If she gives me an out, I'm worried my dumb ass might actually take it, because this is the first time I've had something truly worth not fucking up, and technically I'm already zero for two.

"Wherever you go, I'm going with you. I'll be right there—at your back, by your side, on my knees, whatever it takes. There's nowhere you can go that I won't want to follow."

I don't deserve Emma, not yet, but I can't be without her, and I'll do anything—everything—to make this work.

"Say something," I plead. "Please. Do you need me to beg? I'll fucking do it. Just please, tell me what you need."

"Okay," she says, staring me down. "Kneel."

I blink. "Now?" These are three-hundred-dollar pants.

Her brow arches. "Were you lying to me?"

My heart lurches at her stern tone. "No."

"Then show me. I want you on your knees, Charlie. Don't you want to give me what I want?"

Always.

Holding her gaze, I step forward. I need to be closer.

I need to breathe her in. And just before we touch, I kneel.

"Better?"

My heart is beating so hard, I'm shocked there isn't an echo. The floor is ice cold, and my knees are already protesting, but I'm smiling.

And when she cups my cheek, I remember how to breathe. I cover her hand with mine.

Truth is, I'm cold-blooded. I've been allergic to feelings for as long as I've had them. Getting attached is dangerous for someone who never stays in one place very long. Given the choice, I'd keep my shit locked up so tight the government has it on a watch list. But I never had a choice with Emma.

The whole world is burning, but I am hers until every star turns cold. There's no separating her from me. Me from her.

"Doubt everything else. Hell, question whether the sky is blue for all I care. But there are two things I won't fucking stand for." I count them off. "That you ever doubt how incredible you are, and that you ever have reason to question exactly how far I'll go to prove that to you."

I'll follow her to the ends of the earth. Beyond. Past the mortal coil to whatever exists on the other side. I don't much care how she wants me, as long as it means being by her side.

Heaven. Hell. I'll face it all.

"I want you," I say, pressing her hand more firmly against my cheek. "How ever I can get you. Do you even know what you do to me? All you need to do is walk into a room, and my day is better. It kind of fucks me up when you aren't around. I want everything, Emma. Every smile, every scowl, every debate." The smile that creeps over my face does so unbidden. "All of you. I'd rather cut my own heart out of my chest than have you look at me like I mean nothing to you. You don't even have to do anything. Just be near me, and I'm fucking good. Whatever you want to do, we can make it happen. Anything you want, I want it too. As long as I'm the only one you want. I'm selfish, and I've been a coward, but it's the truth."

"That's a lot to ask for," she finally says, her voice so soft I want to wrap her up and protect her from the world. "What makes you think you've earned it? How do I know you won't get scared again?"

"I can't say I won't ever be scared, but I'm in love with you. Probably have been since the moment you walked into that meeting room. Not being able to admit that to you has killed me. But I can't lose you again. I won't." I swallow around the lump in my throat. "I shouldn't have walked away. I should have stayed and said this earlier. God knows I wanted to. I was terrified. The way you look at me, like I'm everything I could want to be, everything you deserve…" I take a deep breath, ignoring the cold bite of the floor, the ache of my knees, the shadow of Logan in the background. All that exists is her.

"You have the power to hurt me, destroy me so thoroughly there's nothing recognizable left, nothing to put together again, just enough to carry on as a shell of who I used to be. And the thing is? I'll let you. If loving you means the possibility of losing you, of letting you lay waste to everything I am, then it's already too late, because I love you so much there's no room for anything else."

The sadness in her eyes just about breaks my heart.

Emma brings her other hand up to cup my face. "Somewhere, someone convinced you that you're not worthy of love. But I can tell you right now that's a lie. You know how I know? Because you love so beautifully, so completely, that you don't even see it. It's in everything you do, in the way you take care of people. But now it's time for you to let me take care of you. Let yourself be loved, Charlie, please."

"I want you to know, I'm sor—"

She cuts me off, covering my mouth and invading my space. Whatever she wants, she can have, forever, because she's touching me, and maybe it means I haven't completely fucked this up.

"Stand up."

I don't dare to look away as I pick myself up off the floor. As soon as I'm standing, she reels me in by my tie.

CHAPTER 47
TRUST. HOPE. LOVE.
EMMA

The moment Charlie walked in, my breath left my lungs. In fact, my soul may have departed my body as well, because for a series of long, drawn-out seconds, I can't move.

Logan ceases to exist (Charlie has that effect), and as the awe, relief, and sheer thrill of having the love of my life once again within reach sinks in, knowing what it means and—touching my watch again—knowing what he's done for me, I let him talk.

Let him run his mouth as he always does. He needs to, and I've earned it. With every word he says, I only want more, more, more.

"Say it again."

There's no hesitation. "I love you."

"Again."

A dimple appears. "I love you."

"Again."

He's smiling wildly now, his blue eyes bright, and I twist my hand in his tie to pull him closer to me.

"I'll keep saying it, as many times as you want. I'm not going anywhere, and I'm only going to love you more the longer we're together."

"And the rest?" I ask.

"Are you asking me to beg, sweetheart?" And oh, there's the cocky man I know and love. Between that smirk and that single raised brow, he looks all too pleased, even when I tug harder on his tie. "I'll do it. Let me be yours in every way that you're already mine."

And, oh. *Oh.*

I teeter in my heels, his plea hitting me like vertigo.

I've never thought of love as the merging of two halves, and I've never liked the idea of being less than whole. With Charlie, it's so much more than that.

He's been meeting me, matching me, since the day we met.

He's it for me. For the rest of my life, I want to experience everything with him by my side. I want to be loved by him in every way, to give myself over to him, to have him on his knees, by my side, for as long as possible. Longer.

Forever.

CHAPTER 48
I HAVE THE KEY TO YOUR HEART (AND OTHER VITAL ORGANS)

EMMA

A LITTLE WHILE LATER

Good standards should be easily understood and even easier to implement. Ideally, they should be system agnostic (hello, future-proofing), and not—let's say—scrutinized for every available loophole, *Charlie*.

Good instructions are clear, concise, and specific.

Where to click and when, what to expect next, how to triage an issue.

The best kind of instructions aren't instructions at all, but a mutual understanding of what is needed, to be followed with care and without prompting.

That's precisely what life is like with Charlie.

"Are you sure you're okay?" I balance the phone between my ear and shoulder as I toe off my heels, then sink into the couch. "I can come over."

"No, don't," Ivy says. "I'm still a little shell-shocked,

but I've had all day to think about it, and I'm happy. We knew they'd have to choose someone, and I'm glad it was me and not you."

It's been a week since Helix announced a company-wide redundancy. Every day since has been torture, a slow, painful wait to see which of us would get the call.

Ivy got hers twenty minutes after she walked in this morning.

"I haven't told Mom yet. I think I need a few days before I'm ready for that conversation, and if you're free tomorrow, I could really use your help strategizing."

"What about tonight?" I've only just walked in the door, still in my work clothes, but I'm more than willing to head out again.

Ivy sighs. "Tonight, I'm going downstairs to get properly drunk. Living above a bar is so efficient."

My heart hurts for my best friend. "Call me if you need anything."

"Right now all I need is five margaritas and a solid dicking down."

A laugh bubbles out of me. "I don't think I can help with that."

Ivy joins in, and the tight knot in my gut unwinds. Ever since she messaged me the news, I've been worried for her. I already have a list of job options at the ready, and I typed up a reference letter on my phone during my lunch break.

"Come over tomorrow. I'll show you the ridiculously huge package I got. Speaking of which, go be with your obnoxiously obsessed boyfriend."

Ending the call, I leave my phone in the living room

with my shoes and make my way to the bedroom, unbuttoning my shirt as I go. If Charlie is home, he's been unusually quiet.

It's been two months since I moved in, and it was a ridiculously easy adjustment. The biggest issue we faced was dividing the closet.

Even my parents are closer now, living just outside the city, and after roping in Reese and Mae to help them move, Mom offered to volunteer as their stand-in receptionist while they looked for a new one. It's been five weeks and counting.

Now I just need to convince Charlie to put in his notice like he's been talking about. Once that's done, I'll have everything I need.

As I step across the threshold to our bedroom, I crash into the door frame.

Heart leaping right out of my chest, I gape. "Jesus fucking Christ, Charlie."

My mouth is dry. My lungs? A desert. All the liquid in my body has flown south for the winter, and now I'm soaked, because Charlie fucking Walker is sitting naked before me, legs spread, a glinting sliver cock cage between his thighs.

"Fuck."

He looks glorious. A god upon his throne, resplendent and sinful. He knows it too, sprawled casually on the chair, shit-eating grin firmly in place.

My blood is on fire, and he loves it.

"Don't die before you get over here, sweetheart. You'll break my heart."

Sweetheart always sounds good, the way it slips sweetly from Charlie's lips. Sometimes I swear I hear an accent poking through, a remnant of his past, an extra seasoning of personality (which he's already abundant in).

But boss… boss might be better.

There's nothing more exhilarating to me than having his cock in my hand and his will at my call.

Charlie. The man. The menace.

Under my control.

For a moment, I have to brace myself against the wall. I can't move, and I certainly can't look away from him. Not while he's so… beautiful.

"You look incredible."

He spreads his legs wider. "Yeah?"

Only Charlie could be this cocky while locked in a cage.

I drop my head back against the wall, my eyes never leaving his. Each breath is shaky, and I'm not even sure my legs work right now. I'm smiling, overwhelmed and happy and wrecked with want. Every inch of my skin is coated in goose bumps.

"You know you do. Now, where's the key?"

"Next to you. Dresser."

"Good." I pocket it. "Hands on the chair and keep them there until I say so."

He does it, but he's smiling like he has a trick up his nonexistent sleeve. I'm already looking forward to cracking that facade, bringing Charlie to the brink of what he can withstand, then pushing just a little farther, until he's begging me to let him come.

"Yes?" he asks, wagging his brows and grinning. "It looks like you want something."

What I want is to devour him. To strip myself bare and use his tongue as my personal toy. I want to bathe us both in the inferno of my desire until he's a whimpering mess, begging for release.

"You know what I want," I say.

"Do I?"

I push off the wall, stalking toward him.

"Yes, you do."

CHAPTER 49
I'M YOURS (RUIN ME)
CHARLIE

Emma walks into the room, and I have to grip the armrests to keep myself from reaching out, especially when she pulls her shirt out of her pants and slowly undoes the last few buttons in a striptease.

Fuck. This is either the best or worst idea I've ever had.

"Like what you see?" she asks.

Even though she wasn't addressing it directly, my dick twitches like it's trying to answer her.

Her smile is wicked.

She lets her shirt fall to the floor behind her, her nipples peaked and begging for attention. Fuck, I need to get my mouth on those gorgeous tits right now.

"I think I'll leave this here." Emma pulls the key from her pocket and places it on the side table at my elbow. It brings her close enough to touch, and I jump on the opportunity, mouthing at her breast through her bra, licking and sucking one of her perfect nipples into my mouth.

She gasps but doesn't immediately pull away. I switch to the other one.

"Did I say you could touch me?" she asks.

My cock strains at the breathlessness in her voice, throbbing with the need to get harder. I lick a trail up her neck. "You said not to move my hands. You didn't say anything about my mouth."

With a hum, she pulls away and stands between my open thighs. Her gaze touches every inch of me, top to tail, lingering every time she gets to the cage.

I dig my fingers in harder.

"What brought this on?" Emma asks, popping the button of her slacks. She drags the zipper down, bit by bit, and I'm at the mercy of her control. My blood flows like lava in my veins, pooling between my legs.

"You said you wanted to try it, and tonight seemed like a good night."

Like at the office, Emma can push when I want to pull, and vice versa. I don't always need this, to let go so completely, but when I do, she knows exactly how to handle me.

Her pants drop, pooling at her feet. Then she kicks them aside.

My dick kicks up again, attempting in vain to get harder as she slides her panties off. The sound of my nails against the fabric of the chair is loud in the silence.

"You're so fucking gorgeous," I say. "Come over here. I don't need my hands to eat you out. I know how much you love having my tongue inside you."

"Actually," Emma says, dropping to her knees in front of me. Her mouth is so close to my cock, I can feel her hot breath ghosting over it, and I can't stop the noise I make. "It's *my* tongue that you need to worry about."

And then she clasps the cage in one hand and leans down to lick through the gaps between the bars.

"Oh, fuck."

My head hits the chair with a thud. Locked up like this, the head is still mostly covered by my foreskin, and Emma starts there, dipping the tip of her tongue in and under and around the sensitive skin. *Fuck.* My brain is so scrambled, I can't remember what day it is.

She laps up the precum that is leaking out now, her eyes shining bright and wild.

"Remember. No touching until I say you can."

She keeps licking into the cage, moving down to the base, sucking a mark on the inside of my thigh. Both legs are shaking with the effort of not fucking up into her mouth.

"Fuck. Don't stop."

But I'm not in charge tonight; she is.

Emma stands, licking those beautiful fucking lips I'm desperate for, and with a flick of her wrist, frees her breasts from her bra.

She straddles me, pulling a groan from deep in my chest. The scorching heat of her pussy doesn't quite make contact and it's enough to drive a man to the brink.

"Let me touch you." I won't say please. Not yet.

"Do you think you've earned it?"

No, but I don't care. I need to touch her.

"I didn't think so," she says, rubbing herself on the cage.

"Bet I can last longer than you," she teases.

"You like losing, then."

She reaches up to glide her hand through my hair, and pulls.

"That's a whole lot of talking for someone whose cock is locked away."

She's flushed, her hair falling into her face. I'm itching to sweep it away, pull her to my mouth.

I can't move my hands, but I try to meet her thrusts with my hips. I want to watch her get herself off on this, writhing above me like the goddess she is.

Emma moans, the sound going straight to my balls. Fuck.

My fingers flex in place. There's nothing but her word and my will binding me here. "You seem to be struggling with something. I could help with that. If you wanted me to."

She wants to protest, but by the unchecked fire in her eyes, it's clear she wants to get off more.

"I should leave you like this," she says, presenting two fingers to my mouth. "Get them wet for me."

Happily.

I suck them into my mouth, showing her what my tongue could be doing to her clit if she let me move. When she's satisfied, she forces me to watch as she uses her slicked-up digits to rub at her clit.

This is bliss and agony all in one.

"Do you want to touch?" she rasps, head thrown back in pleasure.

"You know I do."

I'm helpless to watch as she writhes and whimpers above me. "Maybe I should fuck you like this, with the cage on. You wouldn't even be able to feel me coming. I could just keep going, getting myself off for hours, and there's nothing you could do."

The moan that rips out of me feels like a roar. "Emma, *fuck*."

She traces my lips with her wet fingers, eyes flashing as I chase them.

She pulls them away before I can properly get a taste. "God, Charlie. Look at you," she breathes, sounding wrecked.

I'm thirty seconds away from losing all control. "Let me. Come on. I know you want it."

Her chest heaves, torturing me with miles of beautiful skin I want to brand with my lips and teeth. "Say it."

"Sweetheart," I say, knowing it isn't what she's asking for.

I hiss as she digs her nails into the soft flesh of my thigh.

"Say it, and I'll let you touch me. *Beg*."

Heat licks up my spine.

"*Please*."

She grabs my wrist and puts my hand between her thighs, and we moan together. With my thumb, I find her clit and circle it the way she likes it.

Head thrown back, she pushes against me. "Make me come, and maybe you can fuck me."

She's gorgeous like this. My sexy, powerful inferno.

"Kiss me," she commands. "Please."

"Only because you asked so nicely."

My palms are damp, but I keep my hands where they are as I lean in to claim her mouth like I've wanted to since she walked into the room.

I lick long and deep, fucking into her mouth the way I want to do to her pussy. In return, she clutches at my face, digging her hands into my hair, my shoulders, my biceps, all the while rubbing herself against the cage.

The steel is slick with arousal and burning hot from friction and our combined body heat.

I keep going, kissing her jaw, licking down her neck, sucking a mark on her collarbone as she arches against me.

She screams out when she comes, shaking over me and riding it out.

Before she can protest, I suck the taste of her off my thumb, straining further in the cage.

We're both panting when she stands, and when she picks up the key and hands it to me, I can't move fast enough.

I miss the lock at first, distracted by the sight of Emma getting on her hands and knees on our bed.

"Now get over here and fuck me into next week."

I have to grip the base of my dick when it's freed in order to stem the immediate and brutal flow of blood, then slip a condom on.

"You got it, sweetheart."

She's so fucking perfect. I love every part of her, the way her mind works, how she's always thinking of solutions to problems, even when they aren't her own. How beautiful she is when she's taking her pleasure.

How fucking gorgeous she looks taking my cock.

I slide in slow, as much for me as it is for her, only stopping when I've bottomed out. Now finally free to touch her, I grip her hips and spread her wide open so I can watch as I fuck into her.

"Charlie, please."

That's the other part of this I love. How smoothly we can hand over control when we need to, giving and taking in equal measure.

"I've got you."

I'm not going to last long. My blood is on fire, and I'm too worked up from her mouth and the squeeze of her cunt. So I don't waste any time pushing deep into her.

"Harder, come on."

Fuck.

She pushes back, meeting me thrust for thrust, hands white-knuckled in the sheets. Without warning, she comes again, and that's it. I'm gone, fucking hard and fast into her as I come.

As I fall to the bed beside her and pull her close, I take in the state of her. Soft and warm and flushed, still with her patented look of determination in her eyes.

I never want to look at anyone else for as long as I live.

CHAPTER 50
TECHNICOLOR DREAMS
EMMA

MUCH, MUCH LATER

Relief is the letting go of the burdens which weigh us down. The slaying of these phantom pressures is enough to free our lungs, allowing us to breach the surface and continue.

I never knew true relief until Charlie came along.

Now? No matter the issue—what to have for dinner, where to spend the day, how to occupy my parents—he has it covered. Before him, I never gave much thought to how much I wanted, *needed*, someone I could rely on.

Tending to my worries the same way he tinkers with his car, checking that we're in safe keeping.

"My life is in your hands," he'll say. "Gotta keep you both purring."

Then he'll throw me a wink, knowing he's only riling me up further. Those nights, he's lucky if he gets to come.

· · ·

Two strong arms wrap around my waist, then Charlie's chest presses against my back. We fit together just as perfectly now as we have for the last ten years. "I love you," he says, kissing the sensitive spot behind my ear.

I lean into him. "I love you more."

"That's not possible."

It's a beautiful night, clear, cool. It's been a long time since I've been in my old apartment, but I miss the sticky, sweaty tangle of limbs when the air conditioning went out.

"Do you remember Venice?" I ask.

"I remember getting fleeced by that guy with the birds."

I laugh. "I told you not to talk to him."

"Yeah, yeah. Basic tourist fail, I know. What made you think about Venice?"

With a sigh, I pull his arms tighter around me. A decade of this, and I still want to soak up as much of him as I can. I want the feel of him burning so deep in my marrow that I can't ever forget it. To take it with me wherever I go.

"Walking through the canals before dawn, it was as if we were the only people there. The only people anywhere. It was so quiet. Kind of lonely too, although it was nice to move through the streets without the crowds. But then you put your arm around me, and it made all the difference. Because you were with me, and I didn't feel lonely anymore."

It's about so much more than Venice, and we both know it.

"Emma," he says, his voice straining the same way my heart is, his hold tightening.

"I'm here." For now and forever.

"Do you know what I realized in Venice?" he asks.

I turn my head to smile at him. "How much better Italian coffee is?"

"That's slander," he teases, bringing his lips to mine. The kiss is deep and slow, reminiscent of a hundred before it, with the promise of a thousand more. "I wasn't sure what I expected to find when we stepped off the train. For so long, I'd been telling myself it would be this incredible place, bigger and better than anything I've seen. But it was just… fine. Cool, yeah, but not mind-blowing. I wanted to be Dorothy, stepping onto the yellow brick road. But it wasn't like that at all. And I didn't want to say anything, because what kind of a dick gets to Venice and is like 'meh'? It wasn't until that night, watching you charm the sommelier at the hotel—fuck, he was so into you. I wanted to throttle him. That stupid accent—"

"Focus, Charlie."

"Right. Anyway, you were magnificent. So fucking gorgeous. You always have been. But you were in your element. Lit up the way you get when you're showing off. I fucking love it. And it hit me. My life turned technicolor the second you walked into it. Everything else pales in comparison."

"Charlie," I choke out, tears stinging the corners of my eyes.

He threads our fingers together, raises our joined hands to his lips.

"That's a nice ring," he says.

"Thanks. Some jerk I used to work with gave it to me."

He chuckles, and I don't think I've ever been this happy. "Lucky guy."

"He really is." I turn in his arms and drag my hands down his chest.

He flexes underneath them, bringing a smile to my face. Show-off.

"Not as lucky as I am, though."

"Wouldn't count on that, sweetheart."

Slowly, I wrap his tie around my wrist and pull him back inside.

THE END

THANK YOU!

My first and largest thanks will always be to you, my wonderful readers.

I absolutely love to hear from you, so don't be afraid to send me a message! Every reaction DM, edit, unhinged ALL CAPS scream, and Dean Winchester gif makes my day.

If you loved the book and want to spread the word, please consider leaving a review wherever you hang out online. Your support means the world to me, and every little bit helps.

Dream big, live loud, create magic.

Dani xo

ACKNOWLEDGMENTS

Thank you to the coffee that got me through drafting.

Thank you to the wine that got me through edits.

Thank you to my besties who listened through many, MANY, hours of voice memos (and still talk to me).

Thank you to Dean Winchester circa Season 1-3, for being as bratty as you are attractive, and thus inspiring Charlie.

Thank you to Ao3 for having some of the best damn stories and authors around. You've gotten me through many sleepless nights.

———

And now, because we all contain multitudes, here are some non-thanks:

Shame to the toy companies who stopped making my favorite vibes. I can't find good replacements and I hope your batteries run out when it's least convenient.

Shame to the depression I fought at the end of 2023 which made writing parts of this book a shit show.

Shame to the partner of my dreams who is still taking their sweet-ass time to find me. Hurry up, babe.

ABOUT THE AUTHOR

Dani McLean is Bi/NB Australian author who writes shamelessly fun contemporary romance with an open-door policy.

She loves coffee, karaoke, and stories that make you kick your feet up in the air.

If lost, she can be found on Ao3, or echo located through her kookaburra laugh.

To stay updated with new releases, giveaways, and more, sign up for her newsletter, or connect with her on social media.

**Find Dani on TikTok and Instagram @danim-
cleanwrites**

ALSO BY DANI MCLEAN

Mortgage of Convenience

———

The Movie Magic Novellas:

Midnight, Repeated

Not My Love Story

A Missing Connection

It Has To Be You

The Forces of Love

———

The Cocktail Series:

Love & Rum

Sex & Sours

Risks & Whiskey